Tropical Liaison

D1732888

A NOVEL BY

Richard S. Hillman

Brighton Publishing LLC
435 N. Harris Drive
Mesa, AZ 85203

Tropical Liaison

A Novel by

Richard S. Hillman

Brighton Publishing LLC
435 N. Harris Drive
Mesa, AZ 85203
www.BrightonPublishing.com

Copyright © 2015

Printed in the United States of America

ISBN 13: 978-1-62183-306-2

ISBN 10: 1-62183-306-2

First Edition

Reviews

"Richard S. Hillman has written an unnerving and irresistible novel of political intrigue and betrayal in the volatile Caribbean. Professor Manny White Vidal is in way over his head but doesn't know it yet. This is a writer who knows how to wield the weapon of suspense and who knows that the only real plot is that nothing is at it seems. Tropical Liaison will remind you of the work of Daniel Silva and William Beck and will remind you as well of just why you started reading stories in the first place—to be transported to a world more vivid and, in this case, a hell of a lot scarier, than the one you're living in."

~John Dufresne

Author of Louisiana Power and Light and Love Warps the Mind a Little, both New York Times Notable Books, among others, including No Regrets, Coyote and The Lie that Tells a Truth.

"Tropical Liaison is a well-written, entertaining, and provocative tale of an American's search for meaning in the midst of an international power-struggle. His journey is perilous, exciting, and illuminating. Richard S. Hillman's attention to detail brings the Caribbean setting to life. Being more than familiar with this region, the novelist knows how to seize the attention of the reader through every page. This enticing fictional journey, with all its merits as a novel, also invites reflection about hemispheric politics. A good read."

~Elsa Cardozo

Author of En busca del Aleph among other political and social studies on Latin America and, particularly, on Venezuelan and hemispheric diplomacy.

"...this brilliantly written story is destined to achieve its place in the literary world."

~Kathie McGuire, director of Brighton Publishing LLC

Dedication

For Audrey, Oliver, Shoshana, and Sydney

Acknowledgments

The list is far too long to include everyone who assisted in my work. And I am solely responsible for any errors or distortions that might appear in Tropical Liaison. However, several individuals and organizations were particularly helpful in the arduous, yet wonderful, process of crafting this novel.

John Dufresne taught me how fiction can tell truths. Kim Bradley, Hector Duarte, Scott Archer Jones, David Livingstone, Peter Mouton, Maureen Mullens, and Christopher Shaun provided critical suggestions and encouragement. Elsa Cardozo, Nicole Caron, Tom D'Agostino, and Robert Hillman commented on early drafts. Brenda Windberg supplied indispensable editorial advice. Don McGuire believed in the value of making my work available to the public. Audrey and Shoshana contributed creative ideas, moral support, and inspiration.

The Taos Summer Writers Conference in Taos, New Mexico; Writers in Paradise at Eckerd College in St. Petersburg, Florida; and The Rosemary Beach Writers Conference in Florida's Panhandle helped me develop my story and writing skills. The Fulbright Scholars Program supported my research in Latin America and the Caribbean.

Prologue

"A CULTURE, WE ALL KNOW, IS MADE BY ITS CITIES."

~ DEREK WOLCOTT

On an otherwise tranquil spring day in 1976 in the tiny Latin American nation of Guarida, a brash knock on the front door distracted Rafael. He looked up from his drawing pad and tried to concentrate on the poster tacked on the wall above his desk. *The beard and beret will be easy,* he thought, *but the fiery eyes will be difficult to capture on paper.*

Rafael was about to continue his sketch when the knocking became more insistent. He dropped his charcoal pencil. *This could be it,* he thought. *Dad is downstairs and will find out what's happening.*

He could barely make out the tinsel tinkling of the dinner bell above the pounding at the door. The bell rang, stopped, rang again, stopped, and then sounded one more time. At dinner, it would have been one continuous ring. He recognized the signal.

Countless times, he and his dad had played the drill as if it were a game. At that moment, despite a year's worth of preparation, his heart beat hard and fast; his hands turned cold. He'd have to complete Che's portrait some other time.

Acting on his father's instructions, Rafael slid his bed away from the wall, pushed open a trapdoor, and snuck backwards into a crawl space. Once inside, he reached out and pulled his bed back into place. Careful not to catch a splinter, he shimmied up into the attic, climbing the rest of the way along the beams to a perch in a dark corner.

Rafael huddled in his hiding place and waited. The attic air felt hot and musty; his shirt stuck to his sweaty back and mucous filled his nostrils. He thought about how Anne Frank must have felt in her hiding place, about how much more real it all felt now than when he'd read her *Diary of a Young Girl* for school. When sound resonated through the air ducts, he held his breath and listened hard.

"Open up," a man shouted in a gruff voice while continuing to beat on the door. Guillermo hoped he would go away if no one answered.

The noise went on, until Guillermo finally yelled, "Just a minute." He placed the dinner bell on the kitchen table and ran upstairs to make sure his son had followed their plan, buying some time for Rafael to get into his hiding place. Then he returned downstairs and told his wife not to worry.

"Now!" the man barked. "I'm not waiting forever."

With his wife at his side, Rafael's father opened the door and saw two men in plainclothes. "Please state your business."

"Security Police." The man showed his badge and motioned for his partner to enter. He cleared his throat and said, "You are Señor Guillermo Vidal, yes? And this beautiful woman must be your señora, Verónica Gutiérrez de Vidal."

"What can we do for you, officer?" Guillermo pulled a handkerchief from the back pocket of his jeans and dabbed the sweat that had begun to bead on his forehead and neck. Only a few days ago, the Guaridan Security Police had ripped apart the home of a suspected subversive, a fellow Guaridan national. Although they found no evidence, they had beaten the man to a pulp.

"You have a nice house here in this lovely part of town," the officer said.

"We call it *El Retiro,*" Guillermo asserted, trying to appear poised. "My wife and I were about to have our supper."

"Ah, yes. The aroma is very pleasant, indeed." He nodded toward the stove, where a typical Guaridan *sancocho* with fish and vegetables boiled in a large pot.

Sweat dripped down Guillermo's face. "May I offer you and your partner—?"

"This is not a social call. Where is your son?"

"Rafael is with his friends on a camping trip. They're in the hills and won't be back for another week."

"So you are all alone, just you and your lovely woman? Very romantic, eh?"

"Please state your business." Guillermo took out his handkerchief again, wiped his face and neck. His hands shook a bit.

"Only following up on information we received from our very reliable sources, Señor Vidal. Be patient. We have a few questions for you."

"Let's get to it then." Guillermo was angry and afraid, yet he knew he had to maintain his composure. He thought about Rafael, felt ashamed that his son had to hide in the attic.

"You aren't being very hospitable."

"I offered sancocho." While he was used to being in complete control in his role as an attorney, all Guillermo could do was go along with this farce, see what would happen next. He was not used to feeling powerless.

"But now you want to get rid of us, no?"

"You were beating down my door. We were about to sit down—"

"Very well, you can start by telling us about your illegal opposition activities and about your scheme to bring down our beloved president, the honorable General Carlos Pérez Santo, and his excellent government that is doing so much for our glorious nation."

"I don't know what you're talking about."

"You are a member of a subversive group, a revolutionary, aren't you?"

"That's ridiculous. I'm well known throughout the Federal District."

"Then you wouldn't mind a thorough examination of your home, Señor Vidal. I am correct in assuming that, yes?"

"What do you think you'll find? We have nothing to hide. You'll answer to the court for this intrusion."

"The court?" The officer spat out the words. Then his expression grew quizzical, as if he were trying to figure out if Guillermo was crazy. He moved closer, studied him. Guillermo's heart beat fast. He knew he couldn't deter the officer. He hoped Rafael wouldn't deviate from their plan.

"Hold the woman." The officer gestured toward Verónica, and his partner grabbed her. She struggled, and he threw her onto the couch.

Guillermo stepped toward his wife. The officer cut him off, stood before him, and said, "Señor Vidal and I will search this magnificent house and see what we might find."

"There's no need to hold my wife, officer. Please, we've nothing to hide." Guillermo felt himself shaking but couldn't stop.

"Hold her nice and tight, yes?" The officer blew a kiss toward Verónica. Then he positioned himself behind Guillermo.

Guillermo's heart pumped as if it were a fist inside his chest. Blood rushed to his head. When he moved to defend his wife, he felt a hard object jammed into his back, assumed it was a gun barrel. He stopped and said, "Don't touch her." He heard his pathetic threat and tried a different tactic. "Listen, I've got some money—"

The man holding her laughed.

"Let's go," the first officer said, and he slid the gun up to Guillermo's neck. The nozzle felt cold and hard against his warm skin. Guillermo had no alternative but to lead the man through the house.

The officer found nothing extraordinary until he reached Rafael's room. There, he stopped in his tracks.

"Now what have we here?" he said with a smile that distorted his stern face. He pointed his gun at the poster on the wall. "Coño… This *hijo de puta* is that infamous Cuban revolutionary, correct? Castro's pal, the *pendejo* who tried to overthrow the Bolivian government—"

"He was Argentine," Guillermo said.

The officer ripped the poster off the wall and slammed it on the desk. He turned and, with the back of his gloved hand, smacked Guillermo across his face. Guillermo stumbled backward, fell, and then scrambled to his feet.

"I'm going to press charges," he said.

The officer laughed without breaking a smile.

Rafael heard his father fall. He held his breath, dared not move. Dad had warned him. *No matter what you hear, son, stay put.* They had rehearsed for an event like this. Yet he was frightened, didn't know what to think. He huddled in the dark, stuffy corner. Tears welled in his eyes.

His father had told him about the government's corrupt activities and arbitrary arrests. In the course of their preparations, they had talked about their family. Rafael's aunt—his dad's sister—and her American husband lived in New York. On his fourteenth birthday, their son Manny, Rafael's cousin, had visited El Retiro. They had become pals, enjoyed roughing it, hiking in the hills, and camping out. Before returning to the States, Manny had given Rafael a Swiss Army knife. Heart racing, Rafael ran his finger over the smooth handle of the knife, a treasure he carried always.

His mother's muffled screaming made him cringe. He heard a struggle, pushing and shoving. Then a thunderbolt-like blast reverberated through the house. The rafters vibrated. Rafael had to stay hidden, no matter what. He longed to go help his parents, but his father's warning loomed large in his mind.

What was that explosion?

He heard his father shout, "Verónica!" The smacking of leather on wooden steps sent chills up Rafael's spine. A terrified shriek like the cry of a wounded animal echoed through air ducts. Another struggle, this time as if every piece of furniture was being pounded to bits. Another explosion—and the struggling sounds ceased.

Rafael covered his face with his hands and cried. He imagined his father protecting his mother, beating away the intruder. He heard shuffling. Then the front door banged shut. Birds, or maybe they were bats, flapped their wings in a burst of commotion, and the light wind outside filtered through the slats in the attic's eaves. Rafael's entire body began to shake. He broke into a cold sweat, and he felt as if he were paralyzed. His own arms seemed like a strait jacket wrapped around his body. A warm stream of urine ran down his pants. He fantasized about the bats, fearsome creatures that would peck his skin if he stayed in the attic much longer. Then cockroaches would crawl all over his body. He shivered, tried to think, to plan. The worst case scenario hit him like a giant wave. His breathing became erratic and he sobbed, his hands jammed into his mouth so no sound would come out.

After an immeasurable amount of time, hearing nothing from below, he forced himself to stand. His legs shook. He took his knife from his pocket, opened the blade, and held it in front of him. He shuffled across the attic and slid through the crawlspace. He unlatched the trap door and pushed his bed away from the opening, then tiptoed through his room and down the stairs.

A horrific sight met his eyes. Bright red blood ran from his parents' bodies, comingling and forming dark pools on the white tile floor. It looked like an oil painting, one of those abstract canvases his mother had shown him at the museum. He gasped for air and slipped on the slick surface as he approached. The acrid odor made him gag, and he covered his nose with his handkerchief.

He sank to the floor next to the bodies of his mother and father, afraid to look but unable to look away. They lay on their backs, their open eyes transfixed on the ceiling as if they were looking through to the attic. Rafael howled like a wolf in distress, let out air that seemed to have been held in forever, and smashed his fist against the floor, again and again. Then his lungs deflated. He could contain himself no longer. He heaved until there was nothing left in his gut, crying uncontrollably for what seemed an eternity. He could hardly breathe.

Just hours ago, before starting his portrait, he had hugged his mom, felt her soft, protective warmth. Now Rafael touched a cold, stiffening remnant—a motionless, lifeless shell. He withdrew his hand from the effigy, folded his knife, and returned it to his pocket. His head hung over his chest. Despite being only thirteen, it was as if all the vitality had been sucked out of his body and the essence of his being had faded away into nothingness.

The odor of gas intermingled with burnt sancocho and the stench of corpses and vomit. Rafael's dry eyes stung and began to moisten again, this time from a cloud of thick smoke filling the room. A purple fire had erupted on the stove. Crackling sparks caught the wall. Orange flames exploded and shot up toward the ceiling as if they were demons.

Suddenly, Dad's image flashed into Rafael's mind. He was smiling, giving him instructions. While it all seemed surreal, Rafael remembered what he was supposed to do, what he had to do. Dad had seen to that.

Rafael dashed up the stairs two at a time to his bedroom. He noticed the poster on his desk, wondered why it wasn't still on the wall. It seemed his entire life had changed since he started the portrait. A flame burst onto the wall, pushing out a wave of heat. He grabbed his backpack from the closet and ran downstairs, almost tripping in the process.

Impelled by a surge of adrenaline, Rafael bolted out of the house and sprinted through the gate in the courtyard wall and out to the road. He stopped and turned around. The cut glass wedged into the top of the wall reflected the red and orange flames consuming El Retiro. Everything appeared to be electrified, as if lightning had struck.

Rafael spun and ran into the hills without looking back. Dad had shown him the way to Gerónimo Esposito's encampment, said he would be safe with the Freedom Front.

Hours later, as he trudged up clandestine paths in the rainforest, the image of Che Guevara flashed before him. The fire in Che's eyes was spreading—the poster probably reduced to ashes. Someday, Rafael swore, he would complete his portrait and resurrect the revolutionary.

Twenty-four years later, in the summer of 2000, Rafael eluded the Security Police by blending in with the crowd in Guarida City's most popular neighborhood. He stood at the entrance to La Trinchera Public School, shoulder-to-shoulder with people dripping sweat, pushing each other and jostling for position on blacktop streets that melted beneath their feet. He saw with his own eyes an event he had doubted would ever take place.

When Rafael returned to the encampment that evening, he told Gerónimo what he had seen and heard: "Two men with badges carried a large wooden box through the mob. One placed the box on a table in the entrance hall. The other remained in the doorway, raised his arms, and shouted for everyone to form a line. He said they would all get a chance to cast a ballot."

Men and women had lined up. Everyone wanted to vote. For the first time in his life, Rafael saw determined citizens with hopeful expressions. They would not be intimidated by the stifling temperature or reprisals from the Security Police, nor would they allow the reelection of Ignacio Báez, the Corrupt Ones' stooge. He had ruled with an iron hand since the coup drove out Pérez Santo twenty years ago.

Only one person was injured when she attempted to break into a block-long line on which voters had been waiting for hours. "A few fainted from dehydration," he told Gerónimo.

"I hope it's all worth it," Gerónimo said without much conviction. "Let's not be naïve—we've never had a real election."

"I saw a group of international observers arrive, accompanied by reps from the People's Democratic Party and the National Party of Guarida," Rafael insisted. He spoke rapidly, his excitement obvious. "The new People's Popular Party and the press were not far behind, and observers checked voter registration cards."

"Don't forget Sánchez and his so-called PPP blame our elites and foreign capitalists for the country's problems," Gerónimo said. "And he's threatened to nationalize oil. The mass turnout must have frightened them. Probably packing for a quick escape from the island if Sánchez takes over."

Rafael hoped that, for many Guaridans, this would be the first legitimate election in their country's history. Now *their* man would take office and things would change for the better. "Never believed I'd see this day," he said.

Gerónimo laid a hand on his shoulder. "Let's see what Sánchez does if he wins."

A week later, Freedom Front comrades gathered around their campfire. Rafael read aloud press reports in pilfered newspapers: "Members of the Electoral Commission, whose loyalty to the regime had eroded, insist on an accurate count. Claudio Sánchez wins by a large plurality. Báez concedes and disappears."

"Now we'll see what happens," Gerónimo said.

After the official announcement was proclaimed on the radio, Rafael ran down the hills to witness the spontaneous procession filling Guarida City's avenues. He slipped into a crowd that slithered through downtown and made its way to the northern zones, where the middle classes observed with quiet disgust.

Veering into the southern barrios, the spectacle was met by thunderous roars. A continuous cacophony of dissonant celebratory reverberations saturated the city. The jubilation was palpable. The drone of clattering pots and pans, vibrating drums and bongos, screeching whistles, and electronic boom boxes would not let up.

Late in the afternoon the parade returned to the central plaza, where a virtual sea of the national colors—green, gold, black, and red—and euphoric triumphant uproars filled its wide expanse. Sweet fragrances of rum and tobacco drifted through the sultry atmosphere. Litter piled up everywhere.

That night Rafael returned to the encampment and watched glaring fireworks ignite the sky. The firecracker blasts were indistinguishable from gunshots that proclaimed exultant victory. According to radio reports, twenty or so individuals were killed, all members of either the PDP or the NPG. Hundreds more occupants of the small island nation sustained bullet wounds, while people of all ages danced with joy.

"We don't live in a democratic culture," Gerónimo lamented.

Rafael shook his head, his hope for positive change dashed. "I hope this doesn't get out of hand," he said.

In the background people chanted a triumphant mantra: "Claudio, Claudio, CLAUDIO... Long live Guarida... Claudio, Claudio, CLAUDIO... Long live Guarida... Claudio, Claudio, CLAUDIO—"

Part One

"WHAT [THE UNITED STATES] DOES WORST IS UNDERSTAND OTHERS."

~ CARLOS FUENTES

Chapter One

Emmanuel White Vidal had re-read some of his best work and thought he was prepared. When the meeting at the State Department's Bureau of Intelligence and Research got underway, however, it seemed obvious that INR analysts had already made up their minds prior to his testimony.

What did they really want from him? His gut told him it was a set-up. Exactly for what, he did not know.

As the meeting dragged on, he sat back in his chair and endured what he believed were fatuous arguments, distorted by clichés. His mind wandered to the good times he had with his cousin when they were kids. Finally, he could stomach no more. He leaned forward, folded his hands on the table, and interrupted. "Excuse me," he said in the most authoritative voice he could muster, "Claudio Sánchez is no threat to American interests. Let's think outside the box on this one."

Everyone at the meeting turned toward him; their faces exuded incredulity, as if he had told an inappropriate joke. Someone blurted out, "And what do you propose, professor? Sánchez has already cracked down on the opposition. He's

1

expropriated and nationalized private businesses and spews anti-American rhetoric."

Play the role, he thought. Being addressed as professor was amusing. Everyone else called him by his nickname. He was just Manny, an assistant professor who considered himself an experienced student. He glanced around the table at the grim expressions. *They're especially cynical,* he thought, *after last year's tragedy at the World Trade Center.*

Manny took a deep breath and let it out. "We're talking about a tiny Caribbean island that needs our assistance. They held a legitimate election; we should abide by the results. Guarida's oil isn't the only issue. The United States should champion democracy and social justice."

His words seemed to hang in the air. A jet roared as it descended toward Reagan National. Vehicles hummed in the surrounding streets. Sirens blared in the distance. At least sophomores took him seriously, he thought, as he peeked at the Tag Heuer watch Dee gave him when they began living together in the Village.

After Assistant Secretary Adam Stark's brief summation, he thanked the participants, adjourned the meeting, and signaled Manny to remain seated. The INR analysts filed out of the Loy Henderson Conference Room. *Like bees swarming to their hives,* Manny thought, as the drone of their chatter faded into the venerable halls of the Harry S. Truman Building.

Stark closed his notebook and looked at him as if studying Manny's face for a portrait. Relieved that he had shaved that morning, Manny tried to remember the last time he wore a tie. Stark smiled, removed his glasses. "Professor," he said, "I asked you to stay after the meeting so we could talk, just you and me."

Manny crossed his arms and leaned back in his chair, figuring he was in for a harangue over his comments during the meeting. "I was wondering why you asked," he said. He respected Stark, considered him an intellectual attempting to survive inside the Beltway.

"Well then, let's cut to the chase." Stark set his horn-rimmed glasses back on the ridge of his nose. "We'd like you to go down to the University of Guarida for a couple of years. We'll pay your way."

"Are you serious?" Manny's smile was puzzled. What was going on? He felt conflicted. While pleased to be considered important, it seemed as if Stark wanted to manipulate him. "I have obligations at NYU, courses to teach. I don't work for the government and I'm up for tenure." Was Stark making a request, or was it something more?

Stark stood and paced the room. He came up behind Manny and placed a hand on his shoulder, and Manny felt his neck muscles tighten. "When have you known me not to be serious?" Stark removed his hand, and Manny relaxed, shook himself a little as Stark walked back to the head of the table. "We just want a presence at the university. It's a hotbed of activism and anti-Americanism. Our people have difficulty penetrating UG. But I've spoken to Alfredo Cardozo; he'll give you a course to teach. And as a civilian, you'll keep us informed. I'll want you to send communiqués through the embassy."

"I thought you brought me in as a consultant," Manny said. "You heard my views." Palm trees, sunny beaches, and red clay tennis courts flashed through his mind. But he also sensed danger, although he wasn't sure why. "With all due respect, sir, you've got trained operatives and diplomats for that sort of thing."

3

Stark thought for a moment, adjusted his glasses. "Your cousin—"

Manny's heart began to pound, blood rushed into his neck. "Died in a fire nearly thirty years ago, along with my aunt and uncle," he blurted out,

"We've reason to believe he might be alive," Stark said, as if sharing a secret.

Manny was speechless. Could Rafael have survived? Where had he been all these years? Wouldn't his cousin have contacted him? He composed himself, studied Stark. "On what do you base that? Is there evidence?"

"I'll get the report declassified for you."

"Yes, please. If he's alive, I need to know."

Stark looked away and moved to get his notebook. "In any event, this is a chance for you to serve your country. And, of course, this is just between you and me."

Manny considered his options. Perhaps he could inject a modicum of reason into his country's policy toward the island. And the revelation that Rafael might be alive definitely hit a nerve. Yet despite everything, Manny wanted to believe he could maintain his integrity, control his own destiny. "I'm sorry," he began.

Stark cut him off, responding over his shoulder as he left the room. "Call me tomorrow. We want you down there now."

Stark entered his office as he always did—through his private hallway door, which hung unsettlingly ajar. He saw Jack Case sitting in his chair with his feet perched on the desk, reading papers in a thick manila folder. Case seemed to materialize whenever there was a crisis of any sort.

Stark closed the door behind him and walked purposefully toward his desk. *Arrogant bastard,* he thought, but refrained from comment. Screwing around with Case would be like playing with fire; Stark was certain about that.

"How did it go, Adam?" Case closed the folder. He brushed his hand over a crew cut that looked like a landing strip on an aircraft carrier. "Mind if I smoke?"

"Hello, Jack," Stark said as casually as he could. "No smoking in the building. New regulations. How did you get in here?"

Case lit up a Marlboro. "I've got my ways. So, what about our Professor Ivory Tower, eh?"

"What do you know about him?" Stark's tone was polite but on edge. The INR meeting was public knowledge, but not his private conversation with Manny. "Is that why you're here?"

Case patted the folder and slowly read the title. He pronounced every syllable as if he were dictating to a stenographer: *"Controlled Unclassified Information — Confidential — (Executive Order 12958, PL 96-456) — Professor Emmanuel White Vidal, AKA 'Manny' — LIMDIS."*

"I told him it was classified."

"It's only LIMDIS—limited distribution," Case said with a smirk. Stark stared at him, hoping his disdain wasn't evident. "He's published extensively on Caribbean politics and especially Guarida." Case quoted a few titles and dates. Apparently he had memorized Manny's history. "He's pretty respected in academia, for what that's worth. Seems he'd rather be on a tennis court, though. Students love him... a couple of times, literally. That's his bête noir, his vulnerability. And he's got a live-in up in New York. The dossier's pretty complete. It's got his cousin Rafael up in the hills with the Freedom Front. He's been there for quite a while. Of course, you've read all of this."

Several scenarios flashed through Stark's mind. There must be a special reason Case had jumped in. Was he planning something as well? There was no sense in derailing himself by competing with him. Perhaps they could help each other.

"I asked him to spend some time at UG," Stark said. "He could let us know what's happening on campus. It's where everything starts down there. By the way, he tried to appear reluctant. And he says he wants to stay out of politics as he tells us how to conduct our foreign policy."

"Typical academic," Case said.

"He did perk up when I mentioned his cousin." Stark removed his glasses and cleaned them with his handkerchief. "No one knows about my plan."

"We'll keep it that way, Adam. This is just between you and me. Do you think he's on board?"

"I don't know. He's up for tenure at NYU. But I'm pretty sure the piece about his cousin hooked him. He might go down there for a while and nose around."

"Good," Case said. "If he does, we'll keep someone on him. We can use a civilian in-country, someone they'd never connect to us. Sánchez has to be contained. Got to protect the supply lines, eh? Let's see how this plays out. Could be a very convenient link, right?"

"We'll have to be careful." Stark put his glasses back on. He thought of Manny as a bright, independent thinker, but naïve—a Boy Scout. Those qualities were elusive in

Washington, Stark lamented, feeling somewhat jealous. "He'll have to be managed."

"No problem. We'll keep this quiet." Case took a long drag on his Marlboro, smiled, and exuded a billow of smoke. Then he waved his hand in dismissal and exited, leaving the private doorway open.

Stark walked around the desk to the door. He watched Case march away, his heels clicking echoes in the long corridor. After the insufferable fellow disappeared, Stark shut the door and locked it. Then he flipped through his file cabinet and found the folder titled *JACK CASE: RESTRICTED INFORMATION.* He settled into his chair and reviewed its contents.

A few years ago, instead of re-upping in the Marine Corps Intelligence Department where he had served for eight years, Case took a position in one of those agencies that doesn't appear on organization charts—perhaps a private contractor, Stark guessed. He was listed as "Intelligence officer working on national security." He had the highest clearance, but no GS rating. Stark doubted Case had taken the Foreign Service exam.

He slapped the folder shut and returned it to the file cabinet. As he prepared to leave, Stark heard the door lock tumble. The door opened and Case stepped into the office. "Still here?"

"What is this?" Stark said. His blood began to boil.

"Just wanted to say good night, Adam."

"I thought you were gone."

"I'll always be around. By the way, I hope you understand how important your cooperation is to us. People in high places are counting on you."

Stark was startled. What the hell was he getting into? Should have used his Ivy League credentials to make big money. After all, he had joined the Foreign Service so he could be a diplomat at State, not get embroiled in covert ops like at the Agency. Public service was supposed to be about serving the common good. Yet here he was plotting with this shady character in the name of national security. Having to deal with Case was like conspiring with the devil. And to add insult to injury, Stark felt guilty about bringing in a non-player like Manny.

"Yes, I think I understand. But I don't appreciate your intrusion into my office." Stark removed his glasses and rubbed the bridge of his nose. "I'm leaving now," he said, and motioned to Case. "Let's go."

They walked out together. Case held out his hand; Stark shook it reluctantly. At the outside door, they parted and went their separate ways.

ᒡᔕ✑Chapter Two✑ᒇᔕ

A t 5:30 p.m., Manny walked up 23rd Street through George Washington University on his way to Georgetown. Twenty minutes later, he ducked into one of the specialty shops at the corner of M Street and Wisconsin. He bought Dee a small jar of chocolate-covered espresso beans, the kind they both loved.

He strolled into the lobby of the Georgetown Inn and grabbed his valise from behind the concierge's counter. He had already checked out before the meeting. He stopped in at the hotel's first-floor restaurant and ordered a tuna salad sandwich. While he downed it along with a large cup of black coffee, he thought about his exchange with Stark.

No way would Manny do the bidding of the government. U.S. policy toward Guarida was wrong. Besides, his appearance before the tenure committee was scheduled for next semester. He couldn't rely on Dean Rhoades. It would be complicated to postpone the delicate procedure and, without the dean's vote, his career could very well be on the line. He shouldn't jeopardize his chances.

A thought tugged at him from deep within. Rafael might be alive—Manny's only remaining family, his only connection to his roots in his mother's country of origin. That was certainly something to think about. Even before meeting

9

with Stark, he had been anxious, although he wasn't sure why, about the course his life had been taking.

Maybe, despite all the risks, getting away for a while would be a good thing.

Around 7:00 p.m., he jumped into his Saturn L100. In five minutes, he was crossing the Key Bridge. He listened to a Manitas de Plata CD on the drive up to New York, tried to slip away from both the traffic and his problems. The riffs and twangs of the classical guitar soothed him immediately.

Watching a long line of semis on I-95, Manny thought about his parents. Their lives, as well as his charmed existence, had ended abruptly when a truck ran a light and side-swiped their MR2, killing them both. His heart began to pump harder and he felt a shiver run through his body. He missed them. How he had loved them.

His dad, an agnostic Jew, had taught Manny to be wary of the conflicts caused by religious fervor. He had counseled his son with Talmudic wisdom: *If I'm not for myself, who will be for me? If I am for myself only, what am I? If not now, when?*

Perhaps as significantly, his dad had taught Manny tennis, a sport that would be a part of him for the rest of his life. *In tennis,* Dad would say, *you try to impose your will. Play the ball, don't let it play you. Try to control each point, but accept a bad bounce or an error or your opponent's better shot.* Manny had learned from his father that elements like the wind or sun can come into play, as can a mistaken tactic or strategy, and he had learned to minimize chance and luck as much as possible. *Make choices and live with the consequences.*

As for her own religion of origin, Manny's mother used to refer to the Catholic Church in Guarida as "The

Church of Pedophilia." She had hated the proselytizing and instilling of fear in children, capturing them for the rest of their lives. She would say that Jesus championed the poor and downtrodden, loved his enemies, and would turn the other cheek in the face of harm. He would have been appalled by the corrupted institutionalization of religion, she had insisted, and its use as a justification for conflict and war.

Manny grew up thinking of himself as a free and independent thinker, a bit different from his more conservative peers. His philosophy of life was straightforward: good choices produce good consequences; bad choices produce bad consequences. At least that was the way it was supposed to work. He began to wonder whether he was making choices or whether the ball was playing him, so to speak.

The stop-and-go traffic gradually became a six-lane speedway as the city lights came into view. Manny sped up and tried cruise control for a while. Then he had to slow down again as he approached I-78 and the Holland Tunnel. Traffic backed up in downtown Manhattan as it emerged from the tunnel. Manny came to a dead stop. His eyes teared up as he inched toward the corner of Erickson Street and Varick Place across from Tribeca Park, the spot where his parents were killed. The incident was out of anyone's control.

Visions of the crash raced through Manny's mind. Although the report indicated only that the truck ran a light and hit his parents' car, he imagined the blood and gore. He could almost feel their pain. He wanted to believe that his parents had died instantly, but other possibilities haunted him. In his mind's eye, he saw his father try to steer away, heard his mother cry out. The truck's brakes screeched. Heavy metal slammed into the tiny sports car, rolling it over, slicing it into pieces, crushing the human beings within.

The thoughts racked his brain, made him feverish. Manny shook his head to clear his mind, only to have the visualizations repeated. The images played over and over like the nightmare that had disturbed his sleep since the crash.

The driver in the car behind him blasted his horn. Manny looked up, startled, and the shock of that moment produced a mystical revelation, a lucid response to his questions. Suddenly he knew what he had to do. It was as if he had no choice. He would call tomorrow and accept Stark's offer. He had to find out what had happened to Rafael.

Bleecker Street was quiet when Manny arrived home at one in the morning. He snuck into the bedroom and slipped into bed without waking Dee.

Though he tried, he could not fall asleep. After lying in a state of semi-consciousness through the night, Manny tiptoed into the kitchen at six and prepared a pot of Blue Mountain. While the coffee brewed, he picked up the *New York Times* from the steps outside his brownstone and glanced at the headlines. *Shit, more of the same,* he thought. He dropped the paper on the living room table, an antique oak he had purchased in a Village garage sale. Through the window, a dark haze obscured the light of dawn.

"Morning, hon." Dee sauntered into the kitchen wearing Manny's terrycloth bathrobe. "Want some breakfast?" She rustled up a couple of toasted bagels with cheese and marmalade.

He kissed his girlfriend on the forehead. "Thanks, Dee."

She poured cups of coffee, and they sat down at the counter that separated the kitchen from the living room. While they ate, they made small talk about the weather and current events. Manny finished his bagel and wiped his mouth with a napkin.

"How was DC?" she asked.

"It was all right."

He grabbed his cup, retreated to the living room, and plopped down at the end of the table. He couldn't get what had happened in Washington out of his mind. Officially, he had neither accepted nor refused Stark's request. Yet he knew that, soon, he would be basking in Guarida's shining sun. *We want you down there now* echoed in his head. Manny looked out the window into the haze. The leaves had begun to turn on the sparse trees that lined the streets of Greenwich Village.

Dee remained behind the counter, rinsed and dried the breakfast plates, too few for the dishwasher. She hummed a tune that sounded like the one about being on your own with no direction home and all that existential stuff. The aroma of the freshly brewed Blue Mountain filled the apartment. She peered over at Manny, smiled, and whispered, "You're like a rolling stone."

Her sotto voce rendition made Manny think about how Bob Dylan's artistic genius captured the mood of the sixties. He watched the tall and limber woman lean over the sink, liked the way Dee's long blonde hair framed her face and fell to her shoulders and down her back. She could have been a flower child.

"Got the espresso beans you like."

"Thanks. Want some?" She picked up the jar.

13

"Not now." Manny stared through the window, this time at nothing in particular. The street light seemed to flicker in the haze.

She placed the jar back on the counter and said, "What's wrong, hon?"

Her Texas drawl seemed more pronounced for some reason. Manny turned back to the table and lifted the first section of the paper. "Look at these headlines, babe." He smacked the back of his hand against the paper and read: *"Nine-Eleven Anniversary Ceremonies in New York, Pennsylvania, and Washington."* Then he dropped the paper on the table, almost knocking over his cup. "Goddamn terrorists. It's been a year, and I still see planes crashing into the towers."

Dee pulled the bathrobe around her waist and tightened the sash. "Gotta let it go, hon."

He sipped the last drops of coffee from his cup. "Want me to put the plates away?"

"Nah." She dried and placed the plates on the shelf above the sink and came out of the kitchen with the washcloth in her hand. She took the seat next to Manny, dropped the cloth on the table, and pulled her hair back. "Let's talk," she said.

Manny had thrown on his warm-up suit and tennis shoes sans socks, and hadn't shaved or combed his hair. Dee once told him she liked the look, it turned her on. But now something else was on her mind.

"What do you want to talk about?" he said.

"Y'know damn well." She picked up the washcloth.

"I really don't have the faintest idea." He picked up the sports section.

"Jeez, you always wanted to talk." She placed the washcloth over the newspaper. "Now you go out and play tennis till you drop."

"It's my way of focusing my mind, Dee. There's only the ball, the geometry of the court—nothing else. No troubles, no past, no future, only the ball. It's like a form of meditation, you know?" Manny noticed that the street light was off. The haze was lifting. "I know why you're upset. I haven't been myself. Even before Stark flew me to Washington, I've felt anxious. I get pissed-off too easily. It's like I'm treading on the edge of a razor. Ever since Mom and Dad…"

Dee put her arm around his shoulders and gave him a hug. "Come here," she said, trying to pull him close.

"I need to get off the edge," Manny said as if he were talking to himself. He gave Dee a weak hug and pulled away. It was hard to make sense of things anymore. His parents were gone, international terrorism had wreaked havoc in his hometown, and the Washington bureaucrats treated him as if his ideas were irrelevant. But they kept inviting him anyway, as if they wanted him to perform like some kind of puppet, for God's sake.

Manny put his head in his hands. He needed to search for meaning, for some sense of order. He compared himself to Larry Darrell, sensing that his path would be as difficult as it was for Somerset Maugham's character.

"Do you love me?" Dee asked.

"What? We've been together for two years. You know how I feel." He did love her, but didn't want to say so at that moment, although he didn't know why. Maybe he didn't like the pressure.

"Say it."

"Didn't I just say it?"

"Not really. I worked my ass off to come up here and be with you."

"You hated the go-sees. You called modeling a meat market, right? And you wanted to return to your studies, get a real job."

"All right, you're a fabulous teacher and I'm so lucky to be working at NYU—at the great Bobst Library."

"Well?" he dropped the sports section on the washcloth and threw his hands in the air.

"I just need to hear it from you, darlin'. I'm not twenty anymore."

"Of course I love you, Dee. But I've got to make some decisions. I'm going to Guarida for a semester or two. Things are happening there. I need to go soon, maybe next week."

"Sonofabitch, so that's it. First I've heard. What happened in Washington? Why don't you let me in, like always, huh? There's got to be more to it. Come on."

"I was told my cousin might be alive."

She grimaced in disbelief and shook her head. "You said he died in a fire."

"I know, but if it's true, he'd be my only living relative."

Her voice softened. "Who told you he's alive?"

"The guy who runs INR. He said it's classified."

"Classified?"

16

"I don't know why. He said he'd get the report for me." It seemed to Manny that finding Rafael would be a key piece of a living jigsaw puzzle. Putting that piece into place would allow all the others to fit, to make sense.

"If your cousin really is alive, where has he been? And what about your tenure—what will leaving now do to your career? What about us?"

"I want you to come with me." He really did, although a part of him was excited about a solo adventure.

Her skeptical look said she wasn't sure he meant it. She folded her arms over her chest and said, "I don't know if I could get the time off. And I'm not sure I want to go to Guarida. Actually, I don't know why anyone would, except for a vacation—maybe a week or two but definitely not a year." She leaned back, studied him. "I thought we were going to think about getting engaged as soon as you got tenure."

"We'll sit down later, when I get back. I really want you to come down there with me, Dee. Think about it, okay? I'll call Washington later." Manny checked the Tag Heuer. "Right now, I've got to get some work done." He grabbed his book bag, made sure he gave her a soulful kiss, and dashed out the door.

Washington Square South was a short walk from Manny's apartment on Bleecker. He entered the atrium that led into Bobst, went downstairs, and found a spot in a dimly lit corner of the stacks in the section housing texts on regions of the world. Scanning the vast number of books on the shelves, he thought about how the Internet had the potential for producing all this information instantaneously.

17

He flipped open to a familiar chapter in one of the books he had written and skipped through the introduction. Maybe the printed page would reveal something, provide insight into his situation. He read his own description of Guarida: *Spanish for "safe haven" or "hide-out," a coral atoll located off the coast of Venezuela that served as a refuge for pirates who controlled the southwestern Caribbean in the early seventeenth century...* Envisioning a tall ship moored off a palm-lined coast, he looked up at the exposed pipes painted the same drab gray as the ceiling.

Manny loved the Caribbean climate, the warmth of its gentle sea breezes, and the brilliance of its sun. His eyes focused on the colorless monotony of the floor, he thought about his previous research, conducted in part because of his mother. She had told him the story of Guillermo, his wife Verónica, and their son Rafael. She suspected the Security Police were behind their deaths. Guillermo had been active in the Freedom Front. Could his cousin have escaped? Surely Stark knew more than he had revealed at their meeting.

"Hi, Professor Vidal—I mean Manny. How're you today?"

Manny's pulse quickened. Holy shit, did she glue on that t-shirt? No bra underneath. Damn, these students became more voluptuous every year. The Free Love Generation—a bunch of Sirens, as far as Manny was concerned. His tryst with an undergrad flashed in his mind: young flesh, supple roundness. Her eagerness, complete abandon, the heat, oh yes, oh no... *Stop thinking this way!* he told himself. "Just fine, Barbara." He couldn't help staring at her breasts. *Continue reading, for God's sake.*

18

Barbara's perfume seemed to call for his attention. Only twice had he succumbed to the temptation. Neither tryst was particularly fulfilling in retrospect. *Jesus, better get back into the book,* he thought. *Discipline!*

But Manny couldn't read. He tried to focus on something else, recalled how the Bureau of Intelligence and Research analysts picked his brain. Although a bunch of bureaucrats, INR was challenging and exhilarating. He peeked at Barbara. The brazen young woman was ogling him. His pulse rose. He felt blood rush through his veins, engorging his sex. *Read, think,* he commanded himself, but it wasn't working.

Barbara closed her book and flashed a seductive smile. "Let's get out of here," she said.

So damned obvious, Manny thought. How did these kids get this way? Maybe just one more time.

He got up. She took his hand and led him to the end of the aisle, hidden from view between the stacks. She moved close to him, and her breasts brushed against his chest. He grabbed her shoulders, pulled her closer, and planted a kiss on her lips. They parted, and her tongue probed the ridge of his mouth. Delicious, but he moved away. *Do not do this,* he kept telling himself.

She grabbed the bottom of her tee-shirt and pulled it up to her neck, rolling it like a body condom. Her young breasts sprung out, nipples pointed at Manny like weapons.

"Let's do it here," she whispered, as if making love with a professor in the university library was the most natural thing in her world.

Manny was more than ready, but he pulled away and stepped back. He shook his head and took a deep breath. "I'm sorry," he said. "I shouldn't be doing this."

"Come on, big boy." She was appealing, but desperate. A hurt look distorted her face.

"You're a beautiful young woman, Barbara, and smart. Focus on your studies," he managed, exercising self-control that had eluded him in the past. Instantly proud of himself, he knew it was the right thing to do, the correct choice.

"Shit!" she said as she rolled down her tee-shirt. "Maybe some other time, huh?" Barbara flashed an affected smile and walked away. Manny felt relieved.

As he gathered his books, he thought about Dee, hoped she would change her mind, and accompany him in Guarida. He sensed, however, that his decision to go would put their relationship on shaky ground. In fact, he was risking everything to follow an impulse—get away, find his roots, his family, himself. It was yet another choice he had to make.

If not now, when?

ᒯᐧᐧ Chapter Three ᕽᑔ

Manny stepped out of the air-conditioned plane that he had boarded at Kennedy. His body thawed as the moist heat engulfed him. He slipped on his sunglasses and looked around.

On the ground, everything seemed to slow down to a meandering pace. No one seemed in a rush to get anywhere, do anything. Those waiting on line blithely stepped and swayed to the intricate salsa beat that provided a background for their staccato-style Spanish.

Manny inhaled the aromas of black beans, rum, and garbage that floated through air so thick you could cut it with a knife. A strange feeling came over him, as if he had morphed into a different person: someone of grander individuality, of greater significance. Was it because he stood head and shoulders above his smaller, darker, and thinner Guaridan counterparts?

On the one hand, Manny wanted to fit in, be considered a local, or at least not stand out like a tourist. On the other hand, he enjoyed his status as an American in the Third World. How could he reconcile the two impulses?

He thought about how Dee insisted that he needed space. She said she would join him later if she could, and she promised she would miss him during his absence. He wished she had come along. He had practically begged her to come. He sighed. Maybe it was better to be alone on this sabbatical, which he thought of as an adventure, a pursuit of meaning. He'd be providing a service to his government, on his own terms, of course, while searching for Rafael. He'd also have a chance to enjoy life in the Caribbean and get some tennis in as well. He had friends at Campo Alegre Tennis Club.

After he cleared Customs, a gauntlet of drivers offered their services. One approached him and said, "Where to?" He reached for Manny's briefcase. Manny stiffened; he was aware of the danger. *Piratas* were not registered cabbies. Some of them robbed and, at times, murdered their fares. Others were just trying to make some extra cash.

He yanked his briefcase out of the pirata's clutch, then walked into a flurry of offers from other drivers. Declining their solicitations, he proceeded to the luggage counter, where he was met by a chauffeur holding a card with WHITE VIDAL printed in large letters. He felt relieved. His baggage and tennis gear appeared after a long wait. The driver hauled his belongings outside to an embassy limousine.

As Manny followed along, he spotted a man eying him from behind his newspaper. The stranger was an atypically tall, wiry individual with a trimmed mustache, well-dressed, a businessman perhaps. Manny shook his head. Probably nothing; locals had a habit of sizing up foreigners, especially at the airport.

Manny got into the limo. When he looked back, the man was gone. He felt a bit foolish, reminded himself he shouldn't let his imagination run away with him. Yet, he was reassured.

The black Cadillac squeezed through narrow streets built for much smaller vehicles. Some streets would not allow the limo to pass. They took a circuitous route to a hotel in the downtown business district of Guarida City.

After settling in, Manny walked over to the UG campus. It was cordoned off by uniformed officers on its periphery; they would not let anyone through the gates. One of the officers informed Manny that students had taken over buildings earlier that day. No one had expected the shut-down.

"Why don't you go in?" he asked one of the Security Police.

"The university's off-limits to us," the officer replied, confirming what Manny already knew—university autonomy enjoyed a long-standing tradition in Guarida, as in the rest of Latin America. But he was still impressed to see it in action.

"We rarely go in," the guard said. "The students act up every so often. The protests will die down in a few days. We won't let it spread beyond campus."

"What do they want?"

"They're demanding an increase in government subsidies, railing against military involvement in classes, and denouncing government corruption."

"It's just the students?"

"Sympathetic faculty and support staff join in. Their salary checks are never on time."

"Do these things turn violent?"

"Only when the *encapuchados*—off-campus anarchists donning hoods and the Freedom Front—infiltrate the demonstrations. Then there are Molotov cocktails, rocks, and many broken windows."

23

Manny could hear the ruckus. Remarkably, there were no serious injuries, but UG was closed for the time being. "How often does this kind of thing occur?"

The officer, frustrated with Manny's barrage of questions, backed off, wouldn't talk any more.

Better to travel hopefully than to arrive, he thought. Robert Louis Stevenson had a point, but Manny had no regrets. Since the university was closed, he'd use his free time to find an affordable apartment. State's stipend was reasonable but not overly generous. He was eager to get out of the small hotel in the business district, where he felt like a transient.

Typical of early February, the temperature was in the mid-eighties. A few ominous-looking clouds floated over the hills, propelled by zephyrs that emanated from the Caribbean Sea. If rain came, it would be a tropical deluge for no longer than an hour. It was a good day to search for an apartment.

Another embassy limousine, this time driven by a dark-skinned Guaridan named Oscar, transported Manny. The first stop was a penthouse in the affluent zone. Oscar informed him that most of the FSOs liked such places, for a price of U.S. $1,000 a month. Guaridans loved to rent to Americans because they always paid on time, he said.

"But there are apartments for half that price in the southern section near the Pérez Santo project, the one the locals call Cell Block Thirteen, or simply the Block. Most of the Americans don't like to go down there," Oscar added.

"Let's take a look." Manny longed to be close to the people. He thought he might find something that was missing in his life, an authenticity that would make him feel more complete.

Oscar's wistful smile reflected in the rearview mirror. Manny interpreted this as an indication he was on the right track. Oscar was perceptive, Manny thought.

The southern section bustled with activity. Specialty shops lined the avenue: beef and poultry shops, liquor stores, and a general *abasto* for groceries.

Manny pointed to a few men in civilian clothing with sawed-off shotguns sticking out of their boots. "Who are they?"

"Private guards," Oscar said. "All the stores employ them. Don't pay any attention to them. For the most part, they're for show."

"Are there many robberies?"

"No. Believe me, the guards just stand around, like a deterrent. Of course, there are occasional incidents, but nothing to worry about."

Manny wanted to believe him, but had his doubts. He'd had enough of the American gun culture to be wary. Not much he could do about it, though.

He noticed a fruit store where people congregated. They sipped juices and engaged in conversation—a friendly place. He stepped out of the limo and sniffed the fresh produce, thought he could distinguish the pineapple and mango aromas from the rest. Forget the guns, this was the real Guarida—a tropical paradise!

"This place is called La Ciruela," Oscar said. "It's very popular. I can show you an apartment in the building next door."

"That would be great." Manny was fascinated with the location. They passed a guard and entered Las Palmas, a medium-sized building of five floors.

Oscar took him up to a third-floor apartment. With a small sitting area, a kitchenette, and an ample bedroom, it also offered a great view of the hills and sat right above La Ciruela. Oscar told him a short walk down the street would bring him to a nice restaurant. "The food is great at El Salón de la Parrilla and the price is right," he said with pride.

"I'll take it. What now?"

"Usually, you'd have to meet with the owner and sign a complex contract. We Guaridans are so formal when it comes to paperwork—reams of papers, stamps, and authorizations—and it doesn't mean a thing at the end of the day."

Manny had no interest in dealing with the bureaucratic crap. He raised his hands and asked, "Do I have to go through all that?"

"Embassy attorneys have worked out the details. All you have to do is sign the contract. Then they'll give you the keys and that's it."

"I appreciate your assistance. Thanks."

"You're quite welcome." Oscar locked the door behind them and then locked the wrought-iron gate. "You know," he said, "your FSO colleagues want an American colonial with a yard, a picket fence, and an armed guard at their gates in the middle of the Third World."

Manny laughed with embarrassment. "Well, you all have guards," he said. But there was a difference. He was ashamed of American behavior abroad; his countrymen acted as if they ruled the world. More than once, he had observed an American tourist shouting heatedly, as if the louder he yelled, the more comprehensible he would be to a national who knew no English.

Manny didn't want to dwell on that depressing topic. And he had more important things on his mind. "How can I find someone in Guarida?" he asked.

"Try the phone book," Oscar said, "or Public Records if the person isn't listed. I'll show you where it is."

Before unpacking his suitcases, Manny went down to the fruit store. Its proprietor, Paulo Ferreira, told him that La Ciruela had the sweetest produce in the Caribbean. The store, perfumed by the aroma of fruits stacked on wooden counters, was a bustling community. People rubbed shoulders while sipping freshly squeezed mango, papaya, guava, passion fruit, or one of the many other tropical delights. Manny sampled a small cup of *guanábana*. Paulo Ferreira wasn't exaggerating.

If this was the Garden of Eden, where was the snake?

The next day, Manny opened the country-wide telephone book resting on the table in his sitting room. Although not a common name, it seemed odd that there wasn't a single listing for Vidal. The Office of Public Records would have an address, he hoped. Thanks to Oscar, he knew it was located downtown, several blocks from the central plaza. He had already observed that it wasn't in a desirable area.

When he arrived at the old run-down building, the clerk—an officious petty official with a large paunch and droopy eyes—sat half asleep at a desk strewn with discolored papers. The office walls needed a fresh coat of paint. Filing cabinets were dusty. And the air-conditioner stuck in a small window sounded like the end of a broken record.

The clerk gazed at Manny through red eyes. Manny made his request. Without another word, the clerk sighed and began filling in a form.

"Excuse me?" Manny said after many minutes.

No answer.

Eventually, without looking up, the clerk pushed a small pile of papers across his desk. He said nothing. It took Manny twenty minutes to complete the forms, sign them, and hand them to the clerk, who put his hand on top of the pile. Finally, after a brief run-through, the clerk insisted that there were no records on file for any Rafael Vidal. Nothing for Guillermo Vidal or Verónica Gutiérrez de Vidal either. *Strange,* Manny thought. It seemed as if his family had been expunged from Guaridan history.

"Please, would you take another look?" he asked the clerk.

"Up yours," the clerk replied. "What more do you want? They don't pay me enough for this shit."

Manny took out a few pesos, offered them to the clerk.

"Won't even cover my bar bill, friend," the clerk muttered while raking in the cash.

Manny put down a few more bills and said, "I really can't afford more than this, sir. Please find the records I asked for, okay?"

The clerk shuffled papers around on his desk, then got up and ambled over to his file cabinet. He opened a drawer, glanced in, and flipped through the folders. He pulled one out, looked at it, looked at Manny, and then dropped it back into the drawer and slammed it shut. "No, nothing in here," he said.

Manny was frustrated by the stonewalling but thought he saw a hint of recognition in the clerk's expression. "May I take a look?"

The clerk shuffled back to his desk, opened a drawer, and pulled out a gun. It looked like a revolver, the kind of six-shooter used in cowboy movies.

Manny stepped back. "Wait a minute," he blurted out.

"Just get the hell out of here. I've taken too much of your gringo bullshit already. I've had enough. Just walk out, and I won't shoot a hole through your head."

"Please, for God's sake, I'm just trying to find my cousin. I mean you no harm."

"There are no records," the clerk responded. Then he spun the gun barrel and inspected its chambers. "Plenty of lead, though."

Manny raised his hands above his head. "Please," he begged, "be reasonable."

"I'll show you what's reasonable." He pointed the gun directly at Manny's chest. "Walk out of here while you still can."

Manny turned, stepped quickly to the door, and departed without comment, shaking as he hurried away. The guy might have been serious.

Manny had better luck at the public library, where he found an *El Nacional* article on microfiche dated Saturday, March 13, 1976. It reported an electrical fire that had destroyed El Retiro, the family's estate. Two bodies, presumably Rafael's mother and father, were found charred beyond recognition. The finding gave him a glint of hope. After the fiasco in Public Records, he valued any sort of information, no matter how minimal.

His mother's story played over and over in Manny's mind. She had left Guarida with her American husband. Her brother and his family had perished in a fire. She suspected foul play. Her brother was involved with the Freedom Front, which had criticized the Pérez Santo regime. The Security Police would not have tolerated that manner of free speech.

Only two bodies were found. Could Rafael have escaped the fire? Stark said he might be alive.

Manny asked the librarian to print copies of the *El Nacional* article. She looked over the microfiche, and her expression changed. She became more serious, as if she were calculating a response. "No sir, we can't do that. Sorry."

"Why not?" Manny was reaching the end of his rope, his nerves wearing thin.

"Library rules."

He was shocked—more resistance. What was going on? If his cousin was alive, why hadn't he contacted him? Perhaps the Freedom Front had provided Rafael refuge up in the hills. Maybe that explained why no one would talk about his family, or El Retiro. Manny knew the Front conducted forays from their base camp, raiding government arms depots and occasionally joining university protests. Despite the danger, he had to explore the hills when he got the chance.

Now he was even more determined to find Rafael. And maybe Stark could supply the information he said he would declassify.

☙Chapter Four❧

The university re-opened after the demonstration ran its course. "These things never last more than a few days," Alfredo Cardozo said when he showed Manny around campus.

"Doesn't seem to be much damage," Manny said. To him, UG seemed like an oasis in the midst of the city. Its tree-lined paths crisscrossed through gardens. The buildings that housed academic departments and classrooms were surrounded by open-air hallways. He immediately felt at home.

Cardozo introduced Manny to a sociologist whose all-black attire made him look like Zorro without the mask. The man shook his hand and asked, "You with the CIA?"

Was Zorro serious? Manny couldn't tell. He shook his head and laughed.

"You're still fighting the Civil War, aren't you?" said a historian with a bushy red beard and a broad smile. Manny faked a grin in response; he was becoming irritated.

An anthropologist who happened to be the spitting image of Indiana Jones joined in and proclaimed, "American Empire's going the way of Rome, isn't it?"

Even if the provocations contained an element of truth, Manny wouldn't take the bait. He said, "I'm here to learn about Guarida, my friends." Their resentment swelled around him. Would the students be as paranoid as their mentors?

"Watch out in class," Zorro cautioned. "Our young people are not as civil and urbane as your new colleagues. They'll squeeze the living daylights out of you."

I will not be provoked, Manny swore to himself. Students loved to challenge authority and expose charlatans—like Zorro, perhaps. Professors should know better than to generalize on prejudiced assumptions. "Thanks for the warning," he said. "I'm aware of how politicized the university is."

"This is where all our revolutions start," the historian added. "At times it's unsafe to tread on our hallowed grounds."

"In this course," Manny said as he began his first class, "we'll analyze the lasting effects of colonialism, the excesses of capitalism, the strictures of communism, and the search for an elusive third path." He paused, looked over the group. They seemed eager and his spirits rose. "The pattern of neo-colonialism has taken on an economic dimension that divides the globe into haves and have-nots. And the have-nots are stuck in a dependent relationship. Guarida, for example, sells its oil to the United States at a good price. But after it's refined, the big oil companies make a lot more. While Guarida appears to prosper, it still has difficulty affording the commodities it must import. Can anyone explain why this is the case?"

"There has been plenty of corruption in Guarida," a student named Héctor said. He was clad in army fatigues.

"Past governments have stolen petrodollars. Our corrupt leaders were in bed with the leaders of powerful countries and businesses. And when economics alone were insufficient to maintain the asymmetrical relationships, then the big powers sent in troops to secure their interests."

"Can you offer examples, Héctor?" Manny said.

"U.S. intervention in the Middle East, Vietnam, Central America, the Caribbean—the list goes on and on..." Héctor spoke in a matter-of-fact tone of voice.

"What about Guarida?" Manny attempted to steer discussion back to the original question.

"As long as we've got oil, we'll be safe." Nicolás was dressed in a shirt and tie but no jacket. Most of the students nodded in agreement. "Guarida's a rich country with large amounts of petroleum deposits, although they're offshore and need refining," Nicolás continued.

"Aren't there ideological reasons for the interventions?" María Pilar asked. She flipped her pen between her thumb and forefingers.

"Good point," Héctor said. "There are ideological rationalizations. Anti-communism and this new war on terrorism are just covers. You'll never convince me that the U.S. cares about promoting democracy or human rights. They have their own interests, and these big powers will support dictatorships when it is convenient. American-made weapons flowed into the hands of Báez and Pérez Santo before him. President Sánchez is trying to do something about all this."

"Hasn't the U.S. contributed more in aid for development than any other country in the world?" Manny knew the answer to his question, but he wanted to see how his students would respond. He was still annoyed by Zorro and his cohorts; he wanted his students to understand the complexity of international relations, rather than reduce analysis to simplistic conclusions.

"With all due respect, professor, as a percentage of GDP, the aid flowing from the U.S. is very small. And I might add," Jorge said, "that it is always designated to countries that possess something the U.S. wants—either a specific resource or product or a market or an alliance. You know, something that will benefit the U.S."

Nicolás blurted, "All countries seek their own self-interest."

Manny could see that the class was divided between a minority who supported the government and a majority who opposed it. These students represented the political vanguard. *Their thinking might reveal where the country is going,* Manny thought. And it seemed to be on a dangerous path.

"I'm not saying it's wrong for a country to seek its own interests," Héctor said. "I just don't buy the camouflage, the holier-than-thou bull crap for pure and simple Imperialism."

Manny noted the change in expression on the faces of several students. They knit their brows and shook their heads, seeming annoyed by Héctor's domination of the discussion. Manny, too, would have liked a more inclusive debate, but he stuck to his Socratic method while calling on others to participate.

"We live in a democracy. I support Sánchez," Héctor replied.

"So do I," María Pilar said. She wore a simple white blouse and slacks, and her dark hair was pulled back from her round face and twisted in a knot. "No system is perfect."

"We're not here to take sides and engage in political battles," Manny said. Recognizing he was in danger of losing control of the class, he tried a different approach. "Is there a third path, one that avoids the excesses of market greed as well as the oppression of authoritarianism? Could there be a path that's neither capitalism nor communism, perhaps? One in which developing countries can compete with developed nations in order to reduce the inequities of the have-nots? Or are we doomed to a future in which the poor will continue to get poorer as the rich get richer? A future of continued violence and warfare as countries jockey for position and strategic advantage? Or, might it not be in all of our best interests to promote development and peace?"

Now the students appeared to be considering Manny's questions, as if he had presented something new and perhaps exciting. María Pilar said, "It would be nice if such alternatives were real. Right now we've got a president who searches for an independent path. He's trying to address our problems."

Héctor nodded in agreement, as did several others. But Nicolás and his group demurred. "This country is going to explode," he said.

The discussion raged on. Manny could see that there would be no closure. Then the students began to close their notebooks, look up at the clock, collect their things, and shift in their seats. *A universal phenomenon,* Manny thought.

"I can see that you're ready to go," he said. "For next class, compare Galeano's assertion that Imperialists suck the blood out of Latin American veins and Vargas Llosa's vehement critique of theories that blame anyone but Latin Americans for their own problems."

This will be a challenging semester, Manny thought.

35

He was relieved—not because the class had ended, but because he felt a sense of fulfillment. He had engaged his students. They were beginning to think outside the box. And the obstacles he faced in finding Rafael, being away from Dee, and working for Stark were on the back burner, at least while he was in the classroom.

The students filed through the door, and María Pilar paused at the door to ask if he would attend the convocation. "Sánchez is going to speak in a half hour," she said.

"Sure," he said, and María and Jorge led Manny to the auditorium, where the president of Guarida was scheduled to open the academic year.

Claudio Sánchez arrived at UG in the midst of heightened security. Guarida Security Police formed a perimeter around the autonomous campus. It was off-limits to them. Sánchez was accompanied to the auditorium by four personal bodyguards.

University officials, concerned that this speech not be marred by dissenters' protests, clustered with University Safety Patrol guards. The students pushed their way toward the front seats, and Manny went along with them. He was excited: he would be in the presence of Sánchez, hear him up close for the first time.

Sánchez stepped to the podium to enthusiastic applause and a few hisses. But, for the most part, the president was well-received by a mass of true-believing supporters. After acknowledging his pleasure at being on campus, he spoke about needed reforms in health care delivery, educational opportunities, and a stronger economy. As he developed these points, he became agitated, waving his arms above his head and drawing out syllables in the traditional style of Latin

American orators. He praised the UG for being a source of innovation and asked for support for his social revolution. He would rid the country of the Corrupt Ones, use the national patrimony—oil—to benefit the masses, and chart an independent course for Guarida. Manny was impressed by the passion Sánchez exhibited in his idealistic articulation of his reform program.

The crowd roared. Manny looked around, observing that enthusiasm for the president was not universal. There were expressions of incredulity, and even hostility, on some faces. A few students laughed sarcastically.

The president diverged into a lengthy diatribe about his humble origins in Cell Block Thirteen. He spoke of his faithful friend and closest advisor, Juan Carlos Guerrero, his catcher on the Block baseball team. "He gave me the signals, but I made the throws," Sánchez said. He then went on and on about shady characters like El Gordo, who played for a rival team and whose career path in and out of the Retén was like a revolving door. Six-two, two-hundred-pound Gordito, as only Sánchez called him, could have made the majors if a life of crime had not claimed the big man, said the president, in order to illustrate the misfortune of life in the Block. "Gordito was a great ballplayer, but few of us make it out of there."

Héctor, who sat in the row behind Manny, leaned over and whispered, "Guerrero's family was prominent until Pérez Santo hanged his grandfather. Juan Carlos grew up with Claudio. They fixed games and bet against their own team."

"What?" Manny said, surprised. "He bet against himself?"

"Everyone knows," Héctor said. Corruption is the norm down here. Sánchez is clever, but his signal became a joke."

"What signal?" Manny asked.

"Claudio would make the sign of the cross three times across his chest," Héctor said, "right before throwing a game. Pretty obvious, no?"

Jorge turned around from his seat next to María Pilar and said, "Knock it off, Héctor. Claudio's our president now. Show some respect." His look was menacing.

"I support him," Héctor said with a broad smile.

María Pilar, who sat next to Manny, gave Héctor a dirty look. "Tell him how Claudio coached Little League, how the kids loved him, you asshole."

The president's human, Manny thought, *a product of the local culture. And just like all politicians, his life is under a magnifying glass.*

After the speech, Manny tried to work his way toward the president. But Sánchez was surrounded by an impenetrable ring of sycophants. As Juan Carlos extricated himself from the crowd, he passed next to Manny, who availed himself of the opportunity to state how impressed he was with Sánchez's remarks. Juan Carlos seemed pleased. Cardozo had introduced him to the American professor.

"Do you think you could arrange a meeting?" Manny managed to get in as Juan Carlos walked past him. He wanted to conduct an interview with the president, speak with him one-on-one. This was an opportunity to see what he was really like and to understand his political perspective. And, Manny might even be able to enlist his support in searching for his cousin. If he could work it in, he would ask about finding Rafael.

Juan Carlos looked back at Manny and nodded.

"Gracias, señor," Manny said. He felt as if he had made an important first step, and he was hopeful there soon would be a breakthrough in achieving his goals. He was determined to find Rafael.

On his way back to the apartment, Manny hopped on a *por puesto.* The privately owned mini-buses, more intimate than the large public *guaguas,* were a cheap means to travel in a city where driving was crazy. The Corolla Manny leased for trips outside the city remained parked in the lot beneath his apartment building.

Inside the por puesto, a small fan attached to a waist-high wall behind the driver blew sweaty body odor through rancid air. Old air fresheners that had lost their potency hung from the rearview mirror along with a large wooden crucifix. Salsa music emanated from a transistor radio perched on a makeshift shelf beside the driver's seat. There was no change machine; people paid what they could afford, usually a few coins, before jumping off.

Manny took por puestos as an opportunity to engage in conversations with Guaridans of the humbler classes. The experience provided the kind of insight into the nation that can't be learned in books. He rarely saw foreigners use this mode of transportation.

"Sir," he asked an old man with a three-day beard, "what are those buildings over there?"

"Those are the headquarters of Petrol International," the man said. "The big American oil company."

"Guarida has a lot of good grade oil offshore," a young woman next to the old man said. "We are a rich country."

A rotund man with a scraggly mustache said, "The country is rich, but we don't know how to share the wealth. A majority of us can't even make a living."

A fat woman holding a large bag of groceries said, "It's the Corrupt Ones. They steal from everyone. They fill their pockets with oil money."

"What do we do about it? Nothing, same thing all the time," said a middle-aged, relatively well-dressed gentleman.

A man in overalls and a carpenter's belt said, "The messiah will save us."

Several passengers nodded. The old man said, "Our messiah will throw out the Corrupt Ones."

The driver turned his head and shouted back to the passengers, "The messiah will deliver us from Babylon."

"Who is the messiah?" Manny asked.

"Claudio Sánchez grew up in the Block. He's a great ball player, pitched for the team; could have made the Bigs. Then he was in the army and pitched for them too. Now he's our president."

Manny felt sorry for them. They seemed to believe in no other recourse than to hope for a miracle, a savior, like something out of a Samuel Beckett play. *It's tragic,* he thought. *They're waiting for Godot.*

Someone in the middle of the bus yelled for the bus to stop. The driver pulled over, slammed on the brakes, and skidded to a stop. El Salón de la Parrilla was just around the corner. Manny angled his way through the crowd and jumped off. He was famished, ready for a nice meal at the restaurant.

People scurried here and there like actors on a movie set, everyone preparing for roles. The whole scene seemed surreal. As he began the short walk through the southern section, he felt like an outsider, an inexperienced extra. He passed school children, businessmen, and housewives. The kids ran through the crowd, the men walked rapidly, and the women strolled. Some stopped in the *abastos,* the cafés, the fruit stores, or the bars. Others were on their way to the restaurants or their apartments.

A display of drawings in the window of a small art studio caught his interest, and he entered the shop for a closer look.

The curator was a short, middle-aged woman wearing a colorful dress. She looked up from her desk and said, "If I can be of any help..."

"Just browsing," Manny said. He was enjoying the bucolic scenes. They reminded him of his camping trips up in the hills. "What are these scenes?"

She rose from her chair and approached the sketches he was looking at. "These landscapes were sketched up in the hills."

"They are quite good, but I don't see a signature. Who's the artist?"

"I don't know, to be honest. A messenger drops them off every so often and takes cash payment for those that have sold. I sell a lot of his—or her—work. Would you like to see the portfolio?"

"Perhaps later, when I have more time. Why does the artist wish to remain anonymous?"

"I don't know, señor. The drawings are popular."

"Thank you, señora. But you must know the artist."

"I wish I did. I could make this person famous."

"Perhaps you could learn the name of this artist. How late are you open? Right now I've got to beat the crowd at El Salón."

She glanced at the clock on the wall. "I close in a few minutes. Why don't you return tomorrow? I'll see what I can find out, although I can't promise anything."

"Thanks. I'll see you in the morning," Manny said as he left the shop.

Manny walked through the gate at El Salón de la Parrilla a few minutes before 6:00 p.m. This typical Guaridan restaurant posted a menu with a selection of grilled meats, yucca, and salad. Most customers drank beer or wine. The open-air setting allowed for people-watching. Manny breathed in the aroma of grilled beef, and his mouth watered. He was ready for a dining experience that lasted a civilized amount of time.

When the host greeted him, Manny pointed to a table next to one occupied by the two attractive, vivacious young women. "May I be seated over there?" he asked, hoping he could strike up a conversation with the good-looking locals.

The host shot Manny a conspiratorial smile and led him to the table. He sat down and greeted the women politely.

"Good afternoon," the women responded almost in unison. One had long black hair; the other was a tall blonde.

After several minutes of small talk, the tall woman excused herself. "It's getting late, and I have to pick up some things. Nice chatting with you, girlfriend. Let's do it again soon. Call me."

The women stood and kissed each other on both cheeks. "Thanks for everything, Evita. I feel a lot better. I'll call." Heads turned as the statuesque blonde left the restaurant.

"May I join you? It seems ridiculous to carry on a conversation from different tables," Manny suggested.

She smiled sadly, tilted her head, and gestured at her plate. "I've finished my dinner, señor. I was getting ready to call for the damages."

"I'm just going to snack on something. Why don't you let me buy you a coffee or some dessert?"

"Please," she waved her hand toward the seat that Evita had abandoned. "Sit. I'll have one cup of coffee, and then I really do have to go."

"Thanks a million. I really appreciate it. I hate dining alone, and you're very nice. Thank you." One hell of an attractive woman, he thought. Her long black hair shone.

People walked up the street on their way home from work. Some held groceries; others carried briefcases. A few wore jogging shorts and cross-trainers. Many residents of this section of the city would go out for a run whenever they could. Most dined at a late hour. Several school children walked by holding cups of fresh juices purchased at La Ciruela up the street. The restaurant was just starting to fill up.

"Allow me to introduce myself. I'm Manny."

They shook hands. Hers felt delicate yet her grip was strong. "I'm Cristina del Carmen Reyes," she said, "but everyone calls me Tina."

The waiter arrived and took Manny's order—a mixed salad, grilled pork loin, and a bottle of Malbec. "Two glasses, please. Tina, would you care to try a glass of wine?"

She shrugged. "Just a sip to see what it's like. It'll be my first Malbec."

"If you like wine, I think you'll appreciate its full body. Not many people know the Argentine wines. The best are from Mendoza. Everyone drinks Chilean."

"So, are you Guaridan, Manny? You know I am."

"My mother was born on the island. She took American citizenship after she married my father, and I was born in New York. So, I guess I'm half Guaridan? He flashed her a grin. "Okay, I'm a gringo, Tina, but it isn't my fault."

"I have nothing against Americans. It's the government I don't like. But I don't much like any government, anyhow. Where did you learn Spanish?"

"Mom tried to teach me. And I took it in school. But I really learned down here on my previous visits. This is where my roots are."

"Roots are important," she said with a laugh. "I love my Guarida. We've got our problems, but doesn't every nation? So, are you on vacation?"

"Oh, no, I'm working. I'll be here for a while. And I'm trying to find my cousin. His name is Rafael Vidal. Ever heard of him?"

"The name sounds familiar."

"Do you know him?"

"I don't think so." Tina's eyes narrowed. She patted her hand on her forehead, seemed to be searching for a connection.

"Have you heard of the Freedom Front?"

"Oh, yeah. They're a bunch of crazies camping up in the hills somewhere."

"You're from the city?" Manny said.

"Heard of Cell Block Thirteen?"

"Pérez Santo's project. Did you grow up there?" Manny knew that the Block, as the locals called the project, was designed for low-income workers who could vote in national elections.

"I'm not ashamed to say so."

"I heard the president speak about his origins in the Block. Are you still living there?"

"With my mother, yes. I take care of her." Tina took a sip of her wine and said, "Besides looking for your cousin, what are you doing in my beautiful country? You're an oil man?"

"God no, not oil. I'm a visiting professor at UG."

"Really?" Tina smiled. "That's a coincidence. I'm part-time secretary in the School of Education. It's a small world, huh?"

"That's for sure. Don't know anyone over in Ed. Except you now, of course."

"What do you teach? And do you like it here?"

"Government, and, yes, I like it."

"So, you're CIA?" She gave him a wink, but he detected a note of genuine curiosity.

"Why does everyone think I'm a spy? It's ridiculous." He laughed and shook his head. "No, not a spy."

"I'm so relieved," she said, and this time he could tell she was joking.

"Good. Now, if you're part-time at the university, what do you do with the rest of your time?"

45

She flashed him a beautiful smile, full of ivory teeth. "I teach in the barrio elementary school."

"No kidding? That's great." Both the smile and the vocation impressed Manny. She was attractive and idealistic, he thought, liking her instantly. Yet, he sensed he should nip this flower in the bud and not allow himself to be drawn into any further interaction. *Just talk, nothing more,* he thought. "How old are the kids and how long have you been teaching?"

"Grade school—and long enough to be weary. I wish it paid a living wage. You really can't make ends meet on a teacher's salary in this country. That's why I have to do the secretarial stuff in the afternoons. Little kids in the morning, big kids in the afternoon, that's my existence."

He sat back and studied her, lifted his wine glass. "Do you like the Malbec?"

"It's nice. But after a couple of beers, I might be getting a little tipsy. I think I'd better leave now."

"Let me order some more coffee." Against his better judgment, Manny tried to buy time. Tina was interesting, and he was lonely.

Tina's eyes lit up, as if the attraction were mutual, but she said, "Thank you anyway. Maybe some other time." She excused herself and stood to go.

"Wait a minute. I'll walk you home," Manny offered.

"You don't want to be anywhere near the Block," Tina said. She sounded sad, and she insisted on walking home alone.

Manny regretfully said goodbye. Tina seemed disappointed as well, but she disappeared into the crowded street. Manny cursed himself for not getting her phone number, but it was probably for the best that nothing came of the encounter. Dee wouldn't have understood, and it wasn't the way to fill the space she wanted him to have. Yet, all he wanted was a dinner companion, someone with whom he could have an interesting conversation, right? Surely, Dee could have lived with that. Or was he in denial, deceiving himself? What did he really want?

Manny decided to stay away from her, and all women, from now on. Who the hell was Tina, anyway?

Chapter Five

Salsa music, barking dogs, and curses emanated from the Block's alleyways, awakening Tina at 7:00 the next morning. She threw off the blanket she'd pulled over her head when gunshots blasted in the middle of the night and got out of bed. That gringo professor could never understand what it meant to live in the Block.

Sancocho sizzled in giant cauldrons in the street, its pungent odor coalescing with the stench of open sewers. Tina grimaced and turned on the exposed electric bulb dangling from the ceiling. She saw her reflection in the mirror that hung above the cot. Pulling her long black hair into a ponytail, she sat on her makeshift seat and thought it clever that the trunk in which she stored her clothes could be transformed into a table or a place to sit.

Tina's meager earnings enabled her to provide for her mother and herself within the confines of the barrio. But on the previous evening, the teachers' union had announced a general strike. Schools would be closed until union demands were met for more equitable pay. Tina knew that salaries would be frozen. To make matters worse, her mother had become ill.

She had always thought of the union as a group that would protect her. That's why she had joined and paid her dues. Now, it seemed as if her membership had put her in jeopardy.

"Mama, I think you were bitten by a *zangudo*," Tina said. "I don't know if yours is the fever that lasts ten days or the more dangerous one." Dengue fever was going around, and the hemorrhagic variety had taken the lives of several of her neighbors. "The public hospitals are backed up for weeks. I need to get you to a private clinic."

"Ay, I feel terrible," her mother sighed as Tina helped her onto the cot in her tiny room.

"Mama," she said, "everything's going to be all right. Remember the time that girl in my third grade class was crying? The one who wouldn't tell me why, and I took her home after school?" Tina knew how much her mother loved to hear about her accomplishments, so she retold the story while her mother listened patiently. The little girl's father had been sentenced to a year in the Retén for petit larceny after stealing food for his family. And the girl's mother had disappeared. Her grandmother cared for her but had no money to buy clothes.

"That poor little girl had to wear the same old dress every day, so I bought her a new one. I took the cash out of our food money, remember? But we got by. Well, she came to class the next day with a smile on her face and she hugged me."

"You're a good girl, my baby, a good girl."

"We'll be okay, Mama."

Tina soaked a towel in cold water and put it on her mother's forehead. *Where the hell will I get the money for a clinic,* Tina thought, *and how will I pay for food or rent?* She

resolved to find another part-time job. At times, the Help
Wanted columns in *El Nacional* listed a few decent
alternatives.

Two days later, after caring for her mother, Tina
headed over to the Boulevard. The popular artery bisected the
city from the southern zone to the northeastern hills. The strip
near the central plaza bustled with pedestrians on their way
back to work or walking to shops, banks, and restaurants.

People stopped for coffee at sidewalk cafés. They
rambled through assorted goods that unlicensed merchants
offered on blankets stretched along the pavement. Hand bags,
belts, clothing, fruits and vegetables, toys, bongo drums, and
guitars were sold on the street. One could even find batteries
and electrical equipment.

Every so often a policeman walked toward the cafés.
The merchants scooped and rolled their goods into the
blankets and scrambled away to another spot farther down the
Boulevard. The process continued each time the policemen
appeared.

Tina took a seat at one of the tables at La Dulce
Pastelería, the largest, noisiest, and most frequented café. Hers
was one of more than a dozen tables on the café's plaza, and
the place was so busy she felt lucky to have a seat. A large
yellow umbrella lodged in the center of her table shielded her
from the sun. She often went there to think in the clamorous
privacy of the outdoor restaurant.

Tina thought about how her pathetic teacher's salary
would be frozen during the strike. *Mama's sick and the
goddamn secretarial pay is never on time,* she muttered under
her breath. *What the hell am I supposed to do?*

The waiter asked if she was talking to him.

"No, just bring me a coffee, please."

He returned with a tiny *café guarideño*, a strong, incompletely filtered brew served like an espresso. Tina sighed, took a sip, lit up a cigarette, and opened the newspaper. She skimmed through the lead story about America's war against terrorism. And she glanced at the title of a long article about the rise in unemployment on the island. No need to read that one either.

The Help Wanted columns had very little to offer. There were a few ads for construction workers, mechanics, and computer techs. Nothing she could pursue.

Maybe I should rob a bank, she thought. Tears collected on the inside corners of her eyelids. Her shoulders drooped and her hands trembled as she dug into her purse for a tissue. She gently dabbed her eyes, covered her face with her hands, and pulled herself together.

She took another sip of the powerful brew, another drag. While exhaling a lengthy stream of smoke, Tina overheard the chatter at nearby tables.

"Another increase in the price of gas," said an elderly woman with a large bag of groceries next to her chair. "It's the Corrupt Ones."

An old man at an adjacent table responded, "Now we'll be paying thirty cents a gallon—almost double."

At a table on the other side of the café, Tina heard two young women complain about the price of food. They said they had to cut back on their basics. "Even products that are grown here are priced too high," one of the women said. "The Corrupt Ones…"

Why, Tina asked herself, *doesn't someone do something about the crap that passes for government in Guarida?* She folded her newspaper with the Help Wanted section on top and was about to stand and leave the café when she felt a presence. She looked up.

"Hello, señorita." He looked vaguely familiar, a handsome man.

"Señor? Have we met?"

He gave a little gentlemanly bow. "My wife works at the university. María Elena is a professor at the School of Education. I've seen you in the office."

"Profesora Torres? She's my boss. I work there part-time, so I didn't recognize you."

"I'm Federico Torres. May I sit?"

"I was just about to leave, Mr. Torres." Tina began to rise.

"Please, allow me to buy you another coffee."

Their eyes met as Tina stood. *What the hell,* she thought. *Someone is always wanting to buy me coffee.* She sat down and nodded toward the chair next to hers.

"Thanks. I've been on my feet all day. You are—?"

"Pardon me. I'm Cristina del Carmen, but I'm called Tina."

She sized him up. The nattily dressed, well-to-do businessman, perhaps an executive at one of the oil companies, had thick, dark hair cut short. Clean shaven, he wore a custom-made brown suede jacket with a dark shirt and a light tie, and he carried a polished leather briefcase.

"It's a pleasure to make your acquaintance, Tina." He settled into the chair and crossed his legs, placing the briefcase within reach.

Tina took out another smoke, and Federico lit it. He looked at the newspaper on the table.

"I see you've got the Help Wanted section. You're looking for something?"

"I'm a teacher. My union is on strike. No pay until the damn thing's resolved. I think they're holding out for thirty percent. They'll never get it. Meanwhile, I'm screwed."

"I know how frustrating that can be, Tina. I might be able to be of assistance. I've helped many UG secretaries, students, even a few professors."

"What do you do for a living, Mr. Torres? You look like someone who has done quite well."

"Oh, yes. I have a business. I've got no complaints. Please call me Federico."

"What kind of business, if I may ask?"

"I'm in the entertainment business."

Tina's eyes opened wide. What kind of entertainment? Did he manage big stars? Was he an agent? If so, how could he help her? She had no special talent as a singer or dancer; not any more than an average Guaridan. She shook her head. "I don't know what you can do for me. I'm just a teacher who needs extra work. I guess I should be getting home now—my mother is sick."

"Before you leave, let me give you something to think about."

She stared at Federico, wondering, *What's this all about? Enough already!*

"Many people in your situation—secretaries, students, teachers—they need to make some extra cash. They like to study or they like their jobs and don't have much time left over. Everyone needs money, for whatever. That's a given." He paused, raised his eyebrows.

Tina pulled her hair back, tried to absorb his meaning. Why was he stating the obvious?

"Secretaries and teachers are paid pitifully in this country," he said. "Actually, that's the unfortunate case in most countries to tell the truth. The most important social functions, like teaching, are undervalued. And people need certain things, but with this economy, it's very difficult to keep up. Am I correct?" He turned to survey the café, then leaned in to her and lowered his voice. "I have a service that allows people in your situation to make a little extra. Actually, a lot extra, if you want."

"What kind of service?" Tina had no idea what he was talking about. "Sounds a bit mysterious."

"It is kind of mysterious. Before you make any judgments, hear me out." Federico focused his eyes directly on hers. "A large number of important people—business executives, politicians, and the like—well, they host functions and parties. They like to enjoy the company of locals who are part of our Caribbean culture. You know, to accompany them, to escort them to restaurants and clubs." He lit up a cigarette and offered one to Tina. She declined. "I help provide for this need," he said. "I run an exclusive, high-quality service. My clientele are among the wealthiest in this country. We assist foreign executives as well. And my escorts are all attractive and well cared for. It's a high class business."

Tina studied Federico's eyes. After a moment, she stated bluntly, "My mother was a whore."

"Tina, this is not that. I don't run a common call-girl operation. Escorting these important people is above board, high quality, and well-remunerated—nothing illicit or illegal. This is a service, and it's in great demand. My employees accompany men seeking the companionship of beautiful women. That's all. Many university students do it."

"Uh, no," she said, and made a move as if to rise from the table.

He held up a hand. "Please don't form an opinion yet." Federico sounded concerned. "Please consider going out a few times to see what it's all about. You might enjoy the experience, usually in the finest restaurants, the best shows, and even sporting events. Sometimes you go to lavish parties in the embassies. There was one at the American Embassy last week. You'd love it, Tina. Just give it some thought. You'd never be obliged to me or anyone else. It's just an easy way to generate some extra cash, my dear. Here's my card. Think it over and give me a call."

Tina took the card, stood up abruptly, and left without saying goodbye. Halfway down the block, she stopped and looked back. Federico, still seated at the table, waved. She didn't return the wave.

She continued walking toward the central plaza. As she passed the old American Embassy building and made her way toward the Block, she thought about Federico's offer. Torn by her belief that the escort business was almost like prostitution and the knowledge that students did it for extra money, she tried to make sense out of the choice she was about to make. She could sure as hell use the cash, especially now. And there was no harm in this, only help. She knew she would do practically anything for her mother, as long as her actions didn't hurt anyone.

She fingered the business card in the side pocket of her handbag. Yes, it could be the opportunity she needed.

ᑦᔐᑯChapter Six᙭ᑐ

Manny felt privileged as he walked past the tired, stoic Guaridans waiting to interview for visas or just holding places in the line. The bulldog-looking Marine in his red, white, and blue uniform inspected Manny's special I.D., compared face to photo, and pressed a button inside the booth. "You're cleared, sir," he said. It wasn't the first time they had gone through the ritual.

As Manny moved through the turnstile into the embassy compound, he passed from one world into another— into a bubble, a sealed-off piece of Americana. It was like exiting Guarida from within and entering a Disney replica of the United States or a national exhibition at the World's Fair. Once inside, he looked at the clean modern edifice with amusement, yet recognized that he felt at home and safe, free from the chaos and illusion beyond the compound's marble walls.

Manny took the elevator to the second floor, cashed a personal check at the embassy bank, stuffed a communiqué to Stark in the diplomatic pouch, and sent a letter to Dee at the APO. Then he took the stairs down to the first floor and entered the cafeteria, which reminded him of the lunchroom at Stuyvesant.

The Spartan cafeteria offered American cuisine at affordable prices. He took a whiff of sizzling hamburgers on the greasy hot table, glanced at the large ketchup and mustard bottles with pump dispensers on top, grabbed a plastic tray, and got into line.

Cultural Affairs Officer Jane Kelley-Noel walked over and stood next to Manny. She wore a tan pants-suit with an orange blouse. Her dirty-blonde hair was pinned up into a bun.

Manny had learned that Janey, the proverbial girl next door, had traveled far from Aurelia, Iowa, the pleasant little town in which she was born and raised. A perceptive and engaging diplomat, an independent thinker rather than a typical bureaucrat, Janey had told Manny that diplomacy and cross-cultural understanding were more effective than military interventions in influencing people and nations. "We can't force democracy and human rights down their throats," she had argued.

Today, however, the topic was more pleasant. "I heard you made the finals at the tennis club," she said as she selected her club sandwich and soda.

"It's on Saturday. Want to come over and cheer for me?"

"I'll be out of town, sadly. I rarely get time off, even on weekends. We're sponsoring a jazz concert down on the coast, bringing in Wynton Marsalis. Tell me about UG."

"My class is supposed to begin at ten in the morning. And it really gets started after we break for coffee, like a social gathering."

"Island time," Janey said. "What else have you been up to?"

"Trying to find my cousin—it seems he's disappeared."

"Have you gone over to Public Records?"

"Nothing there. Not a very receptive clerk, by the way. Pulled a gun on me."

"What? You're kidding, right?"

"We had kind of a misunderstanding."

"Want me to look into it?"

"You'd have to clean up their entire public administration, Janey, but I need to find my cousin. I may have a lead—some unsigned drawings that reminded me of him—but I haven't been able to connect with the artist."

"You think he's an artist? Shouldn't be too difficult to find him; I'll ask around. What's his name?"

"Rafael Vidal. Everyone thought he died years ago when the family estate was destroyed by a fire. But Stark told me he had reason to believe Rafael might have survived. And a news article I located reported that only two bodies were found, probably his parents. Rafael liked to draw. I don't know if he's an actual artist, but I'm betting the drawings are his."

"I'll look into it. If he's in Guarida, we'll find him."

"I'd really appreciate it, Janey. And what can you tell me about the Freedom Front?"

"They're a small group of idealistic guerrillas who live up in the northern hills. They'll occasionally try to blow up a government depot. I don't know what they expect to accomplish, really. At least they haven't killed anyone. Why do you ask?"

Manny recalled his mother's speculation about what had happened after El Retiro burned. He felt a sense of pride that Rafael might be a freedom fighter. "I suspect that my cousin could be with them."

"I'll see what I can come up with." She jotted some notes on the pad she carried in her purse. Then she snapped to the civilian version of attention when a middle-aged man approached their table and paused next to her. "Oh, hello, Mr. Ambassador, how are you today?"

Ambassador Kingfield held a lunch tray in his hands, and Manny saw a bowl of soup and some kind of sliced meat on a roll. He had immediately recognized the tall man with a mane of dark hair that was always ruffled. Kingfield had removed his suit jacket and rolled up his sleeves.

"Very well, thanks. How's Cultural?"

"We're getting by, can't complain."

The ambassador turned to Manny and extended his hand while balancing his tray in the other. "Hello, I'm Frank Kingfield."

"Sorry," Janey said. "Mr. Ambassador, this is Dr. Emmanuel White Vidal. He likes to be called Manny. He's a visiting professor at UG."

"I've heard about your tour here," Kingfield said. "It's good to meet you, Manny. Janey, why don't you set up a meeting so the professor and I can have a little chat?"

"Certainly, sir."

"I'd better get over to a table before my lunch gets cold. Nice to see you both."

"Enjoy your lunch, Mr. Ambassador," Janey said.

60

When he had walked away, she said. "Here's the highest U.S. official in-country in the same cafeteria as janitors, Marines, secretaries, staff assistants, Foreign Service Officers—and even professors."

"Very egalitarian," Manny said. "Wish we lived up to this standard at home."

"We like Frank," Janey explained. "He's a career FSO who rose through the ranks, not one of those parvenus who bought in through campaign donations. You know some of the political appointees can neither speak the language nor even converse intelligently about the country to which they're accredited. Kingfield's fluent in Spanish and can hold his own on Guaridan history and culture. Too bad he's up against so much pressure."

"Seems like a good guy. What's he up against?"

"Washington sees Sánchez as another Castro," Janey said. She gazed out the window, where the island's mountain range could be seen disappearing into the mist in the distance. "Who knows what they're planning up there? You think things are changing in Guarida?"

"How do you define 'things'? If you're referring to Sánchez, he's putting some new programs into action. He's not really a revolutionary. He was elected, for God's sake."

"What do you know about Juan Carlos Guerrero?"

"I've met with him." Manny squinted at her quizzically. "Why do you ask about him?"

"He's Sánchez's chief-of-staff and seems to be the brains behind the operation."

"Guerrero's an interesting guy. His family lost a fortune when Pérez Santo was deposed, something like that. He asked me to advise Sánchez, sit on a committee."

"Are you going to accept?"

"Sure, why not?"

"Be careful, Manny. I've seen innocent Americans arrested or detained just to make a point in the international press," Janey said. "They're accused of spying and who knows what else. It's happened in Cuba, Iran, Venezuela, China, Turkey, Korea."

"Don't worry about me. Let me ask you a far more important question, Ms. Kelley-Noel. Would you be my guest for dinner tonight?"

"I'd love to, but I've got a prior commitment. I'll take a rain check, okay?"

They had dined on several occasions, usually at a formal event, and had become friends. Their outlooks on life, and especially politics, were compatible. Manny was disappointed that she couldn't make it. He liked discussing things with her and hated to dine alone. "Next time I won't take no for an answer," he joked.

"Just don't take your decision to work with Sánchez lightly," she said, tapping her polished nails on the table top. "You have an important choice to make. I have a funny feeling about this."

"I'll think about it, but I'm not buying into all the rhetoric floating around, you know?"

"Be cautious." She laid a hand on his arm. "Guarida can be tricky."

"I will. And I would like to meet with the ambassador. Meanwhile, when I interview Sánchez, I'll have a much better idea about what's going on—and maybe I'll be able to track down my cousin."

Manny normally felt comfortable at Campo Alegre Tennis Club, where rhythmic pings of racquet strings and muted thumps of bouncing balls punctuated the club's sedate ambiance. Today, however, all the side courts were empty while he and Raimundo "Ray" Roldano, progeny of the Guaridan gentry and the club's most eligible bachelor—and top seed—battled on the stadium court. Manny felt like a combatant, sliding and grunting. His effort interrupted their minuet as if to expose the brutish struggle underlying the sport's genteel façade.

The few wispy cirrus clouds floating high above Campo Alegre blemished an otherwise azure sky. Rain would not interfere with the self-important event of the day. The Club Singles Championship was underway.

Unseeded, Manny had prevailed over a tough junior in the first round, a former finalist in the round of sixteen, and strong players in the quarters and semis. In each match, he came from behind. *Never say die* was one of Dad's admonitions, and Ray had coasted into the finals. He played with grace and ease. During the changeovers, he flirted with an entourage of young women who followed all his matches.

Explosive applause interrupted the staid atmosphere. "Bravo, bravo," chanted stylish members in their Ralph Lauren, La Coste, and Fila outfits. The crowd, ordinarily fastidious in maintaining an appearance of nonchalance, cheered every point that Ray won, while Manny's winners were met with silence. He wouldn't let that bother him.

Although he had prevailed in other matches, this time Ray found the answers to Manny's serve and volley attack. Ray danced around the court and came up with incredible shots under pressure. He seemed to be inspired by the crowd of partisans.

Then Ray hit an all-or-nothing running backhand on match point in a third-set tiebreaker. The shot clipped the top of the net and seemed to perch there for a split second, as if deciding on a side. When the ball fell into Manny's court, the crowd, no longer able to feign even a modicum of detachment, went wild. The match was over; they stood, patted each other on the back, and shook hands as they ambled out of the stadium and promenaded over to the club's posh restaurant and bar.

Manny knew that, for Campo Alegre's members, the tiny Caribbean island nation had just defeated the United States of America.

ᑲ Chapter Seven ᑯ

After the match, Manny and Ray strolled over to a table in the club's garden restaurant, where they collapsed into lounge chairs. Ray ordered a pitcher of beer mixed with lemon soda, the so-called champagne of the masses. He poured the concoction into tall glasses filled with ice and offered a toast.

"To el ténis, la plata, and el amor—salud!" They clinked their glasses and took the first, always the best, taste of the popular thirst-quencher.

"You were unlucky today," Ray said with an American drawl he had picked up at UC Santa Barbara. "I was in the zone."

"That last shot could have fallen on either side," Manny said.

"The wind was blowing in the right direction," Ray replied.

"You played well," Manny said. "I don't mind losing a close match, as long as it wasn't on unforced errors." *Don't let the ball play you*, Dad would have said. Players learn that the element of chance can never be denied, notwithstanding talent and effort.

"So," Manny said, "what's happening here in the Land of Sea and Sun?"

"Did you see the news? Sánchez is stirring things up." Ray took a long sip of his drink.

"He seems to have his finger on the pulse of the nation."

"His social revolution is pure bullshit, and you know it, amigo."

"Don't you think people might be better off?"

"It depends on which people you're talking about." Ray smiled reflectively. "You have to come out to my family's *finca,* La Casita Bonita, one of these days."

"Sure, I'd love to, but I'm talking about the vast majority."

"That's pure *mierda,* my friend. You think the economy would be better? Crime is up already. People are being misled."

"Didn't prior administrations engage in corruption?"

Ray looked at the gardens and said, "Did you hear the UN Security Council? Today they found no evidence of weapons of mass destruction or nuclear-related activities in Iraq."

"Let's not argue Iraq. What's happening *here*?"

Ray shook his head. "Let's talk tennis."

Manny leaned forward. "You know some Guaridans believe Sánchez is the messiah."

Ray rolled his eyes. You believe that shit?"

"At least he's made poverty an issue." No need to tell Ray about the advisory committee he was thinking of joining.

"You're not Guaridan, Manny," Ray responded. "You don't have to suffer the consequences of a so-called revolution. You think this country would be better off with everyone poor? There's just so much in the pie. Cut it up equally and no one has anything—at least nothing worth more than a pound of crap. You think Cuba's a good model? Ask the millions who've fled that basket case. And who would buy our oil? Huh? Where's our biggest goddamn market?"

Manny refilled their glasses. "There's a need for education and health care initiatives where poor people would gain the kind of access they've been denied."

"You mean Cuban operatives into the barrios, like in Venezuela? You sound like our little band of rebels," Ray replied. He gave a derisive snort. "As if the Freedom Front has any idea what freedom means."

"I told you my cousin might be with the Front. Whatever you think of them, you've got to help me find him."

A young woman passed their table. She wore a *tanga* that covered very little of her lissome body. The spectacle captured their attention.

"What's your cousin's name?" Ray said as his eyes followed the woman.

"Rafael Vidal."

"Doesn't ring a bell, but I'll check around. Remember, though, you're a naïve gringo and you lost the match. I'm the champ. To the victor belong the spoils."

"Drink up—that's your spoils, champ." They lifted their glasses.

"To Guarida," Manny toasted, "my alma mater, the country where my mother was born." He liked Ray, loved the tropics, but was uneasy with what his friend represented: the same powerful elite that bolstered Pérez Santo and Báez.

"To tennis, tangas, and the United States of America," Ray stated, "an ally that we shouldn't piss off with absurd accusations."

"You love us and hate us, pal." Manny figured Ray's respect for the U.S. didn't extend much beyond its purchasing power. "You condemn American culture for being bourgeois and vulgar, yet you buy all of our products."

"Don't be paranoid," Ray said. "What do you expect? Goddamn golden arches everywhere."

"Why do Guaridans opt for inferior imported whisky or beer," Manny asked rhetorically, "rather than excellent local rums and beers for half the price?"

Ray smiled and drained his glass.

"You've got CitiBank, Chase Manhattan, First Bank of Boston, Bank of America, Wells Fargo—I could go on," Manny said. "And your *cambios* post the latest U.S. dollar exchange rates."

"My family has a substantial amount of capital invested in those banks."

"Guaridans can hardly afford their basics," Manny said.

Ray thought for a moment. "You know what we call the tanga?"

"Dental floss, I know. Come on. Be serious."

"I know what you're thinking," Ray said, "but you should face reality, accept things the way they are, and learn from the past."

"Look at your history, Ray. It's not paranoid for Sánchez to fear interference and meddling. The U.S. supported Pérez Santo until your own military ran him out of the country, the same year the CIA paid truckers to strike against Allende in Chile."

"Your country, just like ours, has interests," Ray said.

"I don't believe in the idea of 'my country, right or wrong.' That sort of patriotism is the last refuge of the scoundrel," Manny said. "We destabilized Jamaica, went into tiny Grenada. Remember? And didn't we march into Haiti, the DR, Nicaragua, and Guatemala, not to mention Cuba? All were on very questionable pretenses."

"Ninety percent of Guaridan oil flows into the States," Ray said. "Washington won't send troops here because they're too concerned with the Middle East."

"Talk about love-hate?" Manny said.

"Sánchez loves to threaten the most powerful country in the world. It's David and Goliath—very sexy, huh? Don't worry," Ray said, "we'll take care of him!"

"What do you mean?"

"Tantalizing scenery, eh?" Ray said as another dental floss bikini passed by their table.

"Don't change the subject."

"Just that Sánchez won't serve out his term. You'll see." Ray gazed at the stadium court. "If you'd won today, we might have needed troops around here."

Manny understood Ray's point of view, but he believed in the kinds of reforms Sánchez was advocating. He worried about the significance of Ray's veiled threat. Would there be a coup? If the country fell into chaos, how would he be able to find Rafael?

Manny resolved to act with dispatch before it was too late.

Manny walked to his office after the second meeting of his class. He dropped his notebook onto his small desk strewn with papers and books, sat back in his chair, and took a deep breath.

Ray's voice echoed in his mind. *We'll take care of him!* What was his friend suggesting about Sánchez?

Within minutes, the telephone on Manny's desk rang. One of Sánchez's secretaries informed him that his interview with the president would take place in one hour. Manny was as surprised as he was nervous. He hadn't expected it to happen so soon.

A plainclothes Security Police officer escorted him from the university gate to the presidential palace. On the short ride, he excitedly jotted down a few questions on his notepad. He also tried to conceive of a strategy to ask about a missing person, since his attempts to locate Rafael had run into roadblocks at every turn.

Juan Carlos Guerrero greeted Manny, led him to the anteroom outside the president's working office, and then took his leave. Left alone for the moment, Manny gazed at his surroundings. Built in the colonial era, the walls of its elegant rooms were paneled with mahogany, giving off a sweet aroma, like chocolate. The floors were inlaid with imported *azulejos,* and Persian carpets covered the ornate Spanish tiles in central areas of the large rooms. Ceilings rose to twenty feet, soaring above the well-preserved antique furniture. Large murals hung on the walls—a glorious battle for independence, a well-known independence leader, a landscape depicting the island's lush tropical beauty.

Manny admired the local art on display in the anteroom—murals and wood carvings of indigenous figures in juxtaposition with photos of oil wells—while he waited for half an hour. He had broken into a cold sweat and was rubbing his hands together when a secretary finally summoned him.

Claudio Sánchez sat behind a huge desk covered with meticulously arranged papers and photographs. A baseball bat leaned up against the side of his desk. The president stood and signaled for Manny to sit in the chair facing the desk. He grabbed the bat and sat down. He caressed the bat, leaned forward, and said, "And what brings you to Guarida, professor?"

"Thank you for this audience, Mr. President," Manny said. "My mother was born on the island, and I've loved the country as if it were my alma mater. I've played some ball in my day, but I'm really a tennis player," he added.

"Tennis is an elite sport, professor. I was MVP on the army's baseball team. I pitched, but could hit as well." Sánchez patted the sweet spot on his Louisville Slugger. "So you left your prestigious post at NYU to come here, to our humble little island?" Sánchez's expression revealed that he was searching for a more penetrating explanation.

"Guarida is beautiful, and it has tremendous potential. And I do love baseball."

"Ah, potential—so you've come to help us develop, eh? That's the term you use, correct? Guarida is a developing area." Sánchez sneered, rested the bat on his lap.

Manny felt uncomfortable, and the bat made him downright nervous. "Every country has problems—social, economic—I don't use development as a pejorative," he said. "It's not necessarily a condescending concept. At least, I don't believe that some nations are better than others."

"That's good, professor. Here in Guarida we are launching a social *revolución,* a complete change in our system. My administration is interested in equity, distribution of our wealth, our petrodollars, to all our citizens."

"That is a laudable goal, Mr. President."

"You know, there are those who are against our agenda, against me." Sánchez leaned back in his chair, his hands behind his head, looking down his nose at Manny.

"Change is always problematical, especially for those who believe they will lose something, like status or power."

"I've read your work, professor. And I must say I'm impressed by your openness, your understanding of Guaridan history. Many of your compatriots think that the American Dream is the only act in town."

"I'm probably not your typical academic," Manny said, "and I'm not always on board with my diplomatic community. But I do love my country. The United States can help foster a more equitable, more peaceful world. Of course, there are always differences of opinion, especially when it comes to politics."

Sánchez looked around his office and absently stroked his bat. It looked as if he were calculating a mathematical equation or searching for the answer to a crossword puzzle clue. He then focused on Manny and said, "How would you like to serve on one of my advisory committees, professor?"

Manny felt anxious and pleased at the same time. He knew that Juan Carlos had suggested this to Sánchez, and there seemed to be no reason why he should not participate in the transformation of Guarida. He believed in the need for this kind of change. It would be beneficial, not only for Guarida, but also for the United States. Yet Manny had misgivings similar to those he had felt when Stark recruited him. And Janey's warning was fresh in his mind.

"What could I possibly offer?" he said.

"Well, you are an expert; we could use your knowledge about the politics and mechanics of socio-political change. We would look to you to help define the change agents and attract the support of your government. Yes, this could be an excellent relationship. Don't you agree?"

"Yes, I'm inclined to accept your offer. To whom should I report back?"

"Juan Carlos will take care of the details. There is a nice stipend, of course. You'll be well compensated."

"Thank you. That's useful, certainly. But my main motivation would be to assist in implementing productive plans for Guarida and bringing our countries closer together." Manny took a deep breath. "There is a personal issue that I would ask that you consider. It might require your assistance, Mr. President."

"What might that be, professor?"

"I'm searching for my cousin, Rafael Vidal. His family perished in a fire in 1976. I believe he survived and is probably somewhere in Guarida."

Sánchez again leaned back in his chair. His brow furrowed and his jaw tightened. Manny perceived a hint of recognition in the president's eyes. He seemed to be seriously considering the request. "Talk to Juan Carlos about this. I'm certain he will help you find your cousin," Sánchez said.

"I was hoping you would intervene, sir." Manny sensed that the president knew something that he would not reveal.

"I look forward to hearing that you will be with us. Talk to Juan Carlos. And thank you for coming in." Sánchez stood, leaned the bat up against the side of his desk, and offered his hand. The interview was over.

After Manny departed, Claudio Sánchez picked up his bat and took a few half-swings. Then he signaled for Juan Carlos to enter his office. The president replaced the bat, returned to his seat, and lit a cigarette.

"How did it go?" Juan Carlos took the same seat Manny had vacated.

"He's searching for his cousin," Claudio responded, puffing smoke in his advisor's direction. "He said something about a fire in seventy-six. That was the El Retiro thing, no? At any rate, I think he's on board. You'll speak with him."

"This is just what we want, Claudio. We can use this so-called professor if and when we need to. Make an example of him," Juan Carlos said.

"That's good," Claudio said.

"We know all about his cousin, by the way. He's a member of the Freedom Front and has been up in the hills since El Retiro," Juan Carlos said.

"He's with the Front, eh?"

"Yes, and the professor is ours, we've got him by the balls. I'll dangle the cousin in his face if I need to."

"Let's see about that. Meanwhile, we can have him followed. Roberto could do it. Or maybe Jorge and María Pilar—they look like students."

"Roberto's been on the professor since he arrived in Guarida. I've already had Jorge and María Pilar enroll in one of his classes." Juan Carlos smiled. "They brought him to your convocation address."

"The professor's an idealist who believes in our revolution. I kind of like him, you know?" Claudio said.

"Yeah, me too," Juan Carlos said. "If only the world were less complicated."

"It is what it is," Claudio said as he grabbed his bat from the side of his desk.

"And by the way," Juan Carlos continued, "he met one of our local beauties at El Salón de la Parrilla. Her name is Cristina Reyes, but she goes by Tina. She works for Federico. We'll enlist her services. Along with Roberto, Jorge, and María Pilar, she could be convenient, eh?"

"Indeed." Claudio Sánchez felt a sense of pleasure. He liked being in control and felt that things were falling into place for him to enhance his personal power. He grabbed his bat and took a few swings.

ᴄ᷍ᴕ᷍Chapter Eightᴕ᷍ᴄ᷍

A fter several dates to see what being an escort was all about, Tina had saved enough money to take her mother to a private clinic and to buy extra food, as well as some new household items. She also bought supplies and treats for her school children and even opened a savings account at the Banco de Guarida. It seemed that her life had taken a turn for the better, like a pleasant dream come true.

On Saturday evening, Tina worked a party at a Nigerian Embassy official's penthouse. She would be the official's date. Decked out in an Oscar de la Renta cocktail dress, she arrived at the party after visiting the safe house and selecting her dress from its vast wardrobe of sizes and styles. As always, Federico arranged everything.

When the party started to break up, Tina caught sight of Akele Mbondo standing on the balcony of his penthouse, where he had a magnificent view of the city's nightlights. He beckoned her to stand near him while he bade farewell to his guests. Mbondo's eyes gleamed through the thin-rimmed spectacles perched on the bridge of his nose. Above his high forehead were rows of wiry black hairs peppered with white highlights. Tina noted that he sported a colorful dashiki that evening, rather than one of the many custom-made Italian business suits he often wore. He told her once that he wore the suits to the embassy where he was a consular officer. She had told him those suits made him look stuffy.

South American, African, and European diplomats thanked Mbondo for a pleasant evening. After all the other guests had gone, he asked Tina to stay for a while. "Let us unwind. The party was grand. Do you not think so?"

"Yeah," Tina said, "though the Brit had a vulgar mouth. I don't speak much English, but I know what 'bloody' means. He propositioned me right in front of the others." She bristled all over again. These higher-ups were no more sophisticated, no better than she, the girl from the Block.

"I will talk to the fool. He will not bother you again," Mbondo said. He poured two flutes, passed one to Tina. Sipping Dom Perignon, they sat back in the plush sofa and relaxed.

"European women are so very sensual," he said. "No hang-ups."

"Guaridans have more rhythm."

"Tina, you are a perfect example of Guaridan pulchritude."

"Thank you, you're very kind. But you exaggerate, to be sure."

"Let us test your theory about Guaridan rhythm." He loaded a CD. "You know, Africans invented the very rhythms that slaves brought into your music. Where do you think the salsa got its beat?"

She listened for a moment and let the beat pulse through her. "This isn't Caribbean. It's African, right?"

"This is the basis for all your rhythm. It's where Brazilian *batucada* comes from. And the Venezuelan *tambores* are direct throwbacks to Africa. It is the basis for merengue, samba, bossa nova, reggae, even American rock, and, of course, jazz. Africa is the earth mother. Life began there. That is an indisputable fact."

Tina rose and moved gracefully to the drumbeat as if the African part of her genetic heritage had become unshackled. Their eyes met, and Mbondo gently brought Tina into his embrace. They danced. The spontaneous choreography felt sensual to her, and she could tell that he felt it too. They paused only to refill their flutes and take a few sips of the champagne.

When Mbondo kissed Tina on the lips, she did not pull away. His hands explored her body. She felt desirable and emboldened. This was nothing like the clumsy experiences she'd had with the barrio boys, and far more refined than the few affairs she had squeezed into her busy schedule while a university student.

Mbondo carefully removed Tina's clothes and set them neatly on the couch. His caresses awakened sensations she had never experienced. It was as if she were liberated from all her inhibitions.

His tenderness and expertise transformed Tina. She learned that lips and tongues were designed for pleasure, that every part of her body, and his, was sensual. She was carried into another dimension. Nothing else mattered. She lived in the moment.

Their bodies coupled tightly, locked together in the primordial dance, riding crests, building, and exploding together. Then there was peace. Then a new wave would form and build to another climax. Each wave seemed to generate more power, more need.

Their love-making lasted for what seemed like hours. Their hands and lips slid over glistening skin, meticulously exploring each other's sweaty bodies, as if charting new territory. The energy she discovered within her was wonderful. Tina would never be the same.

"Do me again, Akele," Tina begged.

On Sunday morning, Tina awakened alone. She felt tiny in the enormous bed. She stretched her limbs and thought about the previous night's activities. Closing her eyes to relax, she felt good for a change, refreshed.

A maid entered, carrying coffee and a croissant on a silver tray. Tina pulled the silk sheet and blanket up to her neck. "Thank you," she said before sampling her coffee.

"At your service," the servant responded with a stern look. Then she left the room abruptly.

A small envelope peeked out from under the cloth napkin on the tray. She opened it. A crisp U.S. $100 bill dropped out. There was also a note:

Tina—

Thanks for a lovely evening. Hope you enjoyed yourself as much as I. Would love to see you again soon. Meetings all day. Stay as long as you like.

Affectionately,

Akele

The money was twice the amount that Federico would deposit into her recently opened account as payment for this date. It must have been meant as a gratuity. Was this to be expected? Although she never entertained the idea of leaving the money on the tray—the maid would have taken it—Tina felt uneasy.

Had she officially become a prostitute? Was she a common whore like Mama? No, this was different. She chose to make love with a dignified gentleman, an international diplomat. She was as much in control as he, and no one was hurt. Quite the contrary, she had thoroughly enjoyed it.

Mbondo had aroused Tina's wildly passionate, almost feral needs. She had surprised herself, taken aback by her newfound knowledge. And $100 American, worth five thousand Guaridan pesos, would go a long way toward resolving her problems.

The maid walked into the room without knocking. "You finished, Miss?"

Tina was confused by the maid's attitude, her scorn. Tina had done her no harm. "I'll be done in a few minutes. I'll let you know when to take the tray."

"All right, Miss High and Mighty."

"Excuse me? You have no right to address me that way. Watch your tongue."

"You're nothing but a *puta*. God will punish you."

Resentment and condemnation enveloped Tina. "Listen, Akele and I—"

"You aren't the first to warm his bed, dear. He did like you, though. I can tell. He didn't tip the others."

"Get the hell out of here," Tina shouted. She spilled her coffee as she jumped out of bed. Mind racing, she dressed quickly and dashed out of Mbondo's penthouse.

Manny stood, elbows resting on a high round table, and listened intently to his colleague's soliloquy. His coffee cup had long ago been drained.

"The Guaridan economy is directly linked to the price of a barrel of oil on the international market," the lanky economist stated. He clutched in both hands hundreds of loose pages, possibly lecture notes or a manuscript. His wire-framed glasses were slipping off his narrow nose. Manny imagined that a strong gust of wind could have dislodged both his colleague's glasses and his dissertation.

"Would you like a clip or a rubber band?"

"No, Manny, I can't let go. Know what would happen if I dropped these papers? *Mierda,* that's what. My career, my life, would be over. Just push my glasses up a bit, would you?"

Manny laughed and fixed his colleague's glasses. Then he caught a glimpse of shiny black hair, its length distinctive. It flowed to the small of the woman's back, just below her waistline. She had to be the one from the restaurant. Tina was her name, he remembered.

Tina turned toward Manny, caught his eye, smiled. He waved to her, and then he focused his attention on his colleague again.

"If I were running the show, I'd use petrodollars for health care and education reforms," Manny said to the economist.

"The Americans will negotiate, or dare I say demand, that the barrel return to around U.S. $28," the economist countered. "This OPEC shit of over $30 can't last. The Guaridan balloon will burst."

"That's the problem with a mono-cultural economy," Manny stated. "Excuse me, please—I think I know someone over there." His colleague waved him away, still smiling and clutching his papers, and Manny strolled over to where Tina stood. "Hello Tina," he said.

"Hi, professor, how are you?"

"Very well, thanks. Why don't we sit down? There's a free table over there."

"Actually, I have some shopping to do." She shook her head, but her eyes were warm; was she playing hard to get?

"Come on, just for a few minutes?"

"Okay then, a few minutes."

They ambled over to the other side of the bar. She reached for the chair across the table from Manny but remained standing. He thought she looked anxious as she swept her hair away from her forehead. "I really have to go," she said.

Manny signaled to a waiter. "Bring us a couple of coffees, please." There was something about this young woman. Was it the idea of forbidden fruit that intrigued him? Dee should have come to Guarida. He missed her. In his heart he knew pursuing Tina was a bad choice. Yet, he felt lonely in this strange land. Chatting with a local would be educational and wouldn't hurt anyone.

"All right, just one cup, *con leche,*" Tina said as she sat down.

"Well, how have you been?"

"Oh, just fine." She swept her hair again, and it fell behind her shoulders in a shimmering wave. "No more problems than usual. And you?"

"I'm good. Hey, that's twice we asked the same question."

Tina shrugged. "You and your friend were solving the world's problems?"

"You knew I was here," Manny said.

"I thought it might be you."

"I'm finished for the day. Every so often a teacher can stimulate some thinking, perhaps move students out of their comfort zones," Manny said. He looked at Tina's eyes. They were large, dark, and staring into his. "I'm certain you've experienced that in your classes," he said, thinking back to the spirited discussion with his students on Perkins' *Confessions of an Economic Hit Man.*

"I'm happy when the little ones listen to me," Tina said. She took the cup of coffee in both hands and blew on it a little before sipping. "Behavior is the challenge in elementary. But I love the kids. They're so innocent. My God, I wish they didn't have to grow up in the world the way it is."

"Yeah, it's tough here on the island. I guess we all have to do what we have to," Manny offered.

"Not tough for you," Tina blurted. "You're a gringo."

Manny was taken aback and wondered what had triggered her hostility. "Hey, wait a minute," he said.

"We come from different worlds," Tina said.

"Was it something I said?" *Are all Guaridans anti-American?* he wondered.

"You Americans think you rule the world. You think Guarida exists to serve you. I can hardly make ends meet. I have to do things you can't even imagine." The words slid off her tongue like a confession of sorts.

"You think that's my fault, Tina? Look, there are some Ugly Americans. But most of us are compassionate. We come from all over the world. I'm half Guaridan." Who was he trying to convince?

"Wait a minute yourself, Mr. Guaridan-Gringo. Come on."

Manny thought for a moment. He wanted to show her that he was different, didn't fit the stereotype. And he hated that his outspoken skepticism was often misinterpreted as arrogance. Manny considered himself humble and empathetic, not dogmatic. "No problem. I'm used to it, being a gringo and all."

"It's not that I don't like gringos."

"Don't worry about it."

"You seem like a really nice guy. I'm not so nice myself."

"Not nice?"

"Never mind..." Tina shook her head.

"We keep bumping into each other," Manny said.

"I didn't know you'd be here," Tina snapped back.

"Oh? Neither did I, but why don't we plan it next time? We could meet at El Salón de la Parrilla, have a nice meal and some pleasant conversation." Dee wouldn't mind, Manny rationalized; it was just so he didn't have to dine alone. Dee would understand. Wouldn't she? Anyway, she'd never know.

Tina flashed her large brown eyes. Manny thought he detected a hint of intrigue in their expression. What was he getting himself into? And why didn't he care?

☞Chapter Nine☜

After two months of negotiations, the teachers' strike was settled by a compromise that satisfied neither the teachers nor the government. Tina was happy to return to the little ones, yet she felt increasingly pressed for time. It seemed as if Federico was calling her much more often than before.

She was sitting alone in El Salón de la Parrilla when her cell phone sounded its salsa tune. She reached into her handbag. Federico again; she almost didn't answer, but cash was cash.

"Hello?"

The normal brief small talk followed. *How pleased the bastard sounds,* she thought. *But I'm not working for his sake. To hell with him—I'm doing it for myself. And I'll make time to see the gringo one of these days.*

"This one's a follow-up, babe," Federico said. "It's with Mr. Wilson. He asked for you. Remember him? And there'll be a couple of my other girls going along as well. He's having a party."

"Him again? Sure, I'll be there," she said. She could actually look forward to a party with Wilson, who had taken her to the opera and treated her well the last time.

Tina arrived at 10:00 p.m. She was always on time and enjoyed dressing for this kind of affair. Feeling elegant in the original Versace that Federico had provided from his large wardrobe, Tina stepped out of the glass-encased elevator into a private area adorned with tropical plants and flowers. Several species of orchids were grafted on dry tree limbs propped against the whitewashed stucco walls around the entrance to the penthouse. Harry Wilson, famous American entrepreneur and oil tycoon, waited at the polished wood doorway.

"How are you doing, beautiful?" Harry said as he kissed Tina lightly on each cheek. A handsome man in his early sixties, his deep suntan and blue eyes dominated his persona. Were it not for his completely white hair, she might guess he was much younger. His fit torso was evident, even in the tuxedo.

"I'm fine. Nice to see you again, Harry." Tina gave him a quick hug. She had accompanied him to Verdi's *Rigoletto* a week ago, and he had comported himself as a perfect gentleman. After the performance, they had stopped for a cup of coffee in the theater café. Then she had his driver leave her at El Salón de la Parrilla and took a cab back to the Block. She didn't want him to see where she lived.

"You look stunning. Please come in, Tina."

As she entered, another woman walked over and stopped next to Harry. "This is my wife, Andrea," he said.

"Oh, hello, Mrs. Wilson," Tina said, taken aback. Why was the wife present? This was a first. A strikingly attractive woman, Andrea Wilson looked much younger than forty-something. Her platinum blond hair was styled in a tight French twist. A silk kimono draped her well-kept figure.

"Oh dear, you're surprised to see me, aren't you?" Mrs. Wilson said.

"Andrea, why don't you see to our other guests? I'll attend to Ms. Carmen Reyes."

Andrea excused herself, and Tina whispered to her host, "I didn't know your wife would be here."

"Not to worry, I've invited a few friends. We're having a little party. It's a nice group, oil execs and a few escorts. You probably know them."

Tina nodded; she had seen other girls at the safe house once or twice.

"I'm certain you're going to have fun," Harry said.

They went into the main room together, where Andrea was mingling with other guests. Harry went to Andrea, drawing Tina along with him, and said, "Too bad McGeorge couldn't be here.

"PI invested millions of dollars in the new oil dock," one of the oil execs chatting with Andrea said. "It's more efficient and closer to the city than the old one."

"Guarida's a safe country," Harry said. "Sure there's some discontent, but the American market keeps this island afloat. The new dock will help."

Tina didn't know what they were talking about. She looked around. She and Federico's girls were the only Guaridans in the penthouse, other than the servants. Although she was getting used to being shown some respect, she didn't like how the maids fawned over her and the escorts. And she would never forget the incident with Mbondo's maid. Weren't they all cut from the same cloth? Again, she asked herself, why was she here? What the hell was going on?

Harry and two of the fat cats were accompanied by their wives. The other three were alone. They made the same points over and over: Guarida was safe, oil deals were in the bag, the island was a great American partner, McGeorge and each of these men stood to make a windfall profit. They would all be billionaires within a year.

Tina refrained from comment. She resented the way these foreigners talked about her country as if it were their personal property. Who did they think they were?

"Guarida isn't part of the United States," Tina muttered under her breath.

"What did she say?" one of the execs asked his host. "Who is she?"

"Miss Tina Reyes," Wilson said. "She's a good girl. Let's not talk business. We're here to relax—have some fun."

Tina moved to the other side of the room and spent the next two hours making small talk with the male guests. At midnight Harry announced that he had a real treat. He grabbed a small silver box and signaled for everyone to gather around. He opened the box and spread its contents, a fine white powder, on the glass coffee table in the center of the living room.

Andrea opened her purse and pulled out her Centurian card. Using the American Express Black, she formed thin rows of the substance on the table. Harry placed a silver tube next to the lines of cocaine. One by one each of the guests inhaled the coke through their nostrils.

Tina was amazed. She felt uncomfortable, yet intrigued. It seemed completely out of character for these gringo businessmen to engage in the kind of behavior she associated with Block youth. And she declined to take a hit. She was flattered by the offer, but she had only snorted the stuff once and knew about the dangers of addiction. She had seen some of her friends fall into the cycle of misery and pain caused by drugs and alcohol.

Harry kept insisting that she join in, persevering to the point that Tina almost yielded in order to shut him up. Instead, she diverted his attention with a few sexy dance steps. With that, the party took a turn. Frank Sinatra was replaced by Fifty-Cent. Curtis James Jackson III rapped about "getting rich or die trying." Sweet incense floated in the air. The men and women tried to boogie, a surrealistic scene reminiscent of images Tina had seen of the hip sixties. She had watched documentaries about Haight-Ashbury on television. Yet these were conservative business people, pallid Americans in their formal attire, writhing ungracefully while the escorts danced provocatively.

Then they all began peeling off their clothes, throwing them onto the sofas and chairs. Tina, who was still sober, was astonished.

Harry still had his pants on; he swaggered over and embraced Tina. "Want to dance?"

She did a few steps with him, then tried to dance apart. He had no rhythm.

"Do you like orgies, my little Guaridan princess?"

Before she could respond, Andrea cut in by inserting herself between Tina and Harry. "Hi, babe." She flashed a come-hither smile at Tina, ignoring her husband.

Suddenly, Andrea embraced Tina, brushed her lips against Tina's, and then probed Tina's mouth with her tongue.

Tina, who felt like a deer frozen in headlights, reacted involuntarily. She felt a tingling sensation rise from her belly up to her breasts. She gave Andrea a long and passionate kiss.

Andrea hugged her, took her hand, and led her to the bedroom. "Good girl," she whispered. Harry, transfixed, followed along like a shadow.

At 4:45 p.m. on Monday, Tina walked from the Block to El Salón de la Parrilla. She arrived at five. Evita, who lived around the corner from the restaurant, was waiting. After exchanging pleasantries, the two women ordered beef tenderloin to be grilled beside their table and a couple of bottles of El Nacional.

"I've had something on my mind for a while," Tina said. She had to decide what to do about a lot of things. Should she continue to work as an escort? Would it be wise to see Manny? But it was her encounter with Andrea that troubled Tina most.

"Spit it out, sister."

"You know I've worked as an escort. I was wondering if we could compare our experiences a little. I hope you don't mind."

"We're friends; you can confide in me. I know exactly what you're going through."

"I'm not so sure about that." Tina glanced around the restaurant. It was only half full. Some people were finishing late lunches and a few had arrived for drinks before an early dinner. Serious dining began well after sunset.

"You want to get out," Evita said, "but need the money. You want what they have and to pick and choose, but they all seem to want sex. Sometimes you don't mind, but you don't want to become a whore. It started out okay, but you're getting sick and tired of the routine. Correct?"

"Actually, the thing is, it can be exciting. And, of course, the money—but you're right. I'm going to end it soon."

"I felt that way for some time: the sooner, the better. 'No glass slippers,' as you've said many times, my friend."

"There's something else." Tina paused, wondered what her friend would think about the real issue on her mind. Should she even tell her?

"What else? There isn't much that will shock me."

"It's embarrassing." Tina surveyed the restaurant again.

"Don't say anything you don't want me to know." Evita smiled and put her hand on Tina's. "Really—"

The waiter served their steaks. They cut into the juicy meat, dipped bites in the red hot sauce and the mild green salsa dressing, had some yucca, sipped the beer. Passers-by ogled the attractive women sitting in the corner, too far away from the sidewalk to hear their *piropos*.

Tina finished a piece of steak, washed it down with her beer, and looked at her friend. She opened her mouth, closed it again, and then blurted that she had an unusual experience. She glanced around the restaurant again, then back at Evita. "It was an oil executive from the States, second time. The first was at the theater. This time he had a party in his penthouse. It got weird. There was coke, but I wouldn't do it. And his wife came on to me."

"I'm not surprised." Evita smiled sympathetically.

"The surprising thing is that I enjoyed having sex with her. Are you stunned?"

A thoughtful expression came over Evita's face. "You little slut," she said with a wink and a laugh. Then she looked into Tina's eyes and whispered, "Listen, I know how you feel. I've been there. And my theory is that anyone can go either way, so don't be embarrassed. The only time I feel real is during sex." She leaned over and kissed Tina on the lips. Scornful expressions appeared on the faces of two elderly women seated at a nearby table.

"I'm Guarideña through and through," Tina said. "And, you know, I actually like my life. I adore you, Evita, and my children will not lose me as their teacher. They need me. Who else would stay with them down in the Block? Who else could?"

Evita brushed Tina's hair from her forehead, caressed her neck.

Tears welled-up in Tina's eyes. She reached over and took Evita's hand, then sighed, wiped her eyes, and smiled. "And there's this guy who invites me to dinner. He's a gringo professor—"

"What the hell is he doing in Guarida? Be careful, honey."

"Yeah, I know."

Evita looked into Tina's eyes again. They both smiled. They held that pose for a prolonged moment, after which Tina ordered another round of beer, this time a couple of Dos Equis. Then they attacked their steaks.

Tina's mind was made up. *Don't jump ship now,* she decided.

ᑫ᠀Chapter Ten᠀ᑫ

A week later, on a Thursday afternoon, María Elena Torres opened her door on the periphery of the secretarial suite and summoned Tina to her office. Tina saved her work, took out a notepad and pen, and walked past the other secretaries. The professor's office was lined by books from floor to ceiling. Papers were strewn all over the small desk, covering it like a blanket.

"No need to take notes; I just need to ask a small favor. My husband called a few minutes ago, he's on his way up, but I have a meeting. Would you let him into my office and arrange for a cup of coffee? I'd appreciate it. I can't get out of this meeting with the dean, we're discussing a new program. I thought I told Federico—he probably forgot."

Tina's smile faded. Why was Federico coming to the university now? How much did his wife know? This might be the right time to end her stint in the escort business.

A few minutes later, Federico walked into the secretarial suite. He wore the same jacket and carried the same briefcase as when he found Tina at the café. He smiled at the secretaries.

"Good afternoon, Mr. Torres." Tina took a deep breath. "Your wife asked me to show you into her office.

Would you like coffee?" She tried to appear calm, collected. Her stomach felt knotted, blood rushed to her head, and her breath shortened.

"Thank you, señorita," Federico stated formally.

Tina was relieved; she didn't want a scene in front of the other secretaries. They were a bunch of gossips.

She pointed to María Elena's door. Federico nodded and signaled for Tina to enter. Then he went in and closed the door behind him.

"Tina, it's good to see you, honey."

"How have you been, Federico?"

"Great. Business is booming. Demand is much higher than supply, though. And when that happens, prices soar. I'm put in an interesting position—"

"Don't go there, Federico. I'm quitting the business." Beads of sweat formed on Tina's forehead, her cheeks flushed. "Why are you here?"

"A special assignment—you were specifically requested, by name. Apparently you've got something special, my dear." He smiled, ignoring her weak attempt to give notice.

"Is it with Mrs. Harris?" Tina asked.

"I know all about that. No, this is with someone who wants your company for an afternoon, day after tomorrow. And *he* must remain anonymous. You'll be well compensated."

"This will be my last, Federico."

"Sure, honey."

That Saturday, Tina settled into the limousine that had come for her and asked the driver, "May I know where we're going, who I'll meet?" Her body was shaking, her nerves getting the better of her. She had no idea what this was all about, not like the usual dates.

"My vehicle is very well equipped," the driver said. "There are refreshments in back. Make yourself at home. We have a two-hour drive."

The leather-upholstered back seat was spacious. Air-conditioning cooled the interior. A mini-bar with a small refrigerator stood behind the driver's forward cabin. Tina tried to get comfortable for the drive to a meeting with an unidentified person at an unknown destination, but her uneasiness would not fade.

The limo sped along the highway along the coast, locals call it the *malecón,* and Tina took a beer from the mini-bar. A few sips calmed her down. She sat back and observed the coves lined by sandy beaches. They passed one after another, each separated by hills with rocky shores. Soon the vehicle slowed down. The roadway, no longer paved, wound around the hills and ended at the water's edge.

"Thanks for the ride, pal," Tina laughed, looking out the window at a Sea Ray Express Cruiser tied to a floating dock. Waves crashed onto massive rocks protecting the shoreline, and the yacht heaved on large swells. She could see two uniformed crew members readying the craft, and one stood waiting where the limo had stopped. "Now what, a boat tour?" she asked her driver.

"I'll return for you after your meeting. Enjoy."

She stepped out of the limo and took the arm of the crew member, who escorted her up the gang plank. He would tell her nothing about her host or the voyage, simply said that she should make herself at home. Once on the yacht, Tina chose to stay on deck. She needed some fresh air. And she wanted to see where she was being taken. She recalled her decision not to jump ship and smiled. *How literal,* she thought.

She wandered into the bridge, where the captain nodded at her as he fired up the engines. "Twin four fifty-four Mercruisers," he boasted. Tina had no idea what he meant. Only once had she been on a boat, and that was a fisherman's skiff with an outboard. The deep rumbling of the powerful engines sounded like an orchestra of muffled bass drums. The first mate cast off the lines, and they set out to sea.

Tina watched the shore line recede into the distance, feeling like a captive. She was heading into deep water and might be in over her head.

The Sea Ray bounced on the heavy chop and rose out of the hole. Then the captain eased off the controls, trimmed onto plane, and announced, "Twenty-two knots at thirty-two hundred RPM. We're at twelve point fifty-five degrees north and seventy-three point thirty degrees west." The vessel left a deep wake for a surprisingly smooth ride.

The outline of what appeared to be a huge, ornate sand castle materialized through the sea mist. As they approached, details of the ethereal apparition came into focus. It looked like Rapunzel's castle, completely out of place on the shores of Tina's humble homeland. The vision brought to mind the fables Mama had read to her when she was a child.

"This is El Palacio Miramar," the captain said. "It was built at the end of this peninsula on the rocky escarpment overlooking the sea. It is accessible only by water, so the rough terrain isolated the bastion from intrusions. Carlos Pérez

Santo built Miramar as a retreat for government officials. This is your destination."

They docked a few minutes later, and an armed guard escorted Tina from the dock to steps leading onto a wide verandah. A familiar figure waited there: the president of Guarida, a broad smile on his swarthy face, his arms outstretched to her. The stocky man wore a silk floral guayabera, casual slacks, and sandals.

"Hello and welcome, Señorita Reyes. I'm so happy you were able to come."

"Hello, Mr. President—thank you," Tina managed. She tried to appear calm, flashed him a bright smile. *My God, she thought, what the hell is going on?*

President Sánchez smiled again in response. "Please call me Claudio. Here we're on vacation. No need for protocol. It's my pleasure to meet you."

"Equally," uttered Tina. She had seen guards, armed with machine guns, on the dock, around the palace, and up on the roof. But none were present on the verandah where she and the president took seats beside a rattan coffee table.

The view of the sea from here took her breath away. Nothing about this place seemed real. It was like a setting for a movie, a fantasy. A waiter appeared and asked what refreshments she might desire.

"Please, request anything you'd like," the president urged her. "We have just about everything here. Would you accept champagne and caviar?"

Tina's mind was reeling. Her body felt as if it were floating. She wasn't really here—she was in a dream that would end abruptly when she awakened. What was Claudio Sánchez up to? "I'll just take a beer, if you don't mind." She wondered if this could be a typical escort encounter. *No, not with the president,* she decided.

"Two Red Stripes, Felipe, and bring the caviar."

She sat primly on the edge of her chair, unable to relax until she found out what was going on. "May I ask why I'm here?"

Sánchez smiled as he scrutinized his guest. "I believe you recognize the duties of citizenship. There are times when we must all make sacrifices for the *patria.*"

Tina was shocked; the dream was over. He questioned her patriotism? She laughed awkwardly and could contain herself no longer. "I love my country."

"Excellent, your patriotism will be an attribute that pulls you through the most difficult times. Now I'll tell you the purpose of our meeting, which incidentally must remain completely confidential." He leaned across the table toward her. "You do understand the need for confidentiality, Señorita Reyes?"

"I'll understand better when I know what you want from me. Please call me Tina, Mr. President—Claudio."

"What I want—what I ask—is simply your patriotic duty, Tina. I brought you here to speak to you in person. I could have had one of my agents contact you, but I wanted us to meet."

Tina curled the ends of her hair through her fingers. Frightening thoughts flashed through her mind, like being forced to become a kamikaze pilot, an Al Qaeda suicide bomber, or something equally outrageous. How was she going to disentangle herself from this muddle?

At least it wasn't about sex, though it would be less complicated if it were, she thought.

"Please don't worry," Claudio said. "All we want is some routine surveillance. We'd like you to report to us about the activities and contacts, and perhaps the ideas and plans, of Professor Emmanuel White Vidal."

"Manny? The professor I met at El Salón de la Parrilla? How do you know about that?"

"Paulo Ferreira is an excellent source of information."

"Paulo? La Ciruela?"

"More importantly, Juan Carlos advises me to keep a close watch on the professor. We've learned that he reports to the U.S. Department of State, which could be a CIA cover, you know. If he's up to something untoward, we must stop it quickly. And he need never suspect that we're keeping tabs on him."

"I don't even know him."

"You will be working for your country. And assuming the professor isn't involved in any subversive activities, nothing will happen to him."

"Why are you interested in him?" Tina held her temples and massaged her forehead.

"He's going to work for me—I put him on an advisory committee," Claudio said with a short, sharp laugh. "We've got him just where we want him."

Tina smiled politely, trying to keep the shock from her expression. *What a ridiculous game they play,* she thought. "So why do you need me?"

"You'll get to know him. Get real close. You're good at that, no? We simply want to know what he's up to, who he meets with and where he goes, that sort of thing." He took a sip of the Red Stripe.

"I don't know..." Tina said.

Claudio pushed back his chair and walked to the edge of the terrace. He stared out to sea, then returned to sit, pulling his chair up next to Tina's knee. "Listen, this is difficult to ask." His breathing was a little rushed. "We don't want your school principal to learn of your employment with Torres, nor about Mrs. Harris's preferences, nor Mbundo's generous patronage—"

Tina was speechless. Her jaw tightened, fists clenched, blood rushed into her head. *Pathetic,* she thought, *the leader of our country stooping to blackmail.* Suddenly a calm feeling overcame the anxiety. She stopped swimming against the stream. The currents were too strong. "Mr. President—Claudio—I want your word of honor that no harm will come to him." Tina stood, crossed her arms over her chest. Although she didn't know Manny well, Tina wouldn't knowingly cause harm to anyone. She had done questionable things, but never with malevolent intentions. She saw her role as an escort as a means to provide pleasure or relief to others. She took a deep breath. "Also, my mother is in need of medical treatment. It's very expensive, you know."

"Certainly, of course, very good, that's very reasonable. We'll take good care of your mother. Please sit down." Claudio gestured toward her chair. "Assuming the professor is innocent—not CIA—he will be protected. Under these considerations you have my word. No one wants to hurt anyone. However, the government must protect itself. And we live in turbulent times, Tina. You understand that, I'm sure."

She nodded, tightlipped, and Claudio rose, paced back and forth. "My administration will change social and economic conditions for the better. Yet there are those who are conspiring to undermine my regime!" He paused and smacked the table in front of them. "My government won't allow the rich elite, the Corrupt Ones, to continue raping the country. Nor will we be a pawn of the United States."

She could think of nothing to say, but she couldn't look away from his intense gaze. "Think about all those who are trapped in the barrios," he said. "What would you say to them if you were in my shoes?" His voice grew quiet, conspiratorial. "Find out what you can, Tina. My assistants will be in touch with you later, but for now, please enjoy the refreshments. Stay as long as you like. When you are ready, my captain will take you back. Thank you for coming, and I apologize that I must leave. I have other matters to deal with."

The president got up, walked away, and picked up a baseball bat that was leaning against the wall next to enormous wooden doors. Tina hadn't noticed the bat until that moment. Claudio Sánchez then disappeared into the interior of the palatial retreat.

She sat and thought for a few minutes, reflecting on her brief conversation with Claudio Sánchez, attempting to put it in some kind of perspective. The encounter was definitely a game changer. Now she was involved in an intrigue she had never imagined—and with the president, no less. She worried that she might not even see the gringo again. Things had gone beyond her control.

While living in Guarida, Manny had spoken with Dee regularly, at least a couple of times a week—until recently. Somehow the frequency of their calls had dropped off a bit. When the phone rang, he hoped it would be Dee. He answered and was instantly cheered by the sound of her voice. After they shared how much they missed each other, she told him that her life had become like a dull routine. Day after day, after working at the library, she simply returned home and watched TV.

"I've been asked out a few times," she said. "I turned them down. Had dinner with Rhoades once, but I don't think he liked hearing about you the whole time." Dee laughed. "He hasn't invited me again."

"How's the weather up there?" Tingling with guilt, Manny attempted to shift the conversation to something other than dinner companions.

"It's getting colder."

"Have you thought about coming down?"

"I'm not sure I'll be able to arrange it. How are you doing with your search? Any leads on your cousin?"

"I saw some unsigned drawings that I think might be his. I've tried to track down the artist, but no luck yet. I'm going to find out what happened to Rafael, mark my words, Dee. Otherwise I'm fine. UG keeps me busy. I've played some tennis, too—I made the finals of Campo Alegre but lost to Ray. I've told you about him. And I've been up to the embassy at least once a week."

"I miss you."

"Miss you too, Dee. I'll call again in a few days."

"Love you."

"Love you too."

Manny sat across from Tina at El Salón de la Parrilla. They had dined there several times since they had met unexpectedly at the university café, eating and talking until both were sated. So far this evening, they had polished off two bottles of Don Miguel Gascón.

Manny and Tina left the restaurant and wandered up the street arm-in-arm, swaying back and forth as if dancing off-balance, stopping and misstepping, attempting to stay on the sidewalk. Manny couldn't walk in a straight line, so Tina guided him. Pedestrians stared at them as they passed. He felt embarrassed to be a bit out of control.

Manny had no idea where they were headed. He hadn't planned anything that evening. They passed La Ciruela, which had closed for the night.

"Where are we, gringo?"

"Right in front of my cave, how do you like that?"

"So this is where the caveman dwelleth—in Las Palmas, huh? Nice digs."

"Come on up," Manny said. "I'll show you my etchings."

They looked at each other and burst out laughing. "Let's see how the gringo caveman lives," Tina said in an exaggeratedly seductive voice.

Manny struggled to find his keys. He fumbled while trying to open the gate. Tina grabbed the keys, opened the gate and the apartment door, and pulled Manny through. As soon as the door clicked shut behind them, she pushed him up against the wall and planted a sloppy kiss on his open mouth. They began groping each other. Both seemed desperate for intimacy, for the feel of human flesh. They pulled off each other's clothes, explored each other's bodies with hot hands and wet lips. Any barriers that had existed between them had vanished.

"In vino veritas," Manny said when they came up for air.

Tina laughed heartily. "That's the truth," she said.

"Well, here we are."

"I thought you'd never ask me up."

He felt as if he were being swept away by feelings and desires that had now been released. Until then, he had sublimated the sexual attraction, pretending their relationship was purely platonic. It was a different feeling than being with Dee. Tina was a compact sex machine who needed little foreplay. Dee's body was larger, her limbs longer. Manny had to work to get Dee ready. Tina shouted; Dee sighed.

As soon as he made the physical comparison, Manny's brain shut down; his body had a mind of its own. He was twenty again, carousing, exploring. His only goal was to score.

They fell onto the living room couch. Tina was hot, moist. Manny was ready. Their sweaty, interlocked bodies moved together in savage unison. They devoured each other, satisfied their hunger—at least for the moment.

Part Two

"THE PROBLEM IS THAT CARIBBEAN REALITY RESEMBLES THE
WILDEST IMAGINATION."

~ GABRIEL GARCÍA MÁRQUEZ

ᑫᕽᎧChapter Eleven᙭ᓬᑋ

After his morning jog, Manny brought up fresh orange and passion fruit juices from La Ciruela. The pungent aromas of a typical Guaridan Sunday-morning breakfast wafted through the apartment. Tina had prepared sausages, eggs, black beans, fried plantains, white cheese and *guayabada,* and coffee. Manny breathed in the scents with pleasure. He had become quite accustomed to having Tina stay overnight. In fact, she had practically moved in.

"How was your run?" she asked. "You took long enough. Breakfast is ready."

"The store was packed—had to wait in line." Manny could have sworn he had seen the businessman from the airport in La Ciruela. But he'd only had a glimpse as the tall man left the store and disappeared into the crowded street. *Small country, but probably not the same guy,* he thought.

After they finished their spread, Manny reclined on the sofa and opened the Spanish translation of *Democracy in America* that he had checked out of the embassy library. Tina cleaned up in the kitchen. Sunlight blazed through the windows. The scene made him surprisingly content.

"It's amazing how perceptive this Frenchman can be. Shit, he got it right over a century ago."

"What? Can't hear you—" Tina shouted. Water pounded on dishes in the sink.

"Nothing, just thinking maybe it takes a foreigner. That would make me an expert on Guarida, huh?"

"Can't hear you." Tina finished in the kitchen, walked out to the living room, and sat down beside him.

"Alexis de Tocqueville wrote about the tyranny of the majority as if he knew the United States would become a bastion of intolerance." Manny thought about the treatment of Mexicans in Arizona and Texas—Dee was sickened by it—and how Qurans were burned in Florida. No one was just an American, everyone had dashes. Italian-American, Polish-American... And every application form had a line for race and ethnicity.

Whenever Manny thought about Dee, he felt pangs of culpability. He tried to assuage his conscience by thinking of his affair as a last fling before engagement. Shacking up with Tina was just an adventure. Latin American men all had mistresses anyway, so when in Rome—

"Enough politics," Tina said, rolling her eyes. "I don't know what you are talking about."

Manny tossed his hands in the air, took a deep breath. "Honey, you do understand gringos."

Tina held up her middle finger. He winced, stretched out on the sofa, and stuck his nose back in the book. His contentment faded.

Tina went into the bedroom, pinned up her hair, and put on a long skirt and a loose-fitting blouse. She had stocked Manny's closet with a few essentials and planned to go out later. She pranced into the living room and flipped on the TV. Given the time of day, Manny assumed she was about to search for one of her beloved *telenovelas*.

The news anchor announced, "Saddam was caught like a rat in a hole."

"They finally got him," Tina said.

"But no WMDs. Should've let the UN observers do their jobs. Leave it on the news for a minute," Manny said before she could switch channels.

The image of a beaming Claudio Sánchez flashed on the screen. He looked like he had just thrown a no-hitter.

Tina raised her eyebrows. Her jaw dropped, and she said, "He's from the Block, you know. I saw him pitch. And I've met him."

"The masses have their champion, their messiah." Manny was intrigued by Claudio Sánchez. *He holds a lot of potential for progressive reform,* he thought. Sánchez ought to tone down his rhetoric, though. Manny had told him so at their last meeting.

"What do I know about politics? I do know that things are different now, Manny. There's a lot of discontent out there."

"Sánchez might be able to make a difference," he said. "But did you hear about the Comidas-en-Ruedas mishap? Members of the group were taken into custody by the Security Police while distributing food in the Block. They were mistaken for subversives."

"Those guys don't create jobs. It's the Corrupt Ones' way of keeping poor people off their backs. This is the first time one of us—like you gringos like to say, a person of color—is in power. You'd never permit it up there, right? You yourself couldn't become president, Manny. Here you're white, but up there you'd be considered a person of color or a Latino, right? It's damn racism. Nothing more, nothing less."

"Things are changing. We've had Colin Powell, and now Carl Pham-Dixon as Secretary of State. But the issue here isn't Claudio's color or class. As much as I sympathize with his domestic agenda, he's challenging the power structure, threatening the United States and international businesses. I'm advising him to be more diplomatic." *She says she knows nothing about politics,* Manny thought, *and then she spouts off about the Corrupt Ones and the United States.* The comments irritated him. "Think about what you're saying, Tina. It's a bit prejudiced and inconsistent."

"Yeah, sure," Tina said. "Listen, I don't want to fight. And if I can't watch my stuff on TV, I'm going over to UG for a few hours. I have some typing that's due tomorrow."

"Today's Sunday."

"I've put these damn reports off and I need to get them in. I'll be back soon."

"Fine. I've actually got some papers to grade anyhow." He rose to his feet and gave her a peck on the cheek. "See you later on. Get your work done. Hurry back."

Good, he thought, *now I'll have a few hours of down-time to accomplish something and get some rest.*

Manny had read through almost half of the student research papers that were due for submission to the department secretary by the following Friday. He'd probably need a week to complete them. He continued reading, but the street noise in the background broke his concentration. He plodded on until the doorbell startled him.

Strange, he thought, *I'm not expecting anyone.* But the timing was opportune; he welcomed the distraction. It was difficult to distinguish one student paper from another. Each one, no matter its primary focus, referred to the strategic value of petroleum, Guarida's possession of large deposits off the coast, and international trade.

He placed the paper he was reading on one of the piles on the sofa, stood up, stretched his arms over his head, and shuffled over to the door. Who could it be? Tina had just left for the university. She couldn't be back yet, and she had her own key.

"Who's there?" Manny said through the closed door. There was no answer. He unlocked the latch and opened the door a crack. He peered through—and couldn't believe his eyes.

"Ta da!" Dee held out her arms, a big smile on her pretty face. It was as if she had miraculously appeared out of nowhere.

Manny froze. His heart felt about to explode as it drove blood into his swirling head. He gasped for air and stared at Dee. She looked good. He opened his mouth and tried to smile. Then he opened the door the rest of the way, unlatched the gate, and took a step back.

Dee stepped into the apartment, and Manny hugged his American girlfriend, his possible fiancée–to-be. She gave him a puzzled look.

"Aren't ya gonna give me a kiss?"

"Of course. You just surprised me, that's all." He gave Dee a warm, soulful kiss and tried to think fast. Tina would soon walk in on them. He would have a lot of explaining to do. This had the makings of a full-blown catastrophe.

Dee glanced around the apartment and tossed her small suitcase on the sofa. It disrupted some of the student papers, which were stacked in categories according to the grades they would receive. "Working?" she said.

"You finally decided to visit."

She frowned. "Aren't you glad to see me?"

"Of course. But when did you decide to come down?"

"Spur-of-the-moment thing—I took a few days off. I've got until Labor Day. Isn't that great?"

"They don't celebrate that down here," Manny murmured. He fought to pull his wits about him. "You must be hungry after the flight."

"I could eat something, darlin'. Then I'm going to attack you."

"Well, come on then, let's go down to the parrilla." He grabbed his phone and his wallet. "Great food, nice place, I'll show you around a bit—"

"What's the big rush?"

"I'm famished," Manny said, thinking about the huge breakfast he'd just finished.

They left the apartment and walked arm-in-arm down the block. The fruit store proprietor, Paulo Ferreira, waved. As they approached El Salón de la Parrilla, Manny steered Dee past, saying there was a better, more intimate, place a few blocks away. He made sure they were seated inside and toward the back. After ordering, he excused himself, telling

Dee he had to go to the bathroom. From inside the men's room, he called Ray.

"I'm in deep shit. Dee just arrived. She's here—she came right up to the apartment. I shouldn't have given her the address."

"Wait a minute. Dee's here?"

"She just showed up. I took her to a restaurant a few blocks from El Salón. What am I supposed to do?"

"Tell her the truth. Where's Tina?"

"She went over to UG. But she'll be back at the apartment soon. You've got to rescue me, pal. Maybe you could come over, take her somewhere?"

"I'm having tapas with my dad, but we're almost done. We aren't far from your place. I'll go over as soon as I can and take her for a walk. But then what will you do? How long is Dee staying?"

"She's here for the week, till Labor Day. Shit, can you just get Tina? I'll figure something out."

"I'll go as soon as I'm done here. I'll call you when I get over there."

"Thanks. You're going to save my pitiful life, my friend."

After Manny returned to the table, he helped Dee decipher the menu and thought he covered his nerves pretty well. She probably wouldn't notice. If he lived through this…

He introduced her to a local dish made with rice, black beans, plantains, and *calalloo*. "It's delicious," she said. He picked at his portion. They had a couple of Coronas and chatted. He would have been happy to be with Dee under different circumstances. His feelings for her seemed to be distant when he was away from home. His initial passionate impulses cooled as the pressure mounted.

When Dee was ready to return to the apartment, where she said she was going to make love to him all night, Manny asked for another beer. "Just one more, honey. Then we'll go." Ray should have gotten Tina out of the apartment by then. If she'd returned on schedule, anyway. *If Ray rescues me from this mess,* Manny thought, *I'll be eternally grateful.*

He paid the bill and they stood to leave. She massaged his neck for a moment and said, "You seem tense, Manny."

Crap! She noticed. He should have known she would. "Nah, just a lot of work lately."

They strolled hand-in-hand back to his building through a circuitous route of busy streets. He pointed out a few interesting stores and a small park. People were coming home from their work. Some had already changed clothes for a jog. La Ciruela was packed. He couldn't avoid Ferreira, since the fruit store was on the way; the proprietor said nothing but winked at Manny.

He decided to make another attempt at stalling. "This is our fruit store, the one I told you about, where everyone stops for some refreshment. Want to try some mango or *parchita* nectar?"

"Tomorrow, babe. Right now we've got more pressing matters."

Manny shrugged and led her back to his place. He fumbled with the keys, his hands trembling; he had trouble opening the wrought-iron gate outside the door. When he finally got it to open, he unlocked the door, then entered the apartment and looked around. Dee stood behind him.

112

"Manny!" Tina shouted from the bedroom. Manny's heart sank, and he tried to block Dee's view. He had already seen what she would see.

"Who is that?" Dee passed Manny and spotted Tina, who stood in the bedroom door wearing panties and nothing else. "Who are *you*?" Dee screamed.

Even with her limited English, Tina understood the full meaning of Dee's question and all it implied.

"Who do you think you are?" Dee stood with her feet spread apart, her hands on her hips; in a cartoon, steam would have been coming from her ears, but there was nothing funny about what was going on. He had to stop it. The two women looked back at Manny, and he held up his hands. "I can explain," he lied, knowing anything he said would just fuel the fire. His face felt as if it had become as red as a Valentine's Day heart.

But before he could open his mouth to try, Tina lunged at Dee. She grabbed Dee's long blond hair and pulled, forcing the tall woman to the floor with a thud. Then, in a rapid movement reminiscent of a wrestler's reversal, she mounted Dee, her legs astride Dee's hips as if on a horse. Manny ran over, tried to pull Tina off Dee. He earned a sharp kick in the groin in the process, from whom he was uncertain.

Oh shit, he thought. *Oh, shit!*

Dee grabbed Tina's long black hair and tugged fiercely. Tina scratched her sharp fingernails into Dee's neck. Dee fought back using her fists. She smacked Tina across the jaw, causing her to fall backward, then sprang forward and got on top of the smaller woman. She held Tina's shoulders to the floor.

This time, Manny attempted to pull Dee off Tina, but was met by Dee's well-placed elbow in his solar plexus. He fell back and gasped for air. Then Dee, with the clear advantage, peered into Tina's eyes and said, "Why the hell are we doing this?"

Oh crap, Manny thought. He stood, holding his side where it ached and feeling like an idiot.

Though at Dee's mercy, Tina seemed to concur. "We should talk," she said.

Dee loosened her grip. Tina pushed her off and stood up. Tina's breasts were bare, nipples erect. She ran into the bedroom, grabbed a black t-shirt, and pulled it over her head. The word *Caliente* glimmered in gold across the front of the shirt.

Dee turned toward Manny, who stood paralyzed. He had no idea what to say or do. He moved slowly toward Dee, but she moved away. When Tina returned to the living room, Dee stared at her, appeared to be summing her up. She took out a tissue from her jeans pocket and wiped her neck. A light splattering of blood—from scratches, rather than a deep wound—dotted her skin.

Almost simultaneously, the two women turned toward Manny. The ice in their stares nearly gave him frostbite. "I can explain," he said, but he almost choked on the words.

"Yes?" Dee said.

"*Sí?*" Tina said.

Manny opened his hands as if holding an imaginary baby in front of him and said, *"Les amo.* I love you both."

Ray arrived just at that awkward moment, passing through the open door and into the weird scene. "Where were you?" Manny said.

"What's going on here?" Ray said, mouth agape.

114

"Who are you?" Dee said.

"Carajo!" Tina said.

Ray introduced himself to Manny's befuddled American girlfriend. They whispered something to each other, and Dee grabbed her suitcase. Then she and Ray walked out of the apartment. Manny was about to follow when Ray turned and put up his hand like a traffic cop. Then Ray guided Dee out the door.

Manny quickly explained to Tina that Dee was an old friend. They weren't together at the moment, he said as a truism, feeling disgusted with himself. He tried to assess Tina's response in her face, her posture. Her brows were raised, mouth open, arms folded. "Be back in a minute," he told her. "Please, just wait. I need to say goodbye." He ran through the door, leaving it open, and flew down the stairs after Ray and Dee.

Ray's arm was around Dee's shoulders as they walked away from the building. Manny followed them. He had to talk to Dee, although he knew he would be at a loss for words. He caught up with Ray and Dee and said, "Dee, please hear me out, honey."

She turned and stared at him. Her eyes were red. Her lock-jawed expression revealed a tortured combination of anger, incredulity, and sadness. She pressed her lips together, shook her head, and walked on.

"I'm a jerk," Manny said. "Dee, I really love you. Please stop. Just talk to me. Let me explain." A dubious look crossed Dee's flushed face. Was this anger, or had it turned to pity? Manny couldn't tell. "Please, Dee. Give me a chance."

She continued walking faster than before. Manny hurried next to her, trying to keep up. People on the sidewalk watched the show.

115

Ray came around from the other side of Dee. "Give it a rest, Manny," he said. "I'll talk to Dee. We'll get together when things calm down."

"Don't waste your breath," Dee said to Ray. She picked up the pace.

Manny jogged along for a minute or so and then stopped. "Please, Dee?" he shouted one last time. He watched them walk away. Then he turned, and with his head hanging down, he wandered back to the apartment. When he stepped through the door, he saw Tina sitting on the couch with her arms folded across her chest. He slumped down on a chair across from her.

"You have to choose." Tina got up and walked over to him, wrapped her arms around his neck, then pulled him close and hugged him for what seemed like a long time. Finally, she looked into his eyes and kissed him on the lips, a passionate kiss to which he slowly responded. "Choose," she repeated as she shed her Caliente t-shirt.

Manny realized in a flash that, by his own stupidity, he'd probably lost Dee. He was living a fantasy, deceiving himself. He really knew it all along. And now he couldn't just go home and pick up where he'd left off. *What a weakling I am,* he sighed to himself. *Brain's in the groin...*

He would make love to her, but he knew the love-making would be purely physical. He grabbed Tina around the waist and flipped her face-first onto the couch. He pulled off her panties and lifted her hips. Then he pushed her forward so that she rested on her elbows and knees. She arched her back and spread her knees apart. He entered with a vengeance.

Manny grunted, Tina moaned. In a perverse way, visions of Tina grappling with Dee fueled him, reflecting the kind of raw sexuality that had defined his relationship with

116

Tina from the start. Afterward, he felt empty, drained, saddened, and confused. He realized this was not what he wanted. He would have to end the fling with Tina and reconcile with Dee. Although a catastrophe at the moment, somehow he would get his life together.

He slept for a few hours, enjoying sweet dreams about Dee, followed by a nightmare in which he was strangled to death by his own hands. He woke on his back, feeling trapped by Tina's leg over his stomach and her hair draped over his shoulder. He didn't move, and eventually he fell asleep again. When he awakened the second time, he found neither Dee nor Tina beside him.

He got out of bed, searched the bathroom, around the apartment, and finally saw Tina perched on the narrow ledge outside the living room window. Nude, she grasped her knees to her chest, looking like a stray cat stuck on a tree limb.

"What the hell are you trying to prove?" Manny called out to her. Tina did not answer. She seemed to be hypnotized. "Come in, please!" No response. "Please, Tina—are you nuts? Come on in and we'll talk. Please!"

Manny couldn't risk trying to grab her through the open window for fear that she would fall. He had to save her. Visions of explaining to the local police what had happened if she fell also entered his mind—it was at least thirty feet down and a fall would certainly result either in death or complete paralysis or something horrible. And he was a foreigner and would instantly be suspect. He pleaded with her again to come in.

Tina turned her head, gazed in Manny's direction. She appeared to be stranded, stuck in a precarious position, unable to move. Her eyes were empty, like a blind person's.

117

At a loss, Manny sat and stared, tried to use willpower to move her in. Tina remained on the ledge.

Finally, after what seemed like an eternity, she inched her way back through the window. As she ambled past Manny, Tina whispered in a hoarse voice, "Choose." His jaw dropped.

She got into bed and slept late into the morning, but Manny couldn't sleep. He sat down in the kitchen and put his head in his hands and his elbows on his knees. His befuddled, tired brain wandered, and he thought, *I must look more like someone suffering on a toilet than Michelangelo's Thinker.* He went to the sofa and straightened out the piles of student papers he was supposed to have read. But he couldn't focus. Instead he roamed around the apartment, gazing out each of the windows at nothing in particular, then sat down again in the kitchen. He had to extricate himself from this unfortunate mess.

Who was he kidding? Sex alone wasn't love.

The apartment seemed empty and almost silent, but not for Tina's raspy snoring. Manny felt drained, depressed, foolish, and alone. Tears formed in his bloodshot eyes.

Somehow, Manny thought, *I have to get Dee to forgive me.*

ᚦChapter Twelveᚦ

A few days later, Manny pushed his way past clusters of students and professors waiting to enter the restaurants and cafés on the narrow streets surrounding the university campus. The UG was quiet.

He had to get out of the apartment, needed to be alone. He ran up the stairs to his office, then turned on the radio and heard a report about UN calls for withdrawal of foreign forces from Lebanon. He switched the station, found the local news.

Gazing out the window next to his desk, he thought about Dee. He had tried to contact her several times since she stormed out of his apartment. She wouldn't return his calls. Manny had been thinking about her more and more often, almost obsessively, since that day.

According to Dean Rhoades, Dee had returned to the Village and was planning a move back to Texas. Did this mean she was leaving for good? His heart pounded. He had to get through to her. Sighing, he contemplated the logistics of a return to the States at least for a week or so, to beg her forgiveness and persuade Dee to stay. Her departure threatened to unravel their relationship, if it still even existed, just as he started to recognize how important she was in his life.

Manny knew he had plenty to sort out. His personal life wasn't the only mess. There were professional issues to deal with, like his tenure at NYU, UG classes, the presidential advisory committee, the INR.

Oh—and he needed to prepare a communiqué for Adam Stark immediately. He jotted down some notes:

1)   Sánchez promises food, price controls, education, health care, national pride.
2)   Idea of "social revolution" resonates.
3)   Will S nationalize oil? Will S use Security Police?
4)   Hope, progress? Follow actions, not rhetoric.
5)   Watch Guerrero.

Manny took a deep breath, looked out from his third floor window. The university's rustic campus was like a refuge within the frenzied city. An enormous tree stood just outside the office. Manny studied the solid trunk and large boughs. Thick, curved limbs hung over the pathway and cast deep shadows. He figured it was a variety of oak, maybe the kind of live oak used for ship-building. The tree must be hundreds of years old, probably had stood during the independence battles and later the riots that ousted Pérez Santo. *A lot of history writ in wood,* he thought.

Just as he turned back to his notes, Alfredo Cardozo stuck his head through the open door. "Come on in," Manny said.

"Good day," Cardozo said.

Manny shook Cardozo's hand. Then he walked around his small cubicle and looked out at the tree. Its boughs bent over the path like a wooden canopy.

"That's the Hanging Tree," Cardozo said. "There's a book on it. Read it when you have a chance. It reveals a lot about our university; it's an interesting story."

"I will," Manny said without much conviction. Reading about trees wasn't his thing.

Suddenly a tropical deluge began to fall, as if the sky had opened. A few professors gathered under the tree, which was like a giant umbrella. Then, just as quickly, the rain stopped, and steam billowed up from the ground.

"You see how the sun has already begun to burn away the puddles?" Cardozo said. "That's how it is in the tropics. The change is abrupt: one minute it pours, the next it's hot and dry."

"Your weather is kind of like your culture, eh? Extreme and uncompromising." Manny smiled, but he wasn't joking.

"We're a passionate people, you know," Cardozo said, "not wishy-washy like some of your compatriots. What the hell is Washington going to do about our beloved leader, huh? He's already nationalized some of your businesses, and I bet he'll go after oil. Then we'll see some action, no?"

"Guarida needs reforms."

"Of course, of course, but that's not the point, my friend. You gringos think there is a solution to every problem. Work hard and everything turns out okay, right? We're a bit more fatalistic, you know."

"I do like many aspects of Guaridan life."

"Is that what Stark sent you down here for?"

"I chose to come. I have to find my cousin."

"If you haven't found him by now, you might want to forget about it, eh?"

"I'll find him." Manny would not give up, despite all the obstacles.

"Well, do carry on in our little paradise. Hope you make the best of it," Cardozo said as he left the office. He paused in the doorway and said, "By the way, how do you like working with Sánchez?"

"We've only met a few times. As I said, the country needs some new programs."

"Be careful, my friend—you're making a pact with the devil. You'll see." He gave Manny a wave and left, his warning hanging in the air, irritating Manny. Why was everyone so afraid of Sánchez?

The professors who had taken refuge under the tree began to disperse. Manny inhaled the humid air and smelled its green, herbal freshness. He sat down, locked his fingers behind his neck, and thought about Rafael.

Find him and get the hell out of Guarida, he thought. *Go after Dee, convince her to come home.* He hadn't heard from Stark; did Stark even read his communiqués?

Adam Stark received a delivery from the White House. It contained a copy of a missive on Petroleum International corporate letterhead. He read silently:

September 8, 2003

President Timothy Harmon

Office of the President

The White House

1600 Pennsylvania Avenue, NW

Washington, DC 20500

Dear Mr. President,

I write to you as a friend and dedicated supporter who is concerned about the political situation in Guarida. As I am certain you are aware, we are importing a large quantity of Guaridan crude. It is refined and distributed throughout the United States. Petrol International is responsible for a significant portion of these transactions.

I believe that the election of Claudio Sánchez on his revolutionary platform poses a threat to the interests of the United States of America. If the Sánchez regime were to reduce the amount of oil that Guarida exports to the United States, it would have a serious impact on our economy. Given the rising global demand, even a small reduction in our supply would cause prices to rise further with concomitant discontent among the American public.

I urge you to consider a course of action that would protect American business interests in Guarida. We need someone responsible to run this country. Claudio Sánchez is not our man.

Sincerely yours,

William D. McGeorge

Chief Executive Officer

Petrol International Corporation

Edificio Torres Grandes

Ciudad Guarida, D.F., Guarida

Stark was annoyed by the letter, which represented the kind of influence that had been increasingly corrupting Washington. Special interests ran the government. Infusions of large amounts of money—like the large amounts McGeorge had given to the president during his campaign—determined policy choices.

He stuffed the letter in his briefcase and left his office. Stark was on his way to an appointment with Excom, the president's executive committee on national security. He dreaded these meetings. Excom, he had come to recognize, was designed to reaffirm the president's preferences, not formulate objective policy. It was all part of the shell game that politics within the Beltway had been reduced to in the modern era.

Stark arrived at the White House at 10:40; by eleven, members of Excom sat on two large sofas in the Oval Office. President Timothy Harmon sat at his desk. He signed a document, looked up, and said, "Okey-doke."

"Yes, Mr. President," sounded a chorus.

"Y'all know that we need to deal with Claudio Sánchez." Harmon drummed his fingers on his desk.

None of the Excom members wanted to be caught off-guard. Stark harbored a not-so-secret desire to be Secretary of State. He knew that David Ramshore, a former Defense Secretary, had political ambitions. Ex-governor of Virginia Robert Muldive, a point man on homeland security, was a party loyalist who aspired to a cabinet post.

Former Army General Bart Kelloring was always cautious and wanted to avoid war if possible. Former CIA Associate Director James Brownfield, who knew the president since they had raised hell together at fraternity parties, was helpful in framing alternative responses. He wanted to help the president.

Elizabeth Gordon-Sparks, a former vice president of academic affairs at Stanford, provided intellectual rationale for the president's visceral policies. She also wished to be appointed Secretary of State. Stark felt uneasy around her. An intellectual snob and a sycophant with an agenda, her articulate justifications for the president's instincts always carried the day.

"Sánchez has allied himself with Cuba," the president continued, "and he's expropriated foreign—mainly American—holdings in Guarida and has begun to purchase arms. I want you to come up with a game plan. This can't be left to politics as usual; it can't be permitted to be talked to death in Congress."

"Sánchez," Stark said, "was elected." He adjusted his glasses. "Preliminary reports show that he received a substantial plurality."

"Since when," the president said, "did an election mean anything down there?"

"Guarida appears to be divided along class lines," Stark continued. "The rich are trying to form an opposition, and the poor have aligned themselves with the new regime. You know what that means."

"My friend Bill McGeorge," the president said, "wrote me a letter. Y'all should have received a copy. With everything that's going on over in the Middle East, gentlemen—and madam—we might be up the creek, so to speak. And y'all know we need to keep the oil coming in, eh?" The president looked around the room. "And we don't need another goddamn Cuba."

The president's confidants shifted in their chairs.

"Warfare," Kelloring said, "is a measure of foreign policy that should be employed only as a last resort and as a defensive response to an imminent threat to national security."

The president's lip curled. The public rarely saw that face. Stark understood his frustration.

Elizabeth Gordon-Sparks said, "At this juncture we're advocating neither war nor a preemptive strike, Bart, but this character can't get to the point of no return. We must be proactive on this. The oil is too important. And anyhow, the U.S. can't be perceived as being dependent on this little banana republic. We need to set things straight, try diplomacy. But when that fails—"

Ram interrupted. "Elizabeth, you say *when* diplomacy fails, and that implies that there's no reason to attempt a rational course. Even if diplomacy proves insufficient, it's a necessary first step. And I don't believe it's a foregone conclusion. We must exhaust all avenues before we resort to military ops."

"I agree," Kelloring said. "Let's not jump the gun. We might want to consider sanctions."

Stark nodded.

The president picked up several reports, pulled them together in his hands, and stacked them like a deck of cards. His face relaxed. Then his lip curled again. "Sánchez is just another Latin American strongman, a dictator with an army and oil, and he's getting weapons. Who knows if he'll obtain WMDs right in our own backyard? I'm open to your recommendations." The president looked up and his lips tightened.

"A preemptive strike is ill-advised," Kelloring said, "as a response to rhetoric and saber-rattling. We need to find substantive aggression on their part."

Stark nodded again.

The president turned to James Brownfield. "Get us some intelligence. The man is dangerous. He's pulling together an anti-American axis. Get me proof. What's in his arsenal? What kind of weapons can he deploy? Connect him with Castro. That will play. Eventually I'll have to take this to the American people. We'll just sit tight for a few weeks, and we'll try diplomacy. Talk to the bastard. Adam, why don't you meet with him? Or send someone. Talk some sense into the maniac."

Stark thought about Manny, but did not want to expose his presence in Guarida at that moment. The professor would remain Stark's secret, and he'd work with Case behind the scenes to assess Manny's value. If he could provide a way out of this mess, Stark's contribution would not go unnoticed. Otherwise, he would have to deny any linkage and leave Manny out in the cold.

The president looked at each member of his team, then continued in a conspiratorial tone: "Meanwhile if the opposition ousts him—there's an opposition on the island, right?—the world will be safer without another goddamn threat." Harmon looked at his watch and said, "I'll be right back, folks." The president got up and left the Oval Office.

The Excom members shot furtive glances at each other.

"What do we have, Jim?" Stark said.

"We can document the Castro connection, expropriations, and threats to cut off the oil. A case could be made that Sánchez now has access to missile silos that were left in Cuba, or their biological weapons. No WMDs, some AK-47s, plenty of inflated rhetoric about defending the goddamn island."

"Not enough," Gordon-Sparks said. "The president won't work with Sánchez. Already made up his mind, sees the region's stability at stake, our hegemony in the area challenged. We need to assess the implications for the national interest. What's our best option? What about Empty Nest?"

"The Freedom Front and Guarida Libre," Brownfield said, "see themselves as opposition movements. The Front has some rebels up in the hills, but doesn't have much of a following. They've taken up arms on occasion, but only for small-scale forays against the Security Police. Now Relleno, Roldano, yeah, Roldano... Guarida Libre. He told Case that Sánchez might be importing yellowcake from Brazil."

"Uranium ore?" Stark adjusted his glasses. *They've got contacts, might know about Case,* he thought. *Do they know about the professor?*

"Exactly," Brownfield bowed his head, "but in order to use this we'll need extensive corroboration. The public would never countenance another Iraq. What we've got now is hearsay proffered by an interested party. We need a clear-cut case—"

"Yellowcake might be what we need," Gordon-Sparks said.

"Liz," Brownfield said, looking up abruptly, "what we need is to generate the legal context, some sort of framework. Let's look at our intelligence. Sánchez purchases arms from Russia and China, also on the free market. There's so much crap being traded out there, it's not funny. This doesn't confirm anything. There has to be aggression. He and his pal Fidel—this could be where we connect Sánchez to WMD, even terrorism. We need to make that case. Yellowcake might not hold up."

"We'll link Sánchez to the terrorists," Gordon-Sparks said. "Get us more, James."

"A hard sell," Stark said. "There's got to be a clear linkage to the network. Sánchez has to have begun developing WMDs. We'll need credible sources."

"Didn't your people in the Company," Gordon-Sparks looked at Brownfield, "already disclose information about the cells operating on Margarita Island?"

Brownfield nodded.

"You're aware that Empty Nest is a covert operation and needs plenty of plausible deniability," Gordon-Sparks said. "No direct American involvement."

Brownfield fidgeted. "There are always leaks, Liz. Adam, we've got to make damn sure that if this goes forward it'll be kept under wraps."

"He wants us to act," Gordon-Sparks said. "It's his show. And you and I both know that his political instincts are what got us here. And if the U.S. doesn't exercise its moral authority?"

Stark removed his glasses. "If it fails, we take the fall."

Gordon-Sparks glanced around the room. "That's always been part of the deal."

"Operation Empty Nest it is," Brownfield said, "if you all agree." Each member of Excom nodded.

"Okay then," Brownfield said, "and we'll pursue the yellowcake."

Stark replaced his glasses and nodded again. He thought about the professor. Maybe he could short-circuit this whole mess the way JFK did when he used Georgi Bolshakov to send secret messages to Khrushchev during the Missile Crisis in '62. He knew it was a long shot, but Stark would get in touch with Professor Vidal. What the hell was he doing down there anyway?

Stark said, "I hope for all our sakes that the nest's emptied without too much fallout."

"President Harmon must have been delayed," Gordon-Sparks said. "I'll report to him that we're dealing with the situation. There's no need to brief him on the details; better that he not know. Good afternoon, gentlemen."

After Gordon-Sparks hurried out, Adam Stark and James Brownfield walked together through the hall of the West Wing.

"What do you think, Jim?" Stark asked.

"This could blow up in our faces."

"Not much we can do now. He's got Liz and the rest of them onboard."

"There's a need for solidarity." Brownfield paused at the door, and Stark noted again the additional guards put in place after 9/11. "After all, we can't divide the Excom."

"Of course. The American public needs reassurance that their captain is navigating the ship of state on a steady course." Stark held up his hand in a farewell salute and took his leave of Brownfield.

ᑫᔑ Chapter Thirteen ᐸᔑ

Tina watched as Ray drove a forehand deep across the court, trying to wrong-foot Manny, who responded with a top-spin down the line. Ray hit a cross court backhand, rushed the net, and positioned for a volley. But Manny was on top of the ball. He drove a backhand out of Ray's reach and closed out the set.

It was Saturday, and there was much activity in the club. Most of the tables were taken. Tina observed their match from one of the tables near the courts as she waited for them.

She had stayed with Manny after the incident with Dee several weeks ago. "I have a past too," Tina told him without filling in the details of her stint with Federico. Nor would she reveal her encounter with Claudio Sánchez.

"All human beings have histories," Manny had responded. He had let her stay. Dee was out of the picture, at least for the moment. Later on, she suspected that he might ask her to leave. It was obvious to her that he still had feelings for the American.

"Nice playing," Ray said to Manny as they sat down with Tina at the table, wiping their faces with their towels.

"You take this much too seriously. It's just a game. There are more important things," Tina said.

131

"Like what?" Ray said. "What could be more important than tennis in the game of life?"

"What happens between those lines is everything," Manny said, smiling for the first time during the conversation. "Seriously, this is really nice. It's like a tropical paradise down here."

"Paradise?" Ray shook his head. "Sánchez has packed congress and the courts, even put his blood-thirsty pals in the government. They've begun to pass laws that support his radical agenda. He's going to take over oil. The guy's nothing but a dictator like his buddy Fidel."

"He can't nationalize the oil industry. He doesn't have the technology," Manny said.

"Your administration is preoccupied with the Middle East. They'll play into his hands," Ray said. "Sánchez continues selling to your PI, while finding alternatives like outsourcing to other companies. And he's building alliances with anti-American regimes."

"Come on, boys." Tina wagged her finger. "No more political bullshit."

"Sorry to talk politics. Just one more point. Sánchez's rhetoric escalates daily," Ray continued. "Now the U.S. is the cause of all our problems. That's popular down here. Anyone who's been successful has sold out to the *Yanquis*. Guerrero is advising our wannabe Big Leaguer to put prohibitions on the press and media. Anyone who criticizes the government is thrown into the Retén."

"Sánchez and Guerrero grew up in the barrio," Manny insisted. "Guerrero's family lost everything after Pérez Santo. The government stole the shirts off their backs. He's bitter. They both are. But, honestly, don't you think there's a need for change? No matter how the vast poverty was created, someone has to address mal-distribution of wealth, lack of education, and issues of basic infrastructure that have crippled the country. I don't like the fact that Sánchez attacks the United States, but our arrogant policies are not complete illusions."

"Typical left-wing academic rhetoric," Ray replied. "You're my friend, so I tolerate your pinko garbage."

"I really hope my views don't affect our friendship," Manny said.

Exasperated, Tina shook her head. "I've told you many times, Ray said, "that some of us in the Third World can discuss issues civilly. The problem is that you will never be in my shoes. So-called revolutionaries never carry through on their promises. These populists dupe everyone. All they want is power. And to maintain it, they become autocrats. And now Claudio Sánchez is going the route of all these tyrants."

"When your class held power," Manny said, "what was done? Sánchez gives hope. No wonder they consider him their messiah."

"He's certainly no messiah," Ray said. "Clever, I'll grant you, got everyone fooled. The barrio programs are window-dressing. Into whose pockets is the oil revenue going? They should've promoted reform when they could. Now the most irresponsible incompetents are in. But the situation will be remedied."

"What do you mean?" Manny asked. He shifted in his chair, and Tina saw the pained expression on his face.

"I mean there are those of us who won't let this abomination persist," Ray said quietly, lowering his voice so that only their table could hear. "And you think the United States will ignore this madman?"

"Sánchez is a character who shoots from the hip and accuses the U.S. of planning a coup," Manny said with a snort. "We've got Al Qaeda, North Korea and Iran, the Middle East about to explode, Hammas, Hezbollah. Could be Armageddon, and Washington will move against tiny Guarida?"

Tina grabbed Manny's arm and held it tight, as if to keep him from doing something he'd regret.

"But won't your country respond to his provocations?"

"Who knows, Ray?"

"One way or the other, we'll take care of it." Ray sounded quite serious, Tina thought.

"Wait a minute, what are you saying?" Manny pulled away from Tina's grasp, stood up.

"Sánchez will never complete a term in office," Ray said.

"What do you mean? Are you saying he'll be impeached?"

"That's not how it works down here."

"You think there will be a coup? You think the military…"

"You're the expert on Guarida, my friend. You tell me."

"That's it," Tina said. "It's time to end all this bullshit. And you guys know damn well that no one ever wins discussions about politics, religion, or sex!"

"Time for a shower," Manny said, and he got up and walked away.

The following day Manny met Tina at La Ciruela for a couple of *parchitas*. Then they went up to the apartment. As he unlocked the gate, he asked why she didn't greet Ferreira. It had seemed odd to him.

"I said good afternoon, didn't I?" she said. "He sticks his nose into everyone's business."

Manny nodded and dropped onto the sofa. Tina turned on the TV and quickly changed from CNN to a local channel with a popular telenovela, the kind of soap opera that appealed to almost all Guaridans. Invariably, the heroine is discovered in bed with her fiancée's best friend; the heroine's father is languishing in jail for a crime he didn't commit; the heroine's mother is hospitalized with terminal cancer; the groom-to-be declares revenge against his best friend, whose wife is seeking a divorce...

"Would you flip it back to the news, Tina, just for the headlines? You can watch your program afterwards."

She sighed but changed the channel for him. On CNN reporters covered the latest outbreak of violence in the Middle East and new scandals in American corporations, while their experts editorialized about Guarida.

Tina plopped into the chair facing the sofa. She sat for several minutes, seemed to be studying Manny, and finally asked, "Are there many CIA agents in Guarida?" Her voice trembled.

"What? I don't know. Why?"

"Guaridans think the CIA is everywhere," Tina said as she turned off the TV.

"I get that all the time, babe." He laughed.

"So there's no truth to it?"

"Oh no, not you too. Are you serious?"

"You're the one who told me they tried to kill Castro. You said that they paid off Noriega and Cédras. You know about all these cases."

Tina was fishing, he thought, and it bothered him. He shook his head and glared at her. "The goddamn Agency has intervened too many times, and mostly for the wrong reasons. But every country has its spies."

"Would you tell me if you worked with the CIA?" Tina's hands were shaking as she lifted her glass of fresh juice.

"So that's it." He sighed and studied her. "I don't know. Agents are sworn to secrecy. Don't know about wives, but operatives wouldn't disclose information to mistresses, for example."

"So, I'm your mistress?" Tina's voice gained strength.

"That was just an example. You're my friend. Come here, babe—let's not get into an argument over nothing, okay?" He sounded calmer than he felt. Maybe he never should have gotten involved with Tina. Dee had truly loved him. Screwed that up, didn't he? Where was all this going, anyway?

"It's not nothing to me." Tina raised her voice. "I wish I knew where we stand. And if you're down here in my country working undercover or something, shouldn't I know?"

"I'm a spook, a super-agent. Bond—James Bond, licensed to kill, and I like my vodka martinis shaken not stirred."

"Just tell me: are you or are you not working for, or with, the CIA?"

"What's this, a shake-down? And who are you, Joe McCarthy? All right, Langley sent me down here to destabilize Sánchez. And I'll do it by defeating him in public debate."

"Manny, please." She looked hurt, but he pressed on.

"I'll deconstruct his arguments to the point that people will laugh at his lack of logic or coherence. I'll single-handedly de-legitimize his entire regime by showing that his positions are neither cogent nor tenable. I'm his nemesis and the Company pays me handsomely, so well that I don't really live in this apartment. I've got a penthouse up there in the hills." Manny pointed at the window, stood up, and signaled. "Let's go off to my mansion and abandon the pretense." His mocking tone masked his anger.

"Manny, I'm sorry, it's just that—"

"And my role as advisor, my academic analyses and writings about the benefits of a reform-minded regime in Guarida, that's my cover."

"Manny, don't—"

"A good cover, don't you think? I'm a sleeper. Problem is, you've seen through me. You've exposed me, put me out in the cold. So where does that leave us?"

"Maybe you should answer the question directly." There was an edge of betrayal to her voice now, and the hurt in her eyes had developed into a brewing storm. "That would end it."

"No."

"No, you won't answer? Or no, you're not CIA?"

"I'm not CIA." Manny slammed his fist on the table.

137

"Thank you," Tina whispered. She let out a deep sigh, and there were tears in her eyes.

There was no love-making that evening.

ᴄ◈Chapter Fourteen◈ᴐ

Finally, Manny had time to accept Ray's invitation to La Casita Bonita. He was aware of the Roldanos' status as descendants of one of the twenty-three Guaridan families that had inherited vast tracts of land from Spanish colonizers in the eighteenth century. Yet, as soon as he entered the grounds, he was overwhelmed by the family's *finca,* with its orchards, vineyards, corrals, and gardens.

The Roldanos had retreated to La Casita, ten miles south of the capital. There, Ricardo, Angélica, and their son, Ray, were watching Sánchez on TV in the comfort and security of their rural home when Manny was ushered in by a servant.

"Welcome," Ricardo said. He was tall and aristocratic-looking, with light skin and wispy hair. He stood and shook Manny's hand.

Ray gave Manny a full *abrazo,* and then Manny approached Ray's mother. Señora Angélica Rosario de Roldano was heavily made-up and statuesque. Manny took her hand and said, "It's a pleasure to know you, Señora Roldano."

"Equally," she said. "Our house is your house. Ray has told us all about you, Manny. Perhaps we'll be able to change your mind about certain things."

Manny smiled and nodded noncommittally, and sat down with them while they watched the rest of the presidential address. After Sánchez's speech, Ray's father and mother looked at each other: Ricardo shook his head, and Angélica fanned herself with an ornate Spanish *abanico*.

"You *are* going to do something about this," she said.

Manny watched Ricardo and listened carefully to his response. "Oh yes, my dear, of course we will take action. No need to worry."

The words struck Manny as conspiratorial and concerned him. He was in the enemy's camp.

Yet, he accepted their gracious hospitality and ended up staying for a few days. His friendship with Ray prevailed over his anxiety. They played tennis on the well-kept grass court behind the pool. And the meals were epicurean delights. Manny vowed to avoid talking politics, and just enjoy himself.

The day after Sánchez's press conference, patriarchs of the Méndez, Gómez-Mora, Hernández, Walker, and Romano-Bello families attended a hastily convened meeting at La Casita Bonita. Manny saw them enter the library. Their mood was solemn, as if a pall were cast over the finca.

"Would you like to sit in, Manny?" Ricardo said. "As an American, you'll be interested, or perhaps you will add another perspective."

"Thank you, sir. I'd very much like to hear what you have to say."

Ricardo introduced Manny to each of his guests. Then he drew a deep breath and began. "Thank you for coming. I know you had only a short notice, and some of us couldn't get out of the city. But you all know why we're here. We can't just sit tight and ride this out. The stakes are too high. We must act. Who else can save our beloved homeland?"

Silence filled the room.

"Obviously," Roldano continued, "this election was a fraudulent exercise in mass participation. What we need here is an electoral college like the Americans." He looked over at Manny, acknowledged him with a nod. "Coño, peasants must be ruled. They're not rulers. This whole mess is like a dirty joke. Those international observers don't know their asses from their elbows. Some of them don't even speak Spanish, for God's sake. They allowed the goddamn peasants, the *campesinos*, to steal this one from under our noses. Sánchez deceived everyone with lies and promises. Neither he nor the peasants have the vaguest notion of what it takes to run this or any other country."

Manny felt uncomfortable and remained silent. What could he say to these people?

Doctor Romano-Bello, a portly man in his mid-fifties, added, "We all heard Sánchez. We have our interests to protect." His fingers twitched as if playing an invisible piano.

Walker, an older gentleman with bushy eyebrows and a bald pate, lit a Romeo y Julieta, held it up to ensure an even burn, and took a long drag. Then he narrowed his eyes and looked at Méndez as he released the sweet smoke from his lips. "We must act," he said.

Manny had read about Walker and Méndez, oil barons whose families made fortunes by operating companies that arranged leases from the government in partnership with

141

major corporations like PI. They provided for extraction of crude from the sea beds and exported it almost exclusively to the United States. There it was refined and sold in the exorbitant American market for energy consumption.

Gómez-Mora spoke up: "I'd like to say something." He took a sip of his Johnnie Walker Blue, which he drank straight up, no rocks. In his late forties, he sported a dark mustache that curved around his hidden lips and descended to a jutting jaw. He had lectured at the university, and it showed in the way he enunciated every word as he spoke. "All of us should know what's happening here, my friends. Isn't this exactly what happened in Cuba and Venezuela? It's not just the oil or even our business interests. And we all have plenty invested. But this is a takeover, a *golpe*. The lower classes want to strip us of our status, our position in society. These peasants, our campesinos, are told *we* are the enemy even after we've protected them and allowed them to be free. Of course we *must* act. The problem is that we won't be able to count on the army as we have in the past."

"There's no telling which way the army will turn," Romano-Bello said. "It's divided. Major Ramírez and a few others recognize their praetorian role, pledged to the defense of the state—the homeland—and will rise to the occasion. What's lacking now is leadership. This whole mess falls on our shoulders. And I might add that the megalomaniac has the balls to appoint Guerrero as his chief-of-staff. Guerrero's family screwed up royally, and Juan Carlos is on a mission to get back what they lost."

"We need a plan," Ricardo Roldano interjected.

Ray nodded. "Why don't we get someone to take him out, eh? Let's lose the bastard," he exclaimed, conscious of being the only representative of the younger generation of elite Guaridans at the meeting.

142

Manny was shocked. He suspected Ray would feel that way, but he didn't think his friend would actually advocate an assassination. Manny knew that if he objected, they would turn on him. So, he said nothing. Sweat began to drip from his brow.

No one contradicted Ray. No one laughed at him. No one told him to desist or that murdering the president was out of the question. In fact, no one said anything in response. There were just knowing smiles.

Manny could contain himself no longer. "Aren't there alternatives?" he blurted out.

"This is Guarida, my friend, not the United States of America," Ricardo said.

"Speaking of the U.S.," Méndez said, raising his abundant eyebrows, "is Bill McGeorge in the capital?"

"What can he do for us?" Doctor Romano-Bello shifted in his chair, as if it was too small for him.

"I don't know," said Méndez, "but he can't be too happy about this fiasco."

"Sánchez has already threatened to nationalize our entire oil business. I wonder what the hell McGeorge is thinking. And the American Embassy, don't you think they'll do something?" Romano-Bello looked at Manny. "They can't let this stand. How the hell are they going to work with a fanatic like Claudio?"

Manny's anxiety level rose. He reached for his handkerchief and wiped his face. He was about to comment when the elder Roldano said, "We cannot wait for them to remedy our problem. This is *our* country."

Professor Gómez-Mora nodded furiously. "Order and stability are fundamental to our traditions and our way of life.

Guarida's in grave danger. It's our civic duty, our sacred trust, to preserve and protect."

"We must defend the homeland," Roldano said. "We can't allow this *fanfarrón*, this clown, to destroy everything we've built here, everything we hold dear."

Manny looked around. There were nods of approval from all present. Now he sensed that the course of history could be determined at this meeting. These oligarchs were hell-bent on eliminating an elected president. And Manny was in their midst. Would he have time to warn Sánchez?

"Except for Ramírez, the military is no longer at our disposal," Ricardo said. "Therefore, my friends, we need to use paramilitary force."

Each man stood and pledged in unison, "Guarida Libre!" Manny stood back next to the wall and observed the time-honored ritual. He had read about elite pacts, yet this seemed surreal. And they didn't care that he—an outsider—was present during their machinations.

Ricardo excused himself, saying he would return in a minute. The others continued their discussion.

"I wonder what Dad has up his sleeve," Ray whispered. Manny's gut told him his friend's father would return with a hired gun.

Indeed, the elder Roldano came back a short time later accompanied by a slight, swarthy man, dressed in a black guayabera, his thick, dark hair slicked back from his face. His dark eyes darted from one object to the next as if he were in constant search of something.

Ricardo locked the door behind them and said, "Pépe can help us. His motivation is similar to our own."

Manny stared in disbelief, despite his prediction. He was frustrated. Why would they allow him, or practically encourage him, to witness this conspiracy?

"Gentlemen," Pépe said, "you got nothing to worry about. Me and my associates will provide the result you desire. You'll see how we accomplish this when we are done. And thank you for your generous donation."

Ricardo did not identify Pépe's origins or connections with the Cuba Guarida National Committee. But the man's Habanero Spanish made that fact obvious, and he concluded by pledging "Guarida Libre! Cuba Libre!"

"Do you think," Gómez-Mora whispered to Roldano, "this little guy knows what he's doing?"

"Major Ramírez recommended him," Ricardo said.

"I hope he is right," Gómez-Mora said.

"Ramírez can be trusted," Ricardo muttered.

Pépe narrowed his eyes. "You got nothing to fear. You leave it to me to take care of this problem."

No one in the group asked for details. Ricardo turned to his co-conspirators and said, "Shall we move forward on this?"

One by one, the oligarchs once again declared, "Guarida Libre."

Ricardo shook Pépe's hand and gave him an envelope. "You know where you'll get the other half," he said as he escorted the man to the door.

"We be in contact," Pépe said as he departed.

After Pépe was gone, Ricardo summoned the head waiter. The group partook of a *merienda*, a light afternoon meal of the finest cuisine. When satiated, the leaders of

Guarida Libre bid their farewells and went their separate ways.

Manny and Ray walked outside, stood for a minute or so, and then Ray said, "I told you we'd take care of everything."

"My God, Ray! This is an assassination. I can't condone murder under any circumstances. You have to stop it. I have no choice but to report this to the embassy, and I'll have to tell the president. I don't know—"

"He knows we're coming after him, Manny. There's nothing you can do."

The night after the Casita Bonita meeting, Ray left Manny at his apartment and then went to Weekends. The regulars were there as well as a large number of people with one thing in mind: they were out to score. Anyone who wanted to hook up for casual sex or buy some dope went to Weekends—secretaries and executives, hustlers and the lonely, young and old. It was a truly multicultural and multiracial lust and thrill-seeking democracy.

Looking across the bar, Ray identified Pépe immediately. He was seated next to an attractive young woman. She looked like a teenager. He had seen her there before as well. Pépe signaled for Ray to join them. Ray held back for a moment—he thought it might be dangerous to be seen with him, yet he wanted to hear his story. So he stood behind their barstools, in the second tier of the crowded bar.

Pépe turned sideways and introduced Yolanda. "Don't worry, hombre, she knows everything," he said in a loud undertone. "The Committee bailed on us. We can't count on those asses for nothing. Yolanda and I, we fly solo."

Ray nodded, aware that the CGNC, concerned with preserving its influence on those legislators sympathetic to its cause, had decided to distance itself from Guarida Libre.

"Mierda, hombre, no problem. We'll pull off this shit, " Yolanda said excitedly. "Only one thing better than coke, *cariño,* is a natural rush. Pure adrenaline." She laughed.

"You one crazy bitch—is why I love you," Pépe said.

"No crazy, Papa hit me, is why I run away," she said. "Love this place. Nothing matter here. Is fun."

Ray could tell that she lived on the edge of reality and was not afraid to fall. "What about you, Pépe? What's your story?"

"I escape from Cuba after police screw me over. I know about Varela Project, but not give up Oscar Payá. All we want is free election."

"What's your plan?" Ray asked.

"CGNC missing the point," Pépe said. "We take out this damn commie over here and Castro loses ally. No more cheap oil for nobody."

"You can count on my ass," Yolanda said.

Pépe whispered, "she love to push envelope, any envelope. It turn her on. I count with it."

Yolanda, Ray surmised, was unable to trace her anger to an abusive childhood.

"You a born rebel, " Pépe exclaimed. His lips quivered and his eyes were misty. "One day, I take you to free Cuba."

Ray looked around to make sure no one was watching them, and then he excused himself. "I was never here tonight," he told Pépe and Yolanda before he left. He scanned Weekends. It was packed. Music blared. Pastel-colored strobe lights flashed on a blanket of smoke that filled the place. Everyone was in the cloud, chatting away with crude intensity that belied any appearance of authenticity and occupied with whatever illicit impulses that had drawn them to the club. No one noticed his quick exit.

This thing's going forward, he thought. No way could he stop it now, even if Manny were right. No, this was what had to be done. This was Guarida's future.

The aroma of fresh coffee and tobacco hung in the muggy air at El Marroncito, one of the cafés on the Boulevard. Bustling sounds of city life—horns, engines, unmuffled exhausts, chatter—mixed with tropical music emanating from ubiquitous sound systems. People strode by in every direction.

Jack Case sat at a table in the corner of the café. He lit up a cigarette; then he picked up the daily edition of *El Nacional.* He glanced at the headlines and saw nothing unusual. *Same old crap,* he thought: unemployment, crime, infrastructural problems, et cetera.

Case adjusted his chair to sit beneath the shade cast by the umbrella lodged through a hole in the center of his table. He waited, reminding himself that nothing was ever on time here. Yet Guaridans always appeared to be at ease. He wondered how they could live this way. Just going into a bank was an adventure.

Americans, he knew, could not tolerate the lack of efficiency, the waste of time, the chaos. But he was patient. Tours in Afghanistan, Somalia, and Pakistan had provided ample opportunity for Case to learn the ropes. He opened the newspaper and perused articles on rising prices. Several columns reported misconduct committed in the capital. The editorials excoriated disloyal political opposition for challenging the glorious social revolution.

One caught his eye:

The Security Police are a sad but realistic reminder of the need for security in Guaridan society and politics. President Sánchez needs this mechanism in order to set into motion needed changes...

He threw the paper down on the table without finishing the article, crushed his cigarette in the ashtray, and was about to light up another when a young woman pulled over a chair from an adjacent table. She threw her shapely legs around the chair with its back-rest in front of her. Her arms grasped the back-rest like a shield.

A pretty face, Case thought. Curly hair tumbled over her shoulders. Around nineteen or twenty, he guessed. She wore tight shorts and a skimpy halter top.

"Hi," she said and smiled.

"Listen, honey, I'm waiting for someone. Sorry—"

"Pépe sent me."

How the hell did she know Pépe? Was she his contact? Case considered the possibility. "I don't know any Pépe. What do you want, Miss?"

"Guarida Libre."

"Who are you?"

"I'm Yolanda."

"Who's Pépe?"

"I'm here with a message."

Case stared at her, lit up another smoke.

149

"I'm your contact. You'll receive instructions from me. When we determine that it's appropriate, you'll transfer funds to a numbered account in the Banco de Guarida—that one over there." She pointed across the Boulevard to a branch office.

Case looked over at the bank. People crowded onto the wide steps. Armed guards were positioned on each side of the enormous doors.

"Give Ricardo Roldano a call. Tell him Yolanda delivered Pépe's message." She got up from the table and disappeared into the crowd.

Case remained seated. He picked up the newspaper and pretended to read. Operation Empty Nest was underway. He smirked. No matter how many black ops Case had completed, his heart would beat faster and he would feel exhilarated every time a new mission began. Now things would get real.

ᴄᵟ Chapter Fifteen ᴄᵟ

Manny accompanied Cultural Affairs Officer Jane Kelley-Noel as they passed several heavily armed guards at the front gate of the ambassador's residence. The compound was surrounded by a high concrete wall topped with barbed-wire and cut glass. Janey told him the U.S. government had purchased and restored the colonial mansion located at the base of the northern hills.

In his open-collared Oxford shirt, Manny was pleased when Frank Kingfield greeted them dressed in a blue *guayabera* and white slacks. At least Manny had chosen appropriately for a change. And now he would have an opportunity to voice his opinion to the highest ranking American diplomat in Guarida.

Kingfield led them through well-manicured gardens. They passed the guest house, swimming pool, and tennis court. Then they entered the compound's main house, walked through an elegantly appointed living room, and out to the verandah.

Bill McGeorge, CEO of Petrol International Corporation, sat at a low rectangular glass table. Kingfield introduced Manny to McGeorge. Janey had met him on previous occasions. McGeorge offered a perfunctory handshake and then glanced at his platinum Rolex. An American flag pin adorned the lapel of his navy blue suit, which he wore with a blazing red tie on a white shirt. His square chin, steel grey eyes, and shiny bald pate were well known. Manny felt a bit intimidated; he'd read about McGeorge in *Newsweek*. According to the article, McBill (as he was called by those who perceived him as a megalomaniac) really didn't control the universe, but he did give it the old college try. McBill had married Mary Catherine Phillips-Moore, an heiress to a tobacco fortune. They were a prominent couple in the City and the Hamptons.

Manny couldn't take his eyes off the spectacular view of the city below. Indirect sunlight illuminated the parks and buildings until sunset, when electric bulbs would sparkle throughout the valley like tiny candles flickering in a sea of darkness. Ceiling fans dispersed the scent of gardenias that grew on bushes scattered throughout the property.

The ambassador took a seat at the end of the table. Janey sat next to him, and Manny took the seat across from Janey on the other side. McGeorge remained at the end of the table opposite the ambassador.

"Bill is here to check things out," Kingfield began. "You know, assure the supply lines and so forth. And I asked Janey to set up a meeting with someone who knows what the hell is going on down here."

The formally attired server, a tall Guaridan with white hair, offered refreshments. Janey asked for lemonade. Manny requested coffee. The ambassador already had an iced tea. McGeorge ordered a glass of Chivas Regal, and Manny figured he was a hard-drinking business type. He wondered how it affected McGeorge's decision-making capacity.

"Thank you for being here," Kingfield said. "The United States has always considered Guarida to be a close ally and trading partner. Of course you all know quite well that we import a significant amount of oil from the island. Petrol International has been our leading corporation in this regard."

The ambassador took a few sips of his tea and said, "Washington is concerned about Sánchez. Janey, what has Cultural come up with thus far? By the way, our discussion will be informal and off the record."

"There's no doubt that Sánchez has captured the imagination of many Guaridans," Janey said. "He speaks to them in their language—that's to say, the language of the streets. And there's an ethnic component, although it goes unstated. They consider him to be one of them."

Kingfield nodded and gestured for her to continue.

"I'm not sure we should be focusing exclusively on Sánchez," Janey added. "Some of the things he and Guerrero and the PPP are saying ought to be taken seriously." She looked over at the PI executive who was sipping his scotch. "It's not just about American access to oil, you know."

McGeorge yawned, glanced at his Rolex. He looked at Manny. "Do you agree?"

"Mr. Ambassador?" Manny said.

"Please, call me Frank. I'd like you all to do so. We're among friends here."

"Thank you, sir. I agree with Janey, but with a proviso. I'd like to start by saying that I sit on one of Sánchez's advisory committees. I agreed to do it—with State's approval, of course— because I think Sánchez has tapped into a deep current of discontent felt by the masses. Sánchez offers hope, a precious political commodity. He's charismatic and articulates the sentiments of the body politic in a way that resonates with everyday problems."

McGeorge tapped his fingers together as if drumming to an imaginary tune. "A typical academic answer, Vidal. You seem to have sold out, eh? And Miss Kelley, what we need to know is what will happen to the price of oil and to our market. That's the issue for the United States of America. This Sánchez is obviously a communist. He's threatening our interests. At least we could deal with Ignacio Báez and his cronies."

"It's Kelley-Noel," Janey said, and Manny couldn't help smiling.

"Please allow the professor to finish, Bill," the ambassador interjected. "As you know, our interests include the maintenance of democracy and human rights."

"That's fine, Mr. Ambassador—Frank," McGeorge said with a dismissive wave. He smiled, took a sip of his scotch, and settled deeper into his chair. "Excuse me for being a realist."

"Excuse me." Janey got up and started toward the bathroom. "Just carry on. I'll be right back."

Manny admired the way Kingfield kept his composure. He knew that McGeorge had contributed a bundle to the president's campaign. Kingfield had to play the game, much as Manny sensed that he disliked doing so. His career depended on it. McGeorge, on the other hand, thrived on exercising his informal authority. To Manny, he seemed like a bully who had to have his way.

"It's the process," Manny argued, "even when Washington doesn't like an elected leader. After all, isn't that what we stand for?"

"Of course," McGeorge said, "but as a precaution, we must develop a contingency plan. Sánchez is threatening U.S.

interests. You're actually in a good position to try to redirect Guarida's path."

"I don't have that kind of influence," Manny said, "and even if I did, I don't oppose the direction Sánchez is taking." He looked at McGeorge and then Kingfield. "Janey has a point."

"Thanks," Janey said as she returned to the table.

McGeorge tapped his fingers on the table, his eyes on Janey. "If we don't get Guaridan oil, we lose a significant amount of strategic resource and weaken our economy and military posture. Another Castro-like regime threatens U.S. hegemony. I've written to Harmon. We have to do something—we can't just sit back and watch the hemisphere sink."

"I hope you aren't talking about covert ops." Manny shook his head and clenched his teeth. *Not again,* he thought. *Haven't we learned anything?*

McGeorge snapped his fingers, pointed to his glass. The waiter appeared at his side and poured another scotch. McGeorge took a sip and said, "All this theoretical posturing is nothing but cowardice. There's really no democracy outside the only true constitutional republic. Mr. Ambassador, I want action. Now!"

Manny shook his head, glanced at Janey, who winced, and then at Ambassador Kingfield, who maintained a blank face. He knew exactly what McGeorge wanted. It would be a shame if the U.S. government capitulated to this kind of pressure.

"I'll get in touch with Washington," Kingfield said. "Your interests won't go unprotected, Bill. Nor will the United States cease to support democratic regimes. Of course, we'll watch Sánchez very carefully. Rest assured, we are on top of this."

Manny felt reassured to hear the ambassador's reasonable summation. *Thank God the McBills of the world don't run the government,* he thought.

Manny listened carefully to the president's television program. "Good morning Guarida, and welcome to *Speak with the President,"* Claudio Sánchez declared. "I'm happy to report that our beloved patria is secure. I've negotiated an arms deal with the Russian Ambassador in which we receive one hundred caches of AK47s, twenty-four tanks, and ten anti-aircraft bazookas. The deal protects us against the inevitable incursion of the Imperialists. Glory to the patria—long live Guarida!"

Manny turned up the volume on his TV. He wanted to hear every word uttered by a man he felt was being unjustly demonized in the United States.

Sánchez fielded questions that ranged from personal ("I've worked in menial jobs, served in the army, and worked my way through, just like you") to policy-oriented ("Yes, I will use our national patrimony to improve our infrastructure and provide needed reforms"). His direct responses impressed Manny.

"Cuban medics," Sánchez said proudly, "deliver health care to those who can't afford the private clinics. They've volunteered as an integral part of their training. And we provide Cuba with petroleum at discounted prices. It's all part of a goodwill exchange between brother countries."

How can this possibly hurt the United States of America? Manny wondered. *Don't we want developed countries on our periphery?*

Sánchez stated that people had lost faith in the old political system; Guarida would continue to export its petroleum; he would negotiate new terms of agreement; and he felt sad for Americans who had suffered electoral manipulations and war-mongering administrations. "We support your ongoing struggles for civil rights and social justice. And perhaps we could assist in showing how people of all races can live together in harmony. Yes, your country could learn something from our small island nation."

Sánchez had broken a visible sweat. He wiped his brow with a handkerchief offered by one of the cameramen. Then he composed himself, smiled, and took another call. "Yes, yes, this is the president."

Sánchez made promises that Manny knew were stretches of the imagination. He wrote them off as hyperbole, the unctuous bravado of political discourse. The country needed fundamental change. Why couldn't businessmen like McGeorge understand this?

Music sounded in the background, signaling the end of the show. Sánchez closed by saying, "It's always a pleasure for me to converse with you, my people, to let you know the state of our great nation and to keep in touch with daily life in all its aspects. I'll continue to work for all of you. And together we'll overcome all obstacles. Long live Guarida!"

Manny turned off the TV. He thought about McGeorge, what the United States might be planning, and the Roldano plot. His allegiances to his country and Guarida were at odds. His friend wanted to murder the president, who Manny was advising, and everyone appeared to know that

157

trouble was brewing. Manny felt like a cue ball careening off billiards in motion. He decided he must warn Sánchez.

After the studio lights dimmed, Sánchez rose from his chair and drained his glass of water. "Let's get out of here. What else do we have today?"

"We return to the palace for a dinner meeting with the Minister of the Interior," Juan Carlos said.

The presidential entourage prepared to exit the television studio. Claudio followed Javier Martínez, his driver and personal friend, and three officers of the Security Police. Juan Carlos lingered behind. They began to walk toward the presidential limousine parked in front of the exit. A crowd of admirers stood behind a roped-off portion of the parking area. Claudio waved at them, and they applauded. He loved the admiration.

When Claudio came into full view, a slight, swarthy man emerged from the crowd, moved forward, and fired three shots. The deafening blasts caused Claudio to cover his ears. He felt a hot sting, like a sharp knife, cut into the flesh of his left arm. Javier fell in front of him.

One of the Security Police was down. The two unscathed Security Police pushed the president back inside the studio door. "I'm not hurt—get the bastards!" Claudio yelled, enraged.

One of the police stayed with Claudio and Juan Carlos while the other ran into the parking area. Claudio heard the screaming from the doorway; he could see the crowd. In the throng, the would-be assassin dropped his weapon and attempted to blend into the crowd with a shapely young woman at his side. The crowd formed an impromptu circle around the perpetrators. Fingers pointed at the couple.

Isolated, they had no choice but to surrender or make a run for safety.

They ran.

One of the police raised his Uzi submachine gun and shouted, "Halt!" The couple continued to run a few more steps, until a barrage of bullets ripped through their legs. Blood splattered around them as they fell hard on the concrete. They were down, not moving.

Claudio watched the drama unfold from the doorway. "Keep them alive," he ordered.

Reporters swarmed into the parking lot, all over the story like vultures on carrion. Claudio was whisked through the crowd to his alternate vehicle without saying a word to them. Then, once inside the car, the president opened the window and looked out at the reporters. "This attempt on my life will not go unpunished. I'll have a full statement for you this evening."

He closed the window, covered his face with his hands. He thought about what he would say to Javier's wife.

Juan Carlos said, "We've got to find out who they were working for."

That evening, after wielding his baseball bat to smash several antique chairs into bits and pieces, Claudio Sánchez prepared to appear on national television. His somber mood stood in dramatic contrast to the upbeat demeanor of his prior appearance.

A reporter stated, "The assassin fired a Rohm RG-14 twenty-two caliber revolver three times in two seconds. None of his three shots found its target. The first bullet hit one of the Security Police in the chest. The second hit Javier Martínez as he jumped in front of President Sánchez. The exploding cartridges killed the police officer and Señor Martínez almost instantly. The third shot hit the armored limousine and ricocheted toward the president. The diverted bullet grazed his left arm."

"Citizens," Sánchez said, "as you can see I am relatively unharmed by the incident. I sustained only a minor flesh wound. However, my dear friend, Javier Martínez—" Sánchez paused, looked down, pressed his hand over his forehead, and wiped his eyes. "Señor Javier Martínez and one of my personal bodyguards lost their lives as a result of this heinous act of terrorism. We already know the identities of the perpetrators. Rest assured that your president is well protected and in complete control. We must defend ourselves. Long live our great and glorious nation!"

After his TV appearance, Claudio directed a brutal interrogation of Pépe and Yolanda by his Security Police. "Carve crosses into the foreheads," he said. "That will make them talk."

"Ramírez!" yelled Pépe. "He supposed to protect us."

When neither Pépe nor Yolanda would incriminate Guarida Libre, claiming they had never heard of Ricardo Roldano, Sánchez ordered his men to cut off their legs.

Pépe and Yolanda bled to death.

Their *cédulas,* or national identity cards, were flashed on every television station and printed in the newspapers the next day. Juan Carlos told Sánchez that there was great public indignation.

Claudio Sánchez knew, however, that some wished the plot had been successful. He would have to be very careful from now on.

160

✑Chapter Sixteen✑

resident Claudio Sánchez felt the need to get away from Guarida, away from the paparazzi. He was sick and tired of the spectacle, saddened by Javier's death, and angered by the loss of his bodyguard. He needed some rest.

A visit to Cuba had been on his agenda for months. He loved rubbing shoulders with the great revolutionary, for whom he had the utmost respect and admiration. In addition to reaffirming the agreement to provide discounted oil to Cuba in exchange for health care and educational support personnel, it was also a symbolic opportunity for the two leaders to show their solidarity in the fight against American dominance.

Claudio arrived at José Martí Airport. From there, he was driven in a shiny pink 1958 Cadillac El Dorado to a nationalized estate about forty-five miles southeast of Havana, between Matanzas and Cienfuegos. He was shown to his room and then seated on the verandah of the main house, where Fidel Castro joined him.

Together, the two national leaders gazed out at acres of rolling hills bounded by mountains in the distance. Sabal, queen, and royal palm fronds swished in zephyrs that conveyed sweet tropical aromas. Claudio felt safe and at ease in the serenity of this bucolic setting.

"First they try to kill me. Then they want to talk," Claudio exclaimed to Fidel. "Can you believe it, comrade? The president of the United States wants to speak with me. My secretary received the call. Incredible, no?"

Fidel lifted his glass of watered-down Havana Club and took a sip. He appeared to have aged rapidly over the past year or so: his thinning beard showed increasing grey, his eyes had lost their luster, appearing strained. He was tiring. Yet he stretched into his tall frame and was as flamboyantly loquacious as always, just slower.

"Claudio, they're playing into your hands, into *our* hands; a typical example of the colossal mistakes committed by the Imperialists. They think they can use the *gusanos,* the worms who fled to Miami, to do their bidding. They think they can control the world." Castro slowly raised his arm, index finger pointing to the sky. "How do you think I've survived for half a century? The embargo has been my strongest ally. Talk to the Cowboy and the press. Let the world know about the clumsy attempt. This is much like the Battle of Playa Girón—what they call the Bay of Pigs—and the countless number of attempts to kill me."

Claudio sipped his straight rum and took a drag on a Cohiba. "Mierda, this is one hell of a good smoke." He immediately regretted mentioning the cigar. It had been many years since Castro's physicians had prohibited him from enjoying the robust Cuban tobacco.

Fidel moved closer, as if to share a secret. "Between you and me, Claudio, if they left us alone, it would be more difficult. They continue to insist that theirs is the only way. I tell you that the Colossus of the North should concentrate its power and efforts in attempting to put its own house in order, to eliminate the rampant racism and crime and greed in that materialistic whorehouse, and to fix its so-called electoral college. Do you think the United States has the right to lecture other countries on democracy? It is the height of hypocrisy. We'll tell the press about the attempted assassination and how the Guaridan people and the Cuban people won't stand for this immoral meddling in our affairs. The international community will stand by us. CIA interventions aren't popular. And covert operations and murder are illegal by any standard. We'll show the historic parallels—"

"Yes, of course!" Claudio said with enthusiasm. "I'm with you one hundred percent." In awe of Fidel Castro, his revolutionary zeal increased with every word the old man uttered.

"As you have most likely found out by now, Claudio, and our agents have confirmed this, there is a major in your army who is a traitor. His name is Ramírez. I'm certain you will take the necessary measures."

"Of course, we know all about him," Claudio said. The Security Police had suspected Ramírez well before the assassination attempt. After their suspicions were confirmed, Claudio had informed Colonel Heráclio Romero y Romero, chief of the Escuadrón de la Muerte, that he personally would participate in an operation to eliminate this threat to national security.

"And you will stop sending oil to the gringos."

"Well, it is a source of great income for us, Fidel. I can get new terms, but—"

"No, I want you to embargo them like they do to me. Coño, this is our opportunity to stick it to the Colossus. This is what you must do, my friend. And use that gringo professor who advises you as a symbol. Make an example of him."

Castro appeared calm and determined, as if he had just issued an order. Yet Claudio was torn. He wasn't ready to give up the money and take a stand. He didn't want to cross his hero, but Castro was asking too much. "I'll work on it; I'll see what Juan Carlos thinks. That gringo might not be a spy, you know. But I've got someone on him just in case. We're following him closely."

"Doesn't matter if he's a spy or not, he illustrates how the Colossus meddles in our affairs."

Claudio contemplated a plan of action. He shifted in his chair, put out the Cohiba, and took a last swallow of rum. "Our economy is dependent on the oil revenue," he said.

"My dear friend," Castro said as he leaned over and put his hand on Claudio's shoulder, "you really ought to think about my suggestion. Think about it very hard. It is the right thing to do, you know." Castro's eyes shone with a steely determination.

Claudio watched the aging legend slowly rise to his feet. Castro stared at Claudio as if to convey the message that he was in charge, that no one defied Fidel Castro. Claudio looked away. Then Castro departed without saying good night.

Claudio went to his room and called Juan Carlos. "He wants us to stop exporting oil to the yanquis. I don't know what to do."

Juan Carlos instructed his president to slow down, not act in haste. They would discuss the issue when he returned to Guarida. There might be alternative sources of petrodollars.

"And he wants us to set up the American professor."

"That's interesting," Juan Carlos said. "I'll put it on our agenda."

Claudio tossed and turned that night, haunted by dreams about Fidel Castro dying in his arms, Timothy Harmon drenched in oil, Manny being crucified, and Ramírez sneaking up from behind him and slitting his throat.

By morning he had decided to take care of Ramírez first, and then figure out how to keep the petrodollars flowing without offending Castro. That wouldn't be as easy and enjoyable as getting Ramírez, but he was certain that Juan Carlos would come up with a plan.

Major Ramírez had double-crossed Army Intelligence by exposing a key contact in the oil industry. He had ruined a deal in which the army was secretly receiving fuel at special discounted rates in exchange for protection. And the Security Police reported to Colonel Romero y Romero that Ramírez had spilled this information to the CIA. More damning, according to Pépe and Yolanda, Ramírez had conspired with them in the assassination attempt. The traitorous major was supposed to have provided cover for their escape. He was an enemy of the state.

Claudio relished the opportunity to be personally involved in this operation. This was payback time. He instructed Romero y Romero's hand-picked team from the Escuadrón de la Muerte to watch the major closely and learn his habits and routines. They staked out his house and waited for the ideal moment.

When the moment arrived, Claudio joined the team. The air didn't move in the room where he was watching the action. It was actually growing hotter, though the sun was far enough in the western sky that the day's heat should be dissipating. He wiped sweat from his face. Waiting for a target was bad enough, but under those conditions it was excruciating.

Claudio raised his binoculars. This time he saw a black sedan pass by the house. The car slowed down but didn't stop. "That's it," he said into the walkie-talkie. "Everybody get ready. The car will come around again and drop off the target."

Clicks came back through the speaker, acknowledging his orders.

"Did anybody see how many were in the car besides the major?"

Two clicks interrupted the static of his radio.

"Second team, Try not to kill anybody yet, especially the major. Just shoot his leg. Cripple him like we did the assassins. I want to talk to the traitor, find out what he knows."

Four clicks.

Claudio watched as the car came back around to the front of the dwelling. He was pleased. This time it stopped. A small man and a very large man, apparently bodyguards, got out of the car and opened the passenger door. The big man looked familiar, even though intelligence reports had never included a picture of him.

Through the binoculars, Claudio watched the major and the bodyguards walk quickly toward the front door of the residence. The big man was about to open the door for the traitor. Claudio turned his binoculars back to the car, which had pulled to the side of the building and parked. The small man, jumped out, opened the trunk, and pulled a black tarp out of the back of the automobile. He covered the car with it.

"Hold," Claudio directed.

One click.

Nothing happened for a moment, and then three short clicks came over the radio. This was the signal to let him know everyone was in position, including the targets. Claudio smiled and clicked the transmit button three times.

The expert marksman on the second team had a high-power M14-style weapon with a scope and silencer. In a prone position, he was capable of ten shots in seventy seconds at one hundred meters. He did not need them. Claudio's man hit the major's leg with one shot, just like target practice.

Finally, a voice came through. "We're ready for you," Roberto said.

Claudio let out a long breath. He grabbed his Louisville Slugger and slung it over his shoulder. He whistled the Guaridan Army fight song, the one the baseball team sang before playing another branch within the military league. The Most Valuable Player headed out the door, down the stairs, and into the street.

When Claudio entered the house, he smelled old dirt and fresh cigarette smoke. He walked into the sitting room, where the major sat in a lounge chair with his left leg resting on a coffee table. A white towel wrapped around his leg was stained bright red, and sweat dripped from the major's face. His mouth was set in a painful grimace.

The bodyguards sat on the couch, their hands tied behind their backs. They looked miserable.

"Major Ramírez, I hope my men were more than gentle with you," Claudio said with a pleasant smile.

The major took a drag on his American cigarette, and Claudio noted how the man's hands shook. "Mr. President, how nice to see you," Ramírez said, as if it were just another normal day. He met the president's gaze coolly, despite the pain on his face. "How are you doing these days? Spending on better girls than usual, no doubt?"

Claudio ignored the jibe and walked over to the couch, stopping in front of the larger man, whose eyes were fixed on the floor in front of him. Blood ran from a nose that appeared to be broken. Claudio leaned on his bat and said, "Look at me."

The man continued looking at the floor.

Claudio swung the bat and hit the floor where the man was looking. "My friend, look at me—or that floor, with your own blood on it, will be the last thing you see." That got the man's attention, and he looked up at the president. "Ah, I knew you looked familiar," Claudio said. "How long has it been, Gordito?"

El Gordo leered, said nothing.

"Come now, no need to hold a grudge. That was a long time ago, and I let you win, remember? I cashed in off that game. Play your position right and I might let you win again, yes?" Claudio signaled to Roberto to loosen El Gordo's hands.

El Gordo's expression changed. His face relaxed and he appeared almost to smile. He shook his hands and head as if loosening up for an at bat.

Claudio turned his attention back to the other man on the couch. "I do not know this man," he said as he pushed the end of the Louisville Slugger into the smaller man's chest. Each of his four team members standing behind the couch took a step back. Claudio got into a baseball stance and lined up his swing on the smaller man's head. He looked over at the major, who tightened the towel around his leg, leaned back in the chair, and took another drag on his cigarette.

Claudio turned his attention back to his swing and noted that a stream of urine was dripping off the couch onto the dirty floor. The small man sobbed the way Claudio had when he found El Duque, his pet hamster, in a state of rigor mortis on the floor of his study.

Claudio turned to look at the major again. "This is who you hire to protect you?"

Major Ramírez shrugged and flicked his ashes on the floor.

Claudio swung.

The sound was sickening, even to him. The small man's skull cracked, but he was still conscious. He looked up at Claudio as his brains slid out the side of his head. Then he fell forward on his face and lay at the feet of the major he had been hired to protect. Blood ran onto the floor but disappeared down the cracks between the floorboards before it reached the major's foot.

"MVP, huh?" Claudio said to his men, who laughed nervously.

El Gordo moved to the end of the couch, away from the body and blood.

"Tough guy, are we still not friends?" Claudio taunted.

El Gordo shook his head. "I don't have no friends."

Claudio relented because he knew El Gordo told the truth. Also, the big man didn't seem to be afraid as much as resigned. He almost looked relieved that somebody was listening to him. "Well, maybe we can change that, Gordito. You like working for this donkey's ass?" Claudio pointed with the bat that now had hair and blood on the sweet spot.

El Gordo shook his head again. "But it's all I know how to do."

Again, Claudio knew the truth when he heard it. "I know, my friend, I know." He turned to the major, who still looked calm. "Who persuaded you to betray us? What gringo piece of shit showed up with a bag of money and a case of Marlboros, like our money wasn't good enough, huh?"

"I don't know what you're talking about."

"I'm talking about the fact that you've been blabbing to those dogs at the CIA. You've been informing, major. And you conspired to assassinate me. Don't deny it; that will only make me angrier."

"What can I say then? I didn't try to kill you. I took the money but didn't tell them anything. They're stupid. I was going to present the money to Juan Carlos next chance I got." The major looked around and smiled. "Well, most of it."

"Really? We'd like our share right now, then. What do you say?"

"I say you should let me go get it."

"How about we have Gordito go get it?"

The major chuckled and said, "What, that pendejo? He shared a brain with that one." The major pointed at the floor with his cigarette. "And now it's on the floor." He broke into laughter, and Claudio's team joined him.

Claudio nodded and smiled along with them until only the major remained laughing. "Major, we've got the money already anyway. We just want to know where the cigarettes are."

The major stopped laughing, all of his attention on Claudio. He didn't say anything for several seconds. Finally he said, "What did you do to my Teresa?"

"Your Teresa? Well, she's everyone's Teresa now, right boys?" The team started laughing again, and this time, Claudio joined them. He put the bat between his legs with the end in the air in front of him and thrust his hips forward and back several times.

The major lunged from the chair. The towel fell from his leg and blood gushed. He grabbed the end of the bat, causing Claudio to lose his balance and fall onto the body at the base of the couch. El Gordo pulled the major off Claudio, and the president stood up quickly, brushed himself off, and reached for his baseball bat.

El Gordo had the major in a hold. Claudio looked around at his team, then he turned to the big man and said, "Kill him, and you have a job working for me."

El Gordo tightened his grasp on the major's torso and squeezed. The major struggled and cried out, but El Gordo's grip was as tight and relentless as a vice grip. The major's screams lasted only until a cracking noise turned them into a gurgle.

El Gordo let the body sag to the floor while he took out his knife. He carved a cross on the major's forehead, and then he looked up at Claudio. Claudio nodded approvingly.

"Welcome to my team, Gordito."

⊘Chapter Seventeen∽

J aney asked Manny if he would like to attend a closed-circuit television session at the embassy. "Harmon's preparing a foreign policy address. His speech writers want to anticipate the Q and A," she said.

Manny was pleasantly surprised by the invitation; this would be a unique opportunity to speak directly with the president. "Are you sure you want me there?"

"I'd like you to come," Janey said.

They took seats in armchairs at the rear of a small room dominated by a large projector screen. The technology provided instantaneous communication between Washington and selected embassies around the world. Twelve FSOs took their seats in front of Manny and Janey. The lights dimmed and the president appeared on screen.

"My fellow Americans," he began, "now more than ever the diplomatic community must articulate the goals and objectives of our great nation."

The president read from a script projected on transparent panels, which made it look like he was talking off-the-cuff. He made the case that the process of globalization had transformed the world. Important economic, social, and technological innovations like jet travel, the Internet, cell phones, instant messaging, and other changes had produced a worldwide community. Ultimately, the president asserted, citizens must remember that the world shared problems and challenges that didn't obey national borders, most notably pollution of the natural environment. Similarly, terrorism had altered the nature of modern military defense systems.

Harmon looked directly into the camera. His expression oozed sincerity. "These are dangerous times." He forced a smile. "Yet we will prevail." His lip curled as he drummed his fingers on the desk.

The president concluded that the form and character of the global society would be determined by choices in the critical decades ahead. "Let me assure you that the United States of America will continue to champion democracy and human rights. We'll oppose dictators and assist countries in the pursuit of their own freedom. These are noble goals, my friends. And we'll pursue them. Thank you—and God bless America."

Manny suppressed a laugh. He saw through the political mendacity. Were people really taken in by such rhetoric?

The first question came from an FSO stationed in Iraq. "Mr. President, when will we be able to draw down our troop levels over here?"

"Just as soon as the Iraqis can provide for their own stability. I'm proud of the brave soldiers who are serving our country, and I know they're in harm's way, but our fellow Americans are safer at home because of them. It's a difficult situation over there, and much more has to be done, but we're making progress."

Again, Manny smirked.

After several questions about the Middle East, discussion shifted to Europe and the UN. Then a few questions and answers regarding narcotics trafficking drifted into the general U.S. position vis-à-vis Latin America. This gave Manny an occasion to take the microphone. Standing at the rear of the side aisle in front of the microphone, he felt emboldened by the impersonal setting. Although he seemed to be talking directly to the president, he was in a dark room thousands of miles away. And he needed to get a few things off his chest.

"I'm Emmanuel White Vidal," he said, "and I'm currently a professor at the University of Guarida on leave from NYU. I'd like to ask you about the attempt on Claudio Sánchez's life. Questions about U.S. complicity have been raised."

The FSOs in the room turned to look at Manny. He continued undaunted. "It's difficult to believe, after so many past interventions, that we haven't committed the same error here in Guarida," he stated. "What do you suggest the Foreign Service and those of us in positions to parley the U.S. position say, in order to set the record straight?"

"Ambassador Kingfield has done a fine job—a fine job—of articulating on this matter," the president stated in an authoritative tone. He leaned closer to the camera. "We regret what has happened down there, but to suggest that the United States of America played any role in that attempted assassination is ludicrous."

"I'm sorry, Mr. President, but that's what people believe. There have been articles in the *New York Times* and the *Washington Post,* written by your own administration lawyers, attempting to justify covert actions and even assassination of enemy leaders." Manny sighed and waited for an answer.

174

The president sat back, looking decidedly unsure of himself. Before he could answer, Manny jumped in again. "It seems obvious that the Cuban exiles were working for Guarida Libre. Did they have our support?"

The president looked away, pursed his lips, then turned back and declared, "Of course the academic community as well as our excellent Foreign Service can provide information to the Guaridan people—those who wish to continue, as we do, our close relationship. We've been good neighbors and friends, and we hope this mutually beneficial relationship will continue."

"Mr. President, with all due respect, that doesn't answer my question."

"Just who do you think—" the president started. He was about to lose his patience, but corrected himself. He leaned back in his seat, smiled, and looked directly into the camera. Then he said, "Next question."

Manny returned to his seat. The president's quasi-responses and platitudes served only to confirm his suspicions. He felt as if he were playing a role in the theater of the absurd.

Janey glared at Manny. "Should have toned it down a bit," she whispered. "I think you just got me into trouble."

The interactive show went on for another fifteen minutes. Then the camera was shut down and the system turned off. Each FSO looked at Manny as they meandered out of the mini-theater.

"He's got a lot of balls," one officer said.

"He's just naïve," said another.

Manny was happy that he had spoken up, and he regretted nothing he had said. But he worried that Janey might be subject to a reprimand for inviting him.

The telephone call from Guarida was put through at 10 a.m. "This is President Sánchez speaking," Claudio said. "Mr. President, I'm responding to your call. What is it that you wish to discuss with me?"

The conversation was strained. Both presidents were accompanied by advisors and translators. Their conversation was taped at both ends.

"Mr. President," Harmon said, "I called to request that you cooperate in our efforts to promote hemispheric security. Specifically, this would mean scaling down your importation of armaments, assisting in the war on drugs, and promoting free trade."

The bastard thinks he can push me around, Claudio thought. He shook his head, looked at his translator, and smiled. "Guarida has allowed the United States to interdict narcotics traffickers through penetration of our air space, and we have exported large quantities of petroleum. You are our largest market. But, Mr. President, Guarida is a sovereign nation. We have every right to buy arms, especially when we feel threatened."

"There's no external threat to your country," Harmon said.

"Then why have the forces of your Southern Command been mobilizing off the coast of Curaçao, Mr. President?" *Let's see what the cowboy says to that,* Claudio thought.

"These're routine troop exercises. But you, Mr. President, have been buying weapons and expropriating and nationalizing foreign holdings."

"Your CIA has been supporting Guarida Libre, correct? They tried to assassinate me." *Fidel was right,* Claudio thought; *they shouldn't be able to get away with it.*

"Ambassador Kingfield has already responded to those allegations."

"You have an opportunity to support me in my quest to chart an independent course for my country." Claudio would show this fool who was more of a statesman. "Of course we wish to maintain a close relationship with you, but not as a dependency. We simply want a relationship among equals."

There was a long pause. The translators had done an excellent job of conveying not only the precise words spoken but also the intonation of each of the men. But the diplomatic parrying got them nowhere.

"Mr. President," Claudio intoned, "there will be changes in the way Guarida conducts its business. I, we, will not allow ourselves to be bullied. Should we determine a need to defend ourselves, we will do so. Would you not do the same? Should we need to shut down over-flights in the name of national security, we will do so also. Would you allow such flights over sovereign U.S. territory? Should we decide to nationalize our oil—"

"I was hoping you wouldn't take that course of action. It wouldn't be good for the future of our relationship. You have to choose between going the Cuban route—look where it's gotten them—and charting a more sensible course. There will be repercussions if you choose the former. I sincerely hope you'll reconsider your position on these issues. If not, there could be dire consequences."

"Guarida does not respond to threats, Mr. Harmon. We are not some backwater leaseholders in your lake. We are a proud nation with resources of our own. Remember who you are dealing with."

"You really ought to consider my offer of friendship, Mr. Sánchez. It might be your last opportunity to foster peace and prosperity for the proud people of your country."

Claudio understood the uselessness of their conversation. There was really no negotiation and therefore no point in continuing. He ended it abruptly by saying, "You should come to Guarida, Mr. Harmon, and learn about our country. Then we can talk."

Stark paced around his office. Agitated, he removed his glasses and gazed out the window. James Brownfield sat in a chair facing Stark's desk, waiting for him to speak.

"Harmon informed me about Professor Vidal's brazen questions and the useless telephone conversation with Sánchez," Stark said. "Harmon's pissed off and wants us to figure something out, create a winning strategy."

"You know the president, Adam. What did you expect?"

"Yeah, I suppose…"

"Who the hell is this professor?" Brownfield said. He didn't mention Empty Nest. "What is he doing down there, anyway? Is he one of ours?"

"His name is Emmanuel White Vidal. He goes by Manny. Case calls him Professor Ivory Tower—pretty funny, huh?"

"So, you know about him? Case is involved?"

Stark nodded.

"Why haven't you briefed me about this? I'd appreciate being kept in the loop."

"From now on you will be, I assure you."

"Ivory Tower?"

"He's at UG. I sent him down there because I wanted a presence at the university. At the time, I didn't have any particular plan; I just wanted to know what was going on. But somehow he insinuated his way onto one of Sánchez's advisory committees. So he has access, and we can use him to communicate with Sánchez. And Liz is insistent that we come up with a strategy—like Harmon says, 'a winning one.' You know what that means."

"Didn't know you had someone in-country," Brownfield said. "What the hell is he up to? 'U.S. complicity,' his exact words, a lot of nerve—"

"He's an outspoken sonofabitch but is positioned well. He's an academic with no government affiliation. Let's fly him up," Stark said. "Keep Liz off our backs. I'll have INR set up a series of sessions on the current situation in Guarida. See if he knows more than what he puts in his communiqués."

"I want to talk to him," Brownfield said. "See what makes him tick."

"He's been here before and knows the ropes. We treat him as an expert," Stark said. "I'm confident the professor will be more useful to us than he has been up to now. He'll be our informal liaison."

Tina had just showered and was drying off. She turned up the volume on the radio. The sweet voice of Omara Portuondo crooned *Dónde está mi amor? Acá, acá, acá.* Tina swiveled her hips to the erotic beat and thrust her hands above her head. The towel tied around her waist dropped to the floor.

"Where's my suitcase?" Manny shouted to be heard above the music.

"Acá, acá, acá."

"Funny."

"Try the top shelf in the hall closet."

"Gracias, gracias, gracias."

"Do you really have to go?"

"I'll be back on the twenty-seventh." Manny had to be in Washington on Monday. He had mixed feelings about the trip. He had always enjoyed acting as a consultant to the INR, despite the bureaucratic officiousness. Yet he sensed there would be more to it this time, especially after his awkward exchange with Harmon. He feared some kind of reprimand. And his work with Sánchez would surely complicate everything. His academic integrity could be put on the line if they wanted to use him as a political operative of some sort.

Don't fantasize, he warned himself. And after the fiasco with Dee, along with Tina's bizarre behavior on the window sill, as well as her accusations that Manny was a CIA agent, he needed to get away. He looked forward to the opportunity to think things through.

Besides, he would contact Dee, try to see her, work things out. He really wanted to get her back. The invitation had come at the right time.

"Why do you have to go up there? You said you weren't a CIA agent."

"Not again, Tina. I thought we put that shit to rest."

"Okay, then why?"

180

"I'll be at the State Department. They need me to set them straight. They think I know what's going on down here."

Tina's towel remained on the floor. She danced over to Manny as he entered the bedroom. He dropped the suitcase, a couple of rackets, and some tennis gear on the bed and studied her body. "I'm going to miss that," he said.

"Here," she said, "take it. You'll need it." She held out her arm and undid the Tag Heuer she had left on in the shower. She hardly ever took the watch off. "What is Washington like?"

"I didn't mean my watch, but yeah. Thanks." Manny placed it on the bed next to his suitcase. Finally he would be able to strap it back on his wrist where it belonged. "Washington is beautiful. And maybe I'll be able to get in some tennis. But the government dominates the place. It's the political capital of the world."

"I hate politics. Don't go." She continued dancing.

"It's just a few lectures and discussions. I'll do my part for what it's worth and return before you know it." Anxiety flashed through him. Maybe he'd be able to convince Stark or some of the INR to consider his take on what had been happening in Guarida. *Got to remain positive,* he thought.

"Are you going to see that bitch?"

Manny studied her. Did she actually have feelings for him? Would it hurt her to know that, for him, their relationship was purely sensual? "Let's meet down at the beach when I get back. I've got the keys to La Promesa; I picked them up at the university. And no, I won't be seeing Dee." Probably never again, he feared. He would try, though.

Regret twisted through him, and he wished Dee had warned him before she showed up at his apartment, what he thought was his hideaway. What was he hiding from? Things could have been different. Yes, he would call her. He had to speak with Dee. And who was Tina calling a bitch?

"I like your plan, Manny. Right now I've got something nice for you." She danced across the room, her skin glistening. She was a Siren, a femme fatale. The lure interrupted Manny's musings. His bag did not get packed for several hours.

Part Three

"WIDE-AWAKE THINKING HAS LED US INTO THE MAZES OF A
NIGHTMARE IN WHICH THE TORTURE CHAMBERS ARE ENDLESSLY
REPEATED IN THE MIRRORS OF REASON."

~ OCTAVIO PAZ

Chapter Eighteen

Manny had stayed at the Georgetown Inn during his previous visits to DC. This time, Stark had reserved a room for him at the historic Churchill.

The Beaux-Arts style hotel's mahogany doors and paneling, crystal chandeliers, and plush carpets contrasted with the contemporary décor of the Sheraton across the street, where members of the public-at-large stayed during their tours of the nation's capital. Manny felt a bit awkward in the halls of the boutique hotel, where he brushed shoulders with visiting dignitaries. He'd try to get used to it, though.

On the first day after his arrival, Manny had an initial meeting with Bureau of Intelligence and Research officials at the State Department. INR provided guidelines for subsequent meetings that were scheduled for the rest of the week.

"We'd like to hear your personal assessment of Guaridan politics with a special focus on what we call 'the drivers'—the forces that move things in that country," an official said.

"I'm prepared to speak about what I've experienced there," Manny said.

"We also want to know if you believe Claudio Sánchez will follow through on his threats to nationalize the petroleum industry. And does he really think the United States will attack Guarida?"

This approach bothered Manny. Of course, for the INR, U.S. interests were primary, but shouldn't be their only concern. He began to wonder exactly what else they might ask of him; he felt uneasy about not knowing exactly what his hosts were planning.

The briefing wasn't what Manny had expected. He was prepared for these questions, but surprised that there was no mention of the attempted assassination. He would have to bring up the delicate subject at some point.

After the meeting, he collected his notes, stuffed them in his briefcase, and was about to leave when one of the INR officials approached him. "Hi, I'm Ted Schroeder, heard you're a player," the man said, flashing a broad smile.

Manny shook hands with Schroeder a bit tentatively. The guy couldn't think he was an insider, a political player— could he? "What do you mean?"

"Would you like to hit a few?"

"Oh, you're talking tennis?"

"Played for the Gators—"

"University of Florida," Manny said. "You're out of my league."

"It's been a few years. I only play once or twice a week now. Come on, we'll have a nice game. I heard you play tournaments. You'll probably run me."

"Doubt it, but I'd love to play. Always travel with my rackets. So, name the time and place, Ted. It would be nice to get out there and hit some. A good break from the ringer you guys are putting me through."

"We need to know what Sánchez will do. His rhetoric is dangerous; he speaks like he's a loose cannon."

What did Schroeder want? Manny wondered if this really was about tennis. He didn't want to appear paranoid, and the guy was friendly. Yes, he would play some tennis. "No shop talk on the court, right?"

"No, man. Let's just play."

When Manny got back to the hotel, he called Dee. No answer. He felt frustrated and decided he would try again later. He had to at least hear her voice, speak with her.

The audiences for Manny's presentations were an eclectic assortment of FSOs, INR analysts, defense and military personnel, "think tank" staff from the Center for Strategic and International Studies, and intelligence community members. Most had no problem in identifying themselves. And Manny was always impressed with their range of knowledge. Of course, their questions were invariably cast in the context of U.S. national interests.

Manny attempted to convince his audience that it would benefit the United States to support Guarida. Despite the incendiary rhetoric on the part of its democratically elected leader, the country had been a strong ally. Even if its oil were nationalized, the U.S. would remain its primary market. Weaknesses in Guarida's socioeconomic structures had caused discontent and instability. Aid for development would bolster the country and strengthen the relationship with its natural partners.

Manny's testimony reflected his hope that the United States would act with magnanimity. He wanted to believe that rational discourse would eventually prevail over emotionalism.

After one of the sessions, Jack Case walked over to Manny. He seemed to appear out of nowhere, an unlit cigarette dangling from his lips so that whatever he said sounded cryptic. "Hello professor." Case extended his hand. "I'm Jack Case."

Manny smiled and shook his hand, noticing the bracelet on Case's wrist. The links looked like human skulls. *Very strange,* Manny thought. "I hope I've done justice to the situation down there," Manny said.

"You did a good job," Case said. "Of course, your perspective's a bit different from mine. *Who is this guy? Take the damn cigarette out of your mouth when you talk,* Manny thought. "How so?"

"You've caught some attention around here. My colleagues see you as a Sánchez sympathizer. You're working for him, aren't you? And your emphasis is on how his so-called revolution has turned the focus onto social problems, as if wealth distribution and health care justify a leftist dictatorship—as if only the right could be corrupted."

Another right-wing fanatic, Manny thought, disappointed that there were so many of them in Washington these days. "I thought my presentation—the data—showed pretty clearly how the right failed to address the basic issues confronting the country. It's a dismal record."

"We don't deny that, professor. But we see Sánchez as another Castro, a megalomaniac. And he's no less crooked than those who preceded him."

Like all the Sánchez detractors, Case assumed corruption without much evidence. Who did he mean by "we" anyway? "Are you with INR?"

"I work with them."

"I see," Manny said. Why was the guy being evasive?

"The United States has interests in Guarida," Case said. "I don't have to tell you that. But you seem to care more about the domestic scene. Gone native, eh?"

"I try to be objective, Mr. Case. I'm a scholar." *He knows about Tina,* Manny thought. *Damn it, she's none of his business! What else does he know? Is the guy spying on me?*

He wondered if Case could throw light on the assassination attempt. He was about to bring it up when Case said, "Of course you—"

"Were we involved in the attempt on Sánchez's life?" Manny asked, cutting him off.

Case studied him but did not answer. Manny sensed that Case wasn't the only one of these bureaucrats who considered him an idealistic professor with little understanding of power, or stakes. Why he had he been invited to Washington? What did they want from him?

Former Secretary of Defense David Ramshore had his secretary call Manny to set up a friendly game. The sport seemed to be a common denominator wherever he went. He wondered if Ramshore was any good. *Should be interesting,* he thought.

187

Manny slid into the limousine parked in front of the Churchill at 9 a.m. The driver took him down Connecticut, past Dupont Circle, and over to Foggy Bottom. The limo pulled up next to a row of cement barriers constructed for security around the State Department. The barricades surrounding the Harry S. Truman Building reminded Manny of mooring blocks, the kind used on docks built for ocean liners, but even larger. He couldn't imagine any kind of vehicle being able to penetrate this line of defense.

Ramshore emerged from a side door of the building, walked past the barricade, and entered the limo, sitting in the seat beside Manny. He looked different in person than on TV—not as imposing. Manny never imagined he would be this close to him.

"Good morning," Ramshore said. His wily grin broke the symmetry of deep lines etched into his leathery face, marks that Manny read as the result of serious contemplation of weighty issues.

"Morning, sir. Thanks for—"

"No need for formalities; call me Ram, everyone does. And we're going out for some nice tennis, anyway."

"And I go by Manny. I really appreciate the invitation, Ram. How did you know that I play tennis?"

"There are no secrets in Washington." Like an orchestrated political leak, word of Manny's tennis game with Ted Schroeder had been disseminated throughout the State Department as rapidly as air escapes from a punctured balloon.

"I look forward to playing with you. It's a beautiful day. I hear Chevy Chase has nice courts."

"You'll love it there. How is INR treating you?"

"Very well, sir. I'm at the Churchill, as you probably know. And the sessions have been stimulating. It's nice to be able to discuss Guaridan politics with so many individuals who are so well-prepared. I really don't know what I can add." Manny was excited to be part of such a formidable brain-trust attempting to serve American interests, yet he was frustrated that the same group could so often obfuscate the very values they were supposed to stand for.

"I hear you're doing just fine. We need every perspective in our analysis of situations like that in Guarida. What do you think we ought to do about Sánchez?"

Manny gave an honest assessment of the need for social change. Ram nodded. He appeared nonplussed. "Manny, you're a patriot, aren't you?"

"Of course I am. I believe in American democracy. It's not perfect, but it works."

"Well, that's good. Naturally, if we're attacked or threatened in any way, you would defend your country, right?"

"Yes, but I'm not one of the 'my country right or wrong' guys. The beauty of freedom is in being able to hold dissenting positions, being able to argue. Conflicting perspectives yield the truth—don't you agree?"

"That's all well and good. Let's say Sánchez takes over Petrol International. What then?"

Manny stiffened. What the hell was this all about? He was about to formulate a response when Ram said, "just think about that." The craggy lines in Ram's face deepened.

On the court, Ram was no competition for Manny. After the match, they sat at a courtside table sipping freshly squeezed orange juice. "That was good. Thanks for the lesson," Ram said.

189

"You defended well and returned a lot of balls." Manny thought it ironic that a former defense secretary had trouble defending on a tennis court.

"I give a lot of advice on defense. I should be able to defend," Ram said with a smile. The creases in his face formed an intricate pattern like a spider's web. "In that context, Manny, we are putting together a strategy to deal with Sánchez. And, since you're so well-positioned on the inside, so to speak, we're hoping to enlist your participation."

Manny's anxiety level rose. "What do you have in mind?"

"Adam will brief you."

So this was the real purpose of playing tennis with the former Sec-Def, Manny thought.

Back in his plush room in the Churchill, Manny dialed room service and ordered a large glass of orange juice and a banana. Then he took a shower, all the while anxious about a scenario that was developing in his mind.

What will I do if they want to use me in a way that contradicts my beliefs? he wondered.

After a long, hot shower, Manny dried off and threw on a soft terrycloth robe emblazoned with The Churchill on the breast pocket. Room service arrived with his order. He closed the door after the waiter and peeled the banana, feeling the most physically relaxed he had been since he had come to Washington. Yet the anxiety was still there, under the surface.

He polished off the banana and tossed the peel into the trash, then dialed Dee's number. She answered after several rings, and he almost forgot what he had planned to say. "Hello, Dee. I'm glad you finally answered. How are you?"

After a pause, she said, "I'm fine, Manny. How have you been?"

"Good. Uh... not good. I'm sorry about what happened." He sank into the wing-back chair, leaned over with his elbows on his knees. "I'm really sorry. Please forgive me."

"Where are you?"

"I'm in DC. I'll come up. We can talk this through."

"There you go again—now you want to talk. Don't bother. And don't come up here."

This wasn't going at all the way he'd imagined. "I've always loved you, Dee. I miss you. My life is empty without you."

"How can you say that? Listen, I'll get over it... *you*, I mean. I'll be okay. And you'll get over me. It was pretty clear to me you already had."

That stung. He stood, started pacing, and paused at the window to look out on DC. "I'm sorry. I love you. That is the truth."

"I'm thinking about going home."

"You mean Texas?"

"Yeah."

"Maybe if you go for a while, it would be a good thing. Then when I get home, we can get together again in New York."

"Manny, what you did—"

"I lost it down there, Dee. Please give me another chance. I've learned about my weaknesses. I won't let anything come between us ever again. Please believe me."

"I can't deal with this right now. You really let me down. How could I ever trust you again?"

"I understand how you feel, but if we could get through this, things might be even better than before. Please don't write me off. I know I don't deserve you, but I'll work very hard to win back your trust, your love."

"Maybe. We'll see." She hung up, and Manny felt his entire body relax, as if he'd just been loosed from a strangling straightjacket. He was relieved; at least there might be a chance for reconciliation. He slept well that night.

Stark, Brownfield, and Case stood next to a Chippendale sofa under Fitz Hugh Lane's *View of Boston Harbor*. The two presidential advisors sipped Jack Daniel's on the rocks while Case held a glass of Bud. They discussed the situation in Guarida.

"There he is," Case whispered. Manny was conversing with someone on the other side of the Thomas Jefferson State Reception Room.

"How did his lectures go?" Brownfield asked.

"He's well-versed and articulate, Jim. Of course, he gave a typical leftist perspective," Case responded.

"He revealed nothing we didn't already know," Stark said.

"As Adam knows, I've been intercepting Manny's communiqués and then forwarding most of them. A few might have fallen through the cracks," Case said.

"Jack, you're in-country—you think he's working with them?" Brownfield said. "You know what I mean... beyond the committee nonsense."

"Nah, his work with Sánchez fits into his do-good dream world. Ivory Tower's just soft on the place. He's shacking up with a hot little Guaridan gal and having a ball down there, but he's no danger to us."

"Lucky bastard," Brownfield laughed. "Too bad the goddamn country's drifting away. Could become serious if Sánchez doesn't back off."

"Ram thinks we can avoid the worst case scenario, Jim," Stark said. "He's got a plan that will avoid another boondoggle like with the Roldanos. Why don't you bring the professor to us, Jack?"

"One Ivory Tower coming up," Case replied.

Case worked his way past the group clustered around Secretary of State Pham-Dixon, over to where Manny and Ted Schroeder stood under the portrait of Thomas Jefferson near the door.

"Federer's the best of all time," Manny was saying. "He's the only current player who could win with wood. Probably the only one not on performance enhancing drugs, too."

"Can I steal away this important fellow for a minute?" Case put his hand on Manny's elbow, and he felt the professor recoil. Case leaned toward his ear and said quietly, "See Stark and Brownfield over there? They'd like a few words with you."

The professor excused himself and followed him. Case pulled out a Marlboro as he led Manny over to the presidential advisors. He stuck the unlit cigarette between his teeth.

193

"Adam, you know Professor Vidal," he said. "Manny, this is James Brownfield. And now if you gentlemen will excuse me, I need a smoke."

Manny noticed that Case hit the speed dial on his cell as he walked away, the cigarette gripped firmly between his lips. "It's a pleasure to meet you, Mr. Brownfield," Manny said. "It's nice to see you again, Mr. Stark."

"We hear that your presentations have been very interesting, even illuminating," Brownfield said.

"Yes," Stark said, "your insight into the dynamics of Guaridan politics will be helpful in our policy-making processes. And we hear that you gave the honorable Ram a good drubbing on the court."

"We had a nice game of social tennis," Manny said. Were they patronizing or humoring him? Stark had requested that he apply to the UG in the first place, but had not replied to any of his communiqués. Manny had to be cautious; they were up to something. "Regarding our discussions, I've tried to illuminate what appears to be going on down there. I'm well aware of the complex set of problems and issues surrounding Sánchez's controversial messages. But I think we should recognize that Guarida is in a social and economic transition. How the United States responds to the situation could be crucial."

"Of course," Stark said.

Brownfield excused himself and walked over to a waiter for another drink. Stark put his hand on Manny's shoulder and steered him toward the corner of the room. They went unnoticed; everyone seemed to be engaged in chatter of one kind or another. Stark cleaned his horn-rimmed glasses with his handkerchief, slid them back on his nose, and looked Manny in the eye. "I trust you've had a good week here. Always exciting in the nation's capital, eh?"

"It's been a very good week, Secretary Stark." *Here it comes,* he thought.

"And we're pleased that you've been present at the university, although I wish you had sent communiqués more often."

"I sent them every week—you haven't responded," Manny exclaimed. "And I sent an analysis of the election results. And—"

"Well, there might have been a breakdown somewhere," Stark said.

"I've been doing my part," Manny said.

"Yes, I can't disagree with that. From now on use my e-mail. It's easy to remember."

"I'll send them electronically from now on. My e-mail is just as easy to remember.

They exchanged email addresses, and Stark said, "Now, Cardozo tells us the students love their gringo professor."

"I've had some good ones." *Why doesn't he get to the point?* Manny wondered.

Stark looked around the room, as if to make certain no one could hear. A group of sycophants surrounded Pham-Dixon. Others clustered around the food and drink. All seemed to be deeply engaged.

Stark turned back to Manny and stated in a low but authoritative voice, "We'd like you to take a message to

Sánchez— off the record of course. You'll act as a kind of liaison for us. We do use informal channels at times."

Before Manny could respond, Brownfield returned with a fresh glass of Jack Daniel's. Brownfield looked around the room in the same way Stark had. "Just between us," Brownfield said, "we won't sit by while the sonofabitch stockpiles AK-47s in Guarida. And if the lunatic won't export his goddamn oil—"

"Who was behind the assassination attempt?" Manny couldn't help interrupting; Brownfield's attitude angered him. Manny thought he knew who was responsible for the attempted coup, but now he needed to get to the bottom of this question once and for all.

"We don't know anything about that," Brownfield said. He and Stark exchanged glances.

"Sánchez seems intent on producing a self-fulfilling prophecy," Stark said. "We'd like to avoid that, professor. He should be aware of what he might be getting into and that there's a way out. By the way, it was Ram's idea for me to approach you on this." Stark put his hand on Manny's shoulder, and Manny took a couple of steps back. He wanted no part of Ram's scheme, whatever his intentions might be.

Stark stepped forward, looked directly at Manny, and said, "You're going back there tomorrow, aren't you?"

"I don't have access to him," Manny said, beginning to feel even more anxious than before. The feeling had been creeping up throughout the week. "I'm not sure I want to act as a liaison. You know my position on Guarida; what could I possibly say to him anyhow?"

"Same message we sent to Raoul Cédras: take the money and run. Don't worry, we'll give you the script."

"I know what happened in Haiti. Listen, I'll go back, finish up my responsibilities at UG, and then I want to find my cousin," Manny said. "I can't guarantee that your message will be delivered." Manny felt like he was being sucked into a vortex that would surely compromise his integrity, and he didn't want to undermine the reform-minded leader. He didn't see how he could convert this into an opportunity to benefit both the United States and Guarida.

"We'll brief you," Stark said.

"I'd appreciate any information you have regarding my cousin, Rafael Vidal. Jane Kelly-Noel found the report you mentioned a while back. It was LIMDIS. Says he's with the Freedom Front. I've searched—"

"I'll get back to you on that," Stark interrupted. "Meanwhile, you'll complete your assignment for us."

Chapter Nineteen

Manny shuffled forward on the line through security checks at Dulles and fumbled for his ticket and passport. He thought about his week in Washington. Thank God that was over.

Acting as a consultant at the State Department had always resulted in interesting experiences. But this time he was troubled by the unexpected request to act as a liaison to the Guaridan president, which was a far cry from sending communiqués. It would mean direct involvement in the affairs of state.

Relieved to get away from Tina for the week, Manny wished he could have convinced Dee to reconcile with him. At least they had talked, and she had left an opening; Manny was grateful for that. He was confident he would win her back.

He handed his ticket and passport to the TSA screener, who said, "Guarida, huh? It's a lot warmer down there. Have a nice flight. Next!"

He found his seat on the Guarida Air 737, fastened his seat belt, opened a magazine, and prepared for the flight.

A tall man dressed in an expensive suit stowed his briefcase in the overhead compartment and took the seat beside him. The man brushed his mustache with his fingers. He looked over at Manny. "I'm Roberto." He offered his hand.

"Hello, I'm Manny." Manny took Roberto's hand in a firm grip. He felt Roberto's calluses as they ended the handshake. That was somewhat surprising, since he figured the man to be a diplomat or businessman, not someone who used his hands for manual labor. The man looked vaguely familiar, but Manny couldn't place him. Manny relaxed when the flight attendants passed by.

He signaled to one of the attendants, "Cup of black coffee, please." Then he turned to Roberto. So how's the weather on the island?" he said.

"Seventy-eight with a lot of hot air from the north—what else?" Roberto said with a smile. Manny liked the man instantly.

The flight attendant served the coffee. Roberto took the cup and held it while Manny took the magazine off his lap and opened the fold-down tray.

"Here you go, *pana,*" Roberto said and passed the cup.

Manny had to smile at the use of the Spanish slang for pal. "Gracias," he replied. He took a few sips, then he set the cup on the fold-down tray and looked out the window. The ground crew pulled away the baggage conveyor belt that led into the plane's hull. The flight attendants began their safety presentation; Manny thought they were mouthing the words. They sounded garbled. He took another sip of coffee, looked at his Tag Heuer, and remembered when Dee had given it to him. He wished he had gone up to New York to see her during the week. A hopeless pang stabbed his heart. Would it have mattered? Would he ever be with Dee again? Then he thought about Tina waiting in Guarida.

Eyelids heavy, Manny felt himself drifting as the plane's engines began to whine. The attendant took the cup and folded the tray. He checked his watch again. The crystal appeared to be glazed over, as if by a warm breath. He tried to clean it with his drink napkin. He moved his hand in front of his face and it trailed. He was dizzy. He closed his eyes, but the cabin kept spinning. Questions swirled in his mind: How did he get drawn back to Washington? Ego? How bizarre was all this? Light dimmed. Sound faded. What the hell was happening?

Ciudad Guarida slept. As the sun peeked over the eastern hills, the morning stillness was broken by rasping engines and hissing air brakes. A truckload of fresh fruit and vegetables had arrived at La Ciruela.

The noise awakened Tina. Her eyes opened before the American in her dream had returned. She grabbed the unframed photo of Manny from the night table and looked at it through moist eyes. She couldn't wait to be with him again.

Her deal with Claudio irritated her. *I shouldn't have told Roberto about Washington,* she thought. Yet, it wouldn't matter anyway, as long as Manny was telling the truth; she had Claudio's word that nothing bad would happen to him if he wasn't a spy.

Sun streamed through the windows. Tina slipped out of bed. Today was the twenty-seventh, and the excitement of Manny's return had kept her up most of the night. She washed her face and pulled back her long black hair to secure it in a way that accentuated her forehead and high cheekbones. *Today will be special,* Tina thought as she gazed at the photo before placing it back on the night table.

She packed a few things, tossed them into Manny's Corolla, and set out on her journey down to the coast. Cars jockeyed for position in order to gain a few extra minutes of weekend partying. "Coño, stay in your lane," she yelled out her open window. Buena Vista Social Club sounded on the radio. Tina turned up the volume and sang along. She loved Cuban music; there was too much American rock these days.

Manny's plane was scheduled to arrive at 2:30, and it was only an hour or so from the airport to La Promesa, the beach house he rented from the university. Tina shivered with anticipation. She wasn't supposed to call Manny unless it was an emergency, but she dialed him anyway. No answer. Then she remembered that his phone had to be turned off in the plane.

Tina never thought she'd be with a gringo. Well, Manny was born and raised in New York, but his mother was from Guarida. He was at least half islander, which, in Tina's mind, explained his exceptional love-making.

A few minutes later, she pulled over to pee. She could avoid the dirty gas station bathrooms by stopping at a small restaurant called El Farol. No other customers were there yet. She ordered a beer at the bar, and, after sipping it for a minute or two, walked to the door with the mermaid carving. El Farol had fish nets on the walls, crab-trap floaters hanging from the ceiling, and an anchor behind the bar. The bartender, a surly old man wearing a captain's cap, disappeared into the kitchen. He doubled as a cook and had to prepare for the dinner crowd.

Returning to her seat a few minutes later, Tina saw a couple of guys enter the restaurant and saunter over to the bar. They appeared to have an alcoholic glow about them. Or maybe they were just relaxed. They reeked of fish and wore khaki pants and marine shirts. The shorter one took a stool; the taller one approached Tina.

"Hey babe, what's up? I'm Álvaro and this little guy is José."

"The sky." Tina remained expressionless, took out a cigarette, and lit it herself. She noticed that Álvaro's shirt pockets were stuffed: a pack of cigarettes in one and a coil of fishing line in the other.

"The sky, huh? That's clever. Ha, ha." He took out the fishing line, coiled it tighter, and shoved it back into his pocket.

"Well, I'm a clever girl."

"How about we step outside, into my truck? We'll see how clever—"

"That will never happen, asshole. Don't mess with me. Okay?"

José stood up, and for a moment Tina thought he might try something. He just laughed. "You eat with that mouth? You're too beautiful to talk like that. Clean up your act, sister. Álvaro just wants you to marry him."

Tina didn't like *piropos,* typical pick-up lines, or condescension. Having struggled through life, she needed respect. Sure, she had done things she might regret, like working for Federico. But a girl had to do what a girl had to do.

Both men backed off when Tina pulled out her knife and let it spring open. She carried the Spyderco switchblade in her handbag for occasions like this. Whether or not these guys would have tried something didn't matter; Tina didn't intend to find out. She strolled backward toward the restaurant door.

The guys broke into hysterical laughter. "Holy shit, one tough bitch! We were just fooling around, you know? You should lighten up, learn to take a joke."

She left the restaurant, got into the Corolla, and pulled away. She saw them through the rear-view mirror. They watched her from El Faro's entrance.

Back on the road she thought about how she needed Manny. Or did she just want him? He respected her, didn't he? The relationship, she reassured herself, had to have something more going for it than just sex. She hoped desperately that Manny had nothing to do with the CIA.

Tina arrived at La Promesa at 3:30. She had picked up the extra key at UG a few days ago, and since the door was still locked, she had to use it. Apparently Manny hadn't arrived yet. She went in, called again. No answer. Maybe the plane was delayed. She walked through the house and could see the beach through the back windows. Gentle waves washed up on the sand. Coconut palms, jasmine vines, hibiscus, and brilliant red-blooming bougainvillea bushes grew next to the house, sea oats near the shore. Brown pelicans cruised above the water, scoping out herring and mullet. When they spotted their prey, it was as if their motion froze for an instant. Time stood still. Then they would drop straight down like dive-bombers, crashing head-first into the brine. On the way back up into the air, fish squirmed in their ladle-like beaks.

Tina recalled telling Manny how these birds dove until the impact of thousands of crashes into the water caused blindness; when finally unable to sight their prey, they retreated to the rocks along the shore and died.

"Probably a myth," he said, "but isn't it like human behavior?"

She wondered what he meant by that as she walked out the back door and down to the water's edge, where she stood motionless. Small swells swept over her bare feet, leaving them partially buried in the sand. She was alone until a young couple came down the beach searching for something.

"Have you seen our dog?" the young woman said.

Tina pulled her feet out of the sand and let the water clean them off. "No, just a bunch of pelicans."

"Well, where can he be? Oh, my name's María Pilar Alonso."

"We're in El Placer, " the boy added. He looked to be twenty, perhaps; no older. "Are you alone?"

"No, I am waiting for someone. We'll be in La Promesa. I'm Tina."

"Oh, sorry, I'm Jorge. Jorge Padilla."

"So, you must be students, right?" Only university people had access to these beach houses.

"Yes, we're at the university. María Pilar studies international relations. I'm in law."

Tina smiled. "If you're in I.R., you must know Professor Vidal."

"The gringo, sure," María Pilar said. "We both took one of his classes. And I accompanied him to see President Sánchez when he spoke at convocation. The professor's really good, very objective. Not like the bullshit artists who pretend to know everything. And he's simpático—he doesn't act like an Ugly American."

"Yeah, that's who I'm waiting for. He should be here soon. I'm a secretary at UG, in the education school, and I teach elementary down in Cell Block Thirteen. You guys know about the Block, right?"

"Yeah," María Pilar said, "we both did some volunteer work there last year. There's been some improvement since Sánchez was elected."

"Hopefully," Tina said, "but I wish our illustrious president would be a bit more diplomatic. Don't you agree?"

"Sánchez understands the popular sentiment, so he has to say the things he does," Jorge responded. He and María Pilar exchanged glances.

"That's exactly what Manny, I mean, Professor Vidal says. You're going to enjoy talking with him. I wish he was here already."

"Why don't you call the airport or the airline or something?" Jorge suggested.

"I called his cell a few times. He's not answering. How'd you know he was flying?" Why did this guy assume Manny had been out of the country?

"Oh, just a guess," María Pilar said with a laugh, but Tina didn't miss the look she gave Jorge. Tina wondered why she seemed upset with him.

Jorge said, "You would have driven down here together—"

"How would you know that, Jorge?" María Pilar said.

"Calm down," Jorge said.

"Hey, you're here on vacation, right?" Tina had enough on her mind. The last thing she needed was a quarrel between these two. "Listen, it's been nice meeting you. I hope you'll come up for a drink after we get settled. We'll be here for the week."

"So will we," Jorge said. "And thanks, we'll take you up on the invitation."

Tina noticed that they returned to El Placer without the dog. Well, it would find its way back. They always did.

She called Guarida Air, learned that the flight had come in on time. Regulations prohibited the release of names. She called Alfredo Cardozo, Manny's department chair, who hadn't heard from him and didn't appreciate the disturbing call from a mere secretary.

She dialed Manny's cell again and left a message: "It's Tina. Where are you? What's going on? Call me, okay?" She tried to speak calmly but knew she sounded desperate.

Manny felt as if he were floating in a cloud. The bits and pieces he saw and heard were a blur in slow motion. When the flight landed, passengers grabbed their carry-ons and stood in the aisle waiting for the attendants to prepare for disembarkation.

"My friend took something... fell asleep... pretty strong stuff... still groggy." It was just snatches of conversation that registered with Manny, apparently coming from his seat mate, talking to the flight attendant. But he couldn't be sure. He felt himself being lifted. His eyes closed as the chair beneath him seemed to move.

Manny awoke to the beating of a bass drum. It was his heart. He must have been dreaming. He tried to move, but some kind of thin string, wrapped around his body, arms, and wrists, cut into his skin. He struggled, couldn't move, went still. Panic gripped him as surely as the string.

Someone dropped a wet cloth on his face. He felt as if he were drowning, couldn't breathe. He held his breath. Many seconds later, just before he started to suck in, the cloth was removed. His eyes felt like they were being pulled out of their sockets. He gasped. All he could think of was getting air into his lungs.

A voice from behind Manny said, "What were you doing in Washington?"

"What?" he sputtered. He remembered boarding the jet at Dulles, chatting with Roberto. He tried moving his arms. The string tightened around him like a Chinese finger trap. The more he struggled, the tighter it became.

"What is Guarida Libre planning now?"

"Agh..."

Again someone covered Manny's face, poured water on another kind of cloth that formed a skintight mask around his eyes, nose, and mouth, clinging like plastic wrap. Again he could not breathe. The capillaries in his nose must have broken, blood trickled into his mouth. It tasted bitter. His vision went black.

Manny felt the cloth being removed just in time. He sucked air into lungs that felt like deflated balloons. His head throbbed. The vessels in his neck were ready to spew boiling blood, splatter everywhere. What the hell was happening? Not a bad dream. This was real. *My God, let it be over.* Manny cried, and the tears burned his eyes. "Stop!" he cried out. "I'll talk." The odor, gas or oil, was sickening. Vomit spilled from the corner of his mouth. He would have done anything to end the torture.

He felt like an inanimate object, powerless, the worst and most frightening feeling he had ever experienced. He was stuck in one of the deepest rungs of Dante's hell. He couldn't see who was doing these awful things to him. He gasped for air when they let him. His fate rested in their hands, whoever they were. He could not move, breathed only on their prerogative, could barely think.

"Tell us who Major Ramírez was working with."

"Who?"

"What is the CIA planning?"

"Please. No more," Manny whimpered. Nothing in his existence had prepared him for this. "I'm... not CIA," he managed to say.

"What about Petrol International? The oil people are involved, no?"

"Please, I really don't—"

"You and Raimundo Roldano are friends, correct?"

"Ray and I... we play tennis. That's all."

"Mr. Professor, listen carefully. We must know when the golpe will occur. You may not agree, pana, but our methods are your methods—extraordinary rendition, enhanced interrogation."

"No, I don't believe in that. I'm against it—"

"Well, your duplicitous government is not. Be that as it may, we know you are a CIA spy."

"I'm not CIA, not a spy!" He was desperate. He couldn't tell them what he didn't know or confess to being what he wasn't. But, he was just about ready to tell them anything he thought they wanted to hear.

"INR is a clever cover. We must protect our nation, our homeland. Now tell us about the next attempt—"

"Yes. No. I really don't know anything. What do you want me to say?"

They dropped another wet cloth over Manny's face. Again, he had to hold his breath. When he could no longer hold it and instinctively tried to take in air, it was blocked by the clinging cloth. Just as he thought he was doomed to die of suffocation and was blacking out again, they pulled it away. Manny wheezed. Then he heard whispering. "No, not again," he pleaded.

"Just leave him. That's enough for now. We'll come back tomorrow. Álvaro, you stay here. He's not going anywhere. Just make sure he remains alive."

It's over, at least for the time being, Manny thought. Barely conscious, he felt some sense of relief. But he couldn't move. They were probably tricking him and would soon continue the ordeal. A bitter odor hung in clammy heat that blanketed him. His limbs had lost sensation, not even pins and needles. He heard water splashing up against something. Seagulls screeched. Then oblivion...

Tina sat on La Promesa's porch, listening to the waves heave, roll, and crash on the beach. The breakers pounded shells and washed them up along the shore. The brine seeped through the crushed shells and filtered into the sand. The undertow sucked water back into the deep. Another wave formed, and the process repeated, as if the sea were breathing.

Tina hadn't slept all night. She saw María Pilar and Jorge bob up and down like corks in the swells beyond the breakers. They battled against the undertow to reach the beach, emerged from their morning skinny-dip, grabbed their towels, and ran across the sand to El Placer. She watched them dry off on their porch, Jorge stroking María Pilar's back, rubbing his body against hers. María Pilar pulled away. She said something to Jorge that Tina could not hear.

The couple entered the cottage, and after a few minutes, came out wearing jeans, t-shirts, and flip-flops. They waved at Tina and strolled down the beach.

Unable to wait any longer, Tina scribbled a note for the students. She grabbed her things and left La Promesa. Before getting into the Corolla, she slid the note under the door to El Placer.

Heading back to the city, if you see Prof. Vidal, please call me on my cell 448-0692. Thanks, hope to see you again. Tina.

She jumped into the car and took off, speeding far beyond the unenforced limit. Fortunately, there was hardly any traffic going back to the city. Almost everyone was headed in the other direction. She needed to get to the apartment in Las Palmas and find out what happened to Manny. Maybe he was still in Washington. They said the flight had come in, but he might not have been on it. Where the hell was he?

Damn tunnel, Tina thought. The light remained red until a lengthy stream of cars, trucks, buses, and motorcycles came through—heavy beach traffic. The light finally turned green, and Tina floored the Corolla. She drove furiously through the maze of unplanned streets and boulevards that constituted the capital city, passing through the squalor of the poor neighborhoods and the opulence of the wealthy zones without taking notice. She screeched around corners. Political banners and graffiti on the sides of buildings seemed to whiz by, all part of a surreal backdrop. She passed armed guards around the central plaza and the boulevard. Large billboards punctured the skyline with pictures of enormous Coca Cola bottles, airplanes with special prices to Miami and New York printed across the sky, and alluring willowy blondes promoting the use of push-up bras or the latest scent. These usually irritated her, but at the moment she wasn't thinking about the landscape.

She parked the car in the subterranean lot, locked the doors, and ran up the steps to La Ciruela. It was already mid-afternoon. "Mr. Ferreira," she said, as calmly as she could when she found him, "I'll have a parchita, please." The freshly squeezed passion fruit juice soothed Tina with its reinvigorating quality. "What's new?" She figured the snitch Ferreira might know something.

"Nothing, same old thing."

"You haven't seen Manny, have you?"

"Not since last week. Why—is something wrong?"

"Ciao," she said.

"Obrigado, let me know when he shows up."

Once settled in the apartment, Tina felt a little better. She napped for a while. Awakened by the noises in the street, she continued to worry about what was happening. She grabbed Manny's photo from the table and gazed at it, and then she looked through the window and saw the usual bustle in the street below. Suddenly she did a double-take, almost certain she saw Jorge and María Pilar on the other side of the street. She tried to clear her head with a quick shake. *Probably just a couple of students who looked like them,* she reasoned as they ducked into the drugstore across from La Ciruela.

Tina took a deep breath. "Mierda," she whimpered. Her day had come and gone. The sun was about to disappear behind the hills to the west of Guarida City. As daylight faded away, she stared at the horizon and wondered where Manny could be.

✑Chapter Twenty✑

On the morning after Tina returned to the city, the sun blazed hotter than usual on the coast. Saba and Aichí had to take a break from kicking their makeshift fútbol back and forth. They squatted down in the open field near to the abandoned oil dock, laughed and sang, felt free as the air. The sweaty children looked out at the sun's rays reflecting off the sea.

"Look how the water sparkles. Let's go in, sis," Aichí called out.

"You go first, little brother. I'll follow."

As they dashed toward the sea, Saba fell behind. She called out, "Aichí, you're only eight and you run like an Olympic sprinter."

The children let the sun dry them after their swim and were about to return to their village. Aichí kicked the ball out in front and then caught up with it and kicked it again. This time he kicked a bit too hard. It rolled over to one of the dilapidated warehouses next to the dock. He jogged over to retrieve the ball, and then stopped abruptly.

"What's that, Saba? Over there, look through the door. Come with me. I don't want to go alone. It could be *duppies*. I'm scared."

"There are no ghosts, Aichí. They're just from grandpa's stories. Don't be afraid. Let's go see."

The children held hands as they approached the abandoned structure and found what appeared to be two spiritless bodies. One was bound to a board. The other was lying on the sandy floor. Neither moved. Saba and Aichí jumped away. Aichí picked up the ball and, with Saba not far behind, dashed back to their village without looking back.

"Mamá," Aichí shouted when they reached their home, "there's something scary at the dock."

"You and Papá must see," Saba said. "Please come with us. Come, come now. Please hurry!"

Barely conscious, Manny could not open his eyes. There was no sensation in his body, like he was frozen. He couldn't move, but he could hear noises.

Something, or someone, stirred very close to him. There was a rustling of feet. "Aah, aah..." It was a person, a man, perhaps a guard. He sounded as if he had just awakened and was stretching.

Manny, afraid that he would be tortured again, remained silent. *Play dead,* he thought; it was his only defense.

"You look nice and comfortable, pal," said the man. "You're not going anywhere. I'm going for a plunge to cool off, but don't worry, I'll be right back." Why was he talking to a corpse?

After a few minutes, Manny changed his mind and managed to whisper, "Please help me..."

There was no response. The man must have gone out for his swim. There was nothing Manny could do now, except just try to keep breathing.

Manny was barely breathing and delirious when Saba and Aichí returned with their parents. They quickly cut the fishing line that bound Manny's limp body, scraped together a makeshift travois, and dragged him to their village. He heard a child's voice say, "The other body must have been taken by the Great Spirit to the Land-Beyond-the-Clouds."

Once in the village, members of the tribe began nursing Manny with methods that dated back centuries. After a while the organic herbs, and perhaps the tribal elders' incantations, seemed to work miracles. Manny's eyes, which felt like they had been glued shut, finally managed to open. The blurred apparitions of two small beings appeared before Manny, but only in his right eye. Slowly, as if adjusting a camera lens, his eye focused on Saba and Aichí. Manny was speechless. Was this a dream?

For what seemed like days, he was barely aware of the children watching him. They were present when he finally uttered, "Where am I? Who are you?"

Manny couldn't understand their native language, but Saba flashed a broad smile filled with shiny white teeth and said, *"Por fin te has despertado, señor."* She explained in broken Spanish that she and her brother had found him, and their tribe was bringing him back from the Land-of-the-Dead.

Manny lay in a hut with a thatched roof, smelled herbs, heard birds chirping, and again thought he was dreaming. Although frightened that he had lost vision in his left eye, he was happy to be alive. Agonizing over what had happened, Manny speculated that his captors were terrorists or maybe mercenaries. Did they mistake him for someone else? They had asked about a coup against the government. Wouldn't the Security Police have taken him to jail? What about Roberto? Was he involved? The message he was supposed to deliver to Sánchez could have figured into this mess. Were they going to follow him? They said they would return.

"You're safe with us," the folk-healing *curandero* proclaimed as if he could read Manny's mind. "We have guards and traps hidden in the forest to protect our village from the barbarians." The children's parents, tribal elders, and the curandero nursed Manny for the next two weeks.

"I'm grateful to you, my friends. Saba and Aichí saved me, you all did."

Manny looked around, accommodating to the loss of peripheral vision on the left side. Hopefully, modern medicine could restore his full vision. For now at least he was alive and could see.

He had struggled to provide the tribe with some sort of explanation for his strange situation. *Start at the beginning,* the curandero had said. So, for hours each day he had recounted his story. It was all he could do to piece things together. The elders had listened patiently.

"God is with us, Emmanuel. It is the meaning of your name," the *cacique*, their tribal chief, said. "You're on a journey. It's one that will mark your destiny. Your ideals will sustain you as the conditions of life teach cruel truths. The world is full of challenges and deceit. We can only make small changes. Much is beyond our control."

"Please," Manny said, "accept my watch as a token of my gratitude." Somehow the Tag Heuer had remained in place through Manny's ordeal. "It's all I have to offer." He had lost his wallet and cell phone. His luggage was probably stored in the airport.

"We measure time in a different way, one that is guided by the sun and stars," the curandero said.

"Keep your watch, my friend. You'll need it," the cacique said.

"Thank you. It was given to me by someone close to my heart." Manny would have done anything to be at home with Dee. After all he'd been through, the mere thought of his normal life tormented him. Where was she now? Would he ever see her again? Someday, he hoped (without much conviction at the moment), they would be together again. He had to extricate himself from Guarida first and foremost.

The cacique drank water from a *porrón*. He moved from Manny's left side to face him and offered the leather decanter... Manny thanked the cacique and took a long sip. The cacique said, "We are Arawaks. The outside world mistakes us for savages and treats us like chattel. They take our homes for what they call development. They take our ancestral lands and pollute Mother Earth. And they do it by serving their master, the black mud that we use to caulk our canoes. It's their source of energy and wealth. Yet their Tower of Babel will fall."

The cacique paused, studied Manny, and then continued. "We're all part of the oneness. We treat our living surroundings as an extension of ourselves. The land, the vegetation, the animals are as sacred as the water we drink and the air we breathe. The Great Spirit has endowed us with inner strength to endure. You see this in us. And through the Great

Spirit we will point you in the right direction. There's much that awaits you on your mission, my friend."

The cacique's dignity, self-awareness, and inner peace impressed Manny. His powerful words inspired a sense of awe, humbling Manny in his presence. "I wish I were as certain," he said. "I carry a message to your president. I have doubts…"

Saba and Aichí came over to sit next to the adults. When their mother told them it was time to sleep, they hugged Manny good night, giggled, and scampered away.

"He's not *our* president," said the cacique. "We don't trust him."

Manny wished he could find some hope. Didn't Sánchez do some good, like provide better health care and education? He needed something to believe in, and he didn't want to give up, not even now. The cacique was probably right, though.

"The politicians' promises are always broken. You will see, Emmanuel. You will see. Get some rest. We have more to discuss tomorrow. Soon you will be ready for your trek back into your world. When you are strong enough, you will carry your message. You will always remember us. And you will go in peace."

"Where the hell is he?" Claudio shouted as he rose from his desk. He picked up his Louisville Slugger and strode over to stand before Roberto and Álvaro.

"He was tied to a board, Mr. President," Roberto said. "When we went back for him, he was gone. Álvaro left him for a few minutes. He just went in for a quick dip."

"I want you to find him, bring him in alive." Claudio tapped his bat on the floor and looked toward Juan Carlos, who remained seated.

"Álvaro," Juan Carlos said, "obviously you've screwed up. How could you leave the professor unguarded?"

Claudio raised his bat and walked over to Álvaro, who began to shake. "The prisoner couldn't move," Álvaro said in a weak voice. "It was a thirty-pound test line. I just jumped in the ocean for a few minutes. No one was within miles of the dock."

"What about the Indians?" Claudio said.

"I didn't think—"

"Exactly, Álvaro, you didn't think," Juan Carlos said. "But now you can rectify this situation. And there will be no need for violence."

Claudio swung his bat gently in the air. Then he said, "I've talked to his girlfriend, Cristina Reyes. She'll deliver him to us if we don't find him with the Arawaks."

Juan Carlos smiled menacingly at Álvaro and Roberto and said, "Meanwhile, we'd like you and José to meet with Jorge and María Pilar, find Miss Reyes, then bring in the professor, eh? And don't mess up this time."

Saba and Aichí held Manny's hands as they led him into the rainforest and showed him the trail to take. He thanked the children, gave each a long hug. They grasped him around the waist, held tight, and would not let go.

"I must go now," Manny said. "Your cacique is right. I'm on a mission. Stay with your parents and your tribe. I'll return."

The children dropped their arms from around Manny and pointed to the east. Then they waved goodbye. *Like little angels,* he thought. He looked back a few times, waving and watching them grow smaller in the distance. He had to adjust to monocular vision. It was not as difficult as he'd expected, but he wondered, with a pang of longing, how it would be on a tennis court, if he were ever to play again.

When he could see Saba and Aichí no longer, Manny turned and started his trek. He walked for miles, had no idea where the trail was leading, hoped he would find a town or village, eventually the city. Somehow, he would contact Janey. The embassy should be informed about what had happened to him. And he knew he would need safe haven; he couldn't risk returning to the apartment.

The trail remained close to the shore. He heard the surf crashing on the rocks and the screeching seagulls. He caught glimpses of the ocean through the trees and vines.

Manny tired. His hands shook. He pushed on. At least he was alive. He emptied the small water pouch the children had given him. His throat was parched, and his shirt was drenched with sweat. He began to see double. He shook his head to clear his vision. On he walked, for hours and for miles, seeing no signs of civilization, peering up at the staring faces of immense ferns. The trail curved around bogs, boulders, and gargantuan trees. Spanish-moss and vines hung from their branches, forming an eerie canopy that filtered the strong sun.

Manny stumbled into an opening and saw a huge waterfall, perched himself on a flat rock at its base, and felt the cool spray. He filled the pouch and sipped cold water. Then he got up and started to walk. When the roar of the waterfall faded away, he heard a wild clattering that could have been club-winged manakins performing their mating calls or bats beating their wings to escape from cave rats. Then

Manny thought he heard something else—footsteps—behind him. He picked up his pace. The footsteps continued and again he thought someone, or something, an animal perhaps, followed him. His whole body shook and sweat poured from his forehead. A black snake with a red line on its back slithered across his path, turned its triangular head, and showed its split tongue.

Was someone on Manny's trail? He feared being tortured. Never again, he swore. He began to run, had to keep his mouth closed to avoid swallowing a swarm of buzzing gnats. Breathing hard, he pushed forward on adrenaline alone. Mist rose from the forest like ghosts. They spoke to him through the voices of wind, rustling leaves, hooting owls, and screeching gulls. He didn't know what they were saying. He felt disoriented and frightened, just as he had when his childhood friends dared him to enter the Tunnel of Horror in Coney Island.

The trail crossed a shallow river atop a natural rock bridge. Manny staggered over and reached for the water pouch. It was gone. He must have dropped it along the way. He looked back but kept going, stumbling on, driven by anxiety and fear.

Then he heard the drums. Their poignant beat echoed ahead of him. Manny recognized the sound of the tambores. African slaves of long ago had carved the drums out of tree trunks and used them to send messages. Their descendants kept the rituals alive. Manny ran toward the beating, drawn by its hypnotic pulse. His feet shuffled through soft ferns. He jumped over dead tree trunks that crossed the dirt path. The dense rainforest surrounding the trail seemed to part, revealing another clearing ahead.

The blaze of a campfire burning in the center of the glade illuminated a wizened man's long white beard and colorful robe. He held a live chicken by its legs. Women, whose sweat-drenched black skin reflected sparkles exploding from the flames, danced in a circle around the old man. A woman who looked like Tina jumped into the center of the circle and received the chicken. She clutched the animal's legs and held it above her head, and its wings flapped in a futile attempt to escape. The man chanted incantations, grabbed a bottle, and poured a clear liquid into her mouth. A fat woman puffed cigar smoke around her face.

Manny's mouth dropped open. Could that really be Tina? She released the chicken and ripped off her clothes. All the women were nude, their drenched bodies gyrating to the rhythm of the tambores. A few of the dancers fell out of sync, as if in convulsions. The earthy sensuality of the startling scene grabbed Manny's puerile attention, rapidly overcoming his initial repulsion.

The chicken tried to escape from the circle, but the women drove it back and the man caught it. He clutched its neck with one hand, then whipped the bird around in a rapid circular motion above his head. Feathers flew. Its neck snapped. The chicken danced its last pathetic steps before the man chopped off its head with a machete. The headless creature continued to move around, finally dropping into a pool of its own blood.

The woman—he knew now it was Tina—lifted the bird to drink the vital fluid flowing from its neck. She wiped the blood on her face, breasts, and stomach and then offered the carcass to the old man, who partook of the privilege.

As the old man drank, his dark skin turned white and his robe green with blotches of brown and grey, like combat fatigues. He stripped off the camouflage. Blue and red veins bulged on the ethereal soldier's chalk-white skin. He hoisted Tina by placing his hands under her buttocks. She shrieked as she rode his red, white, and blue torso. They writhed in concert with the frenetic drumbeat. Their insane laughter was soon replaced by pleasurable groans. Then the man threw her to the ground, kicked her in the ribs, and walked away.

The next morning, Manny awoke alone, nestled in a bed of ferns under a large tree next to a clearing in the midst of the tropical rainforest. There were no signs of chicken blood, only dying embers and ashes within a circle of stones. What had happened last night? His mind must have been playing tricks on him. It had to have been a hallucination provoked by fear, dehydration, and fatigue. But what did it mean? Did he think Guaridans were primitive and superstitious?

Manny began to shake. He stood and massaged his temples. Then, as if receiving a message from himself, several lines from Homer's *Odyssey*, once memorized in college, popped into his mind: *Dreams surely are difficult, confusing, and not everything in them is brought to pass...*

How could he have remembered that? Was he going crazy? Was all this really happening? Was Tina nothing more than a good lay? Was the United States screwing Guarida?

Manny's gut told him it was all true. He decided to keep his wits about him, break with Tina once and for all, and convince Stark that his ultimatum to Sánchez would be self-defeating. But first, he had to find his way out of this forest and back home.

⋐⌐Chapter Twenty-One⌐⋑

A United States Marine, decked out in his dress blues, waved members of the Excom through the well-guarded entrance to the White House. Security had been beefed up since 9/11. Adam Stark was one of the last to arrive.

Stark entered the West Wing, took an elevator to the basement, and proceeded past a duty officer of the current watch team. Once in the Situation Room, he took note of the wood-paneled walls, behind which were secure communications systems. *Here we are careful about what we say,* he thought.

President Harmon had summoned the Excom for a special meeting. David Ramshore, Robert Muldive, and James Brownfield were seated in chairs facing the president. Bart Kelloring and Elizabeth Gordon-Sparks sat at opposite ends of the rectangular table, while Secretary of State Carl Pham-Dixon sat next to the president in the center. Stark took a seat next to Brownfield.

Kelloring got up and walked slowly to a glossy map of the Western Hemisphere that hung on a stand to the right of the table. All eyes turned toward him. He used a magic marker to draw a line on the map. Stark watched intently and wondered if any of the others in the room knew in advance what this was about.

"This line represents the twelve nautical mile territorial limit recognized by the United Nations Convention on the Law of the Sea," Kelloring stated. "As you can see, it is off Guarida's southern shore. This morning, I received word that one of our surveillance boats, a PT boat based in Bonaire, was hit by hostile fire. I'm sorry to report that it went down. The boat was somewhere in this vicinity." Kelloring drew a triangle that covered the line he had previously drawn. Now Stark began to sense where this was going. "This triangle is our boat. It was on a routine mission, but might have wandered into Guaridan waters during a storm. In fact, radio contact was lost prior to the incident. The Guaridan government claims that the U.S. launched an invasion. Sánchez is charging that a military vessel within territorial waters without clearance constitutes an act of war."

"Nonsense," Pham-Dixon said.

Stark nodded.

Harmon's lip curled, and he drummed his fingers on the table. "An act of war has been committed, general, but not by the United States of America. The enemy attacked us. We cannot allow this sort of aggression to stand."

"Mr. President," Pham-Dixon said, "this whole incident is really a case of bad weather compounded by mistaken judgment. It's an unfortunate situation. There doesn't appear to be any imminent threat." Pham-Dixon spoke with his usual confidence.

"I agree, Mr. President," Kelloring said.

Stark said, "I do as well."

Ramshore, Muldive, and Brownfield remained silent. However, Gordon-Sparks contended that, no matter what the cause, a United States vessel was attacked and sunk by a hostile regime. "We must respond to this," she said.

The president's lip relaxed.

"This smacks of another Tonkin Gulf." Stark pushed his glasses to the bridge of his nose and leaned forward. "And we all are well-aware of the quagmire that got us into." He thought about Ramshore's plan and wondered what the hell had happened to the professor. No communiqués, no e-mails, nothing since his last visit to Washington. Stark had sent e-mails and tried calling him. Neither Cardozo nor anyone at the embassy knew where he was. He seemed to have disappeared, fallen off the face of the earth.

"Well, if Sánchez is importing yellowcake," the president intoned, "if they're building WMDs, we can't just stand by and watch. They took down one of our boats, for God's sake."

A palpable unease invaded the Situation Room. Stark was sure each member of the Excom knew what the Commander-in-Chief wanted. No one responded until Gordon-Sparks broke the silence.

"What we have here, gentlemen, is an act of aggression that requires an immediate response. A limited military retaliation would be appropriate. There's no need for a congressional declaration; it can be accomplished by executive order. We use our forces already in place. This operation would require nothing more than a quick invasion and occupation on the order of an Operation Urgent Fury. We remove Sánchez in the process. We'll get in and out fast, just like our intervention in Grenada. This is what I advocate, Mr. President."

"Thank you, Lizzy," the president said. "I'll bring in our Secretary of Defense and the Joint Chiefs, and we'll see what they have to say."

Despite serious skepticism expressed by Pham-Dixon and members of the Excom, Stark knew that the president had already come to a decision.

The next day Secretary of State Pham-Dixon stared directly into the television camera. He placed his hands together as if he were about to pray and squinted into the lights.

Stark turned to scan the group that President Harmon had assembled for Pham-Dixon's press conference. Surrounding the Secretary of State, who sat at his desk, were the Secretary of Defense, Chairman of the Joint Chiefs of Staff, Director of Central Intelligence, and presidential advisors Ramshore, Brownfield, Muldive, Kelloring, and Gordon-Sparks, as well as Stark himself. American flag pins were stuck neatly in each person's lapels. On the wall behind them was a huge American flag that served as a background, a portrait of American power projected on television screens throughout the nation and the world.

Stark liked Pham-Dixon, the son of a Marine Corps captain and a Vietnamese seamstress. He had risen to the rank of brigadier general prior to his selection first as Chairman of the Joint Chiefs of Staff and then as Secretary of State. He was a good soldier. Yet Stark could sense Pham-Dixon's inner turmoil.

Pham-Dixon tensed his brow, tightened his lips together with the corners turned down, and fidgeted in his chair. Then he stacked the papers on his desk into a pile, sat forward, patted the sides of the pile, and looked up. "Ready," he said.

The cameraman signaled: "Five, four, three, two... Okay, let's roll."

"My fellow Americans," Pham-Dixon began, "the United States and Guarida have had a long and amicable relationship. Recently, however, Guarida has embarked on a course that has compromised its fledgling democracy. Claudio Sánchez has censored the press, expropriated businesses, appointed only his supporters to positions of authority, and wants to eliminate institutional opposition. As if that weren't enough to cause us to reevaluate our relationship, terrorist cells have been operating on Venezuela's Margarita Island, with possible linkages to Guarida."

Pham-Dixon took a deep breath and gazed at his papers. Then he knit his brow, clenched his teeth, and proclaimed that Guarida had imported yellowcake uranium from Brazil. "Yellowcake," he said, "is essential for only one purpose. We believe Guarida wants a nuclear capability." He stated that WMDs would contravene the Rio Treaty as well as the Arms Control Agreement. Therefore, the United States—along with its allies in the region—must strongly oppose this development.

Stark removed his glasses and pressed his hands on his temples. He watched Pham-Dixon point to a map of the Western Hemisphere. The secretary drew concentric circles emanating from Guarida to major cities in the U.S., representing distances with vulnerability to an intercontinental ballistic missile, places likely to be hit, and time-to-target of a potential detonation.

This is a repeat performance of the Cuban Missile Crisis, Stark thought. Yet he knew that it would take many years before these weapons could be made operational.

"We must build a coalition of Latin American nations, take the case against Guarida to the OAS and the UN, and mobilize U.S. troops in the Southern Command," Pham-Dixon concluded. Sweat had formed on his broad forehead and was running down the sides of his face.

Stark replaced his glasses. Then he dropped his head shaking it in despair.

Manny had been walking for three days, following the trail through the rainforest. He ate nuts and berries, drank from streams, and slept at the base of trees. He was obsessed with his dream about the powerful United States raping his little island paradise, his Guaridan lover abused by an American military figure. Or, Manny thought, was it he who was screwing the country? Or was the country screwing him? He wondered if he would ever find Rafael.

He thought he heard a humming in the distance, a buzzing sound, and he stopped in his tracks. He cupped his ears and listened. It sounded unnatural, incongruous. Was his mind playing tricks on him again? Could it really be cars or trucks? He prayed and kept moving.

As if out of nowhere, a layer of crushed rock covered by cement crossed his trail. The apparition didn't look real—the roadway seemed as out of place as the sound of vehicles. Yet civilization's paved thoroughfare loomed before him, a neat swath cut through the jungle.

Manny felt a burst of energy. He scampered up the soft shoulder onto macadam as if emerging from a prehistoric netherworld into the contemporary world. The nightmare was ending. He tried to wave down one of the few cars that sped by. It didn't even slow down. Then another, and another. Why wouldn't anyone stop? He must look like a vagrant, he realized. Would he be stranded in the middle of nowhere after all he had been through? Manny sat down on a log beside the roadway.

Finally an old truck with wooden slats around its bed halted about thirty yards ahead. Manny jumped up, shuffled to the side of the truck, and asked the driver where he was headed. Where was the nearest village?

"Get in. I'll take you as far as I'm going," the driver said.

Manny climbed into the truck. With the vision gone in his left eye, he had to turn his head far to the left in order to see the driver. The old man smoked a dark cigar that Manny could tell was good tobacco, a maduro. His face was craggy with the lines of a tough life. A farmer, Manny thought, then spotted plantains, grapefruits, tomatoes, and cabbages piled in the truck bed.

"Going to market?" he asked, relieved to be sitting in a moving vehicle, no matter how slow. The man drove at a snail's pace.

"Yes, señor," the old farmer replied respectfully. The taciturn man asked nothing about Manny, where he had been or where he was going.

They passed a sign that identified the two-lane road as National Highway Route 1-A. Manny remembered that it led into Guarida City from the northwestern coast. A sign indicated that Pueblo Pequeño was twenty kilometers from where the truck was poking along at around ten kilometers per hour. At normal speed, the capital was an hour or so beyond the town. At this rate it would take at least three hours.

"I've been on a trek through the forest," Manny said to break the ice. "I reside in the capital—"

The man interrupted. "Stay away from La Ciudad."

Manny assumed this was an expression of the usual disdain the campesinos harbored for the pollution, congestion, and criminality of city life. When the man went on to explain that the Americans had invaded, Manny's mouth dropped open. He massaged his forehead, took a deep breath, and shook his head. Was his dream coming true?

Why had the military preempted his message to Sánchez? What happened to the plan? In a way, Manny felt relieved. He'd never wanted to be involved anyway. But what was he supposed to do now?

"The Americans don't like President Sánchez. He won't sell out to the yanquis. They attacked just like our president said they would. The city is dangerous." The man took a long pull on his maduro.

Manny muttered, "How did they attack?"

The man puffed out a billow of smoke. "They tried to parachute in," he said. "Our forces shot them out of the sky like sitting ducks. My own son is in the army. He told me." The farmer tilted his head upward, grinned, and took another drag.

"Guarida is defeating the Americans?"

"They landed troops from the sea. Now there's fighting right out in the streets. I'll go up there," the old man boasted, "if the patria summons me."

Manny scratched his bearded face. He hadn't shaved since before that fateful flight. And now, things didn't add up. He got out of the truck when the farmer turned off the main road, thanked the man, and waited for another lift. He would have liked to return to his apartment, but it was too risky. Whoever was responsible for his capture was probably still looking for him and would pursue him again. The thought of another torture session sent chills down his spine. And there was fighting in the city, according to the farmer. Manny decided to try to make it to the embassy. He would seek safe haven there.

He walked along the main road for ten minutes before a young couple in a Ford Focus pulled up and took him into Pueblo Pequeño. There he learned that all the phones in town were dead. He walked back to the highway and waved down another ride that took him the remainder of the way to the outskirts of Guarida City.

"Thanks," he said to the middle-aged woman as he stepped out of her car.

"Be careful," she said. "Don't go near the palace—I hear there's been a lot of shooting there."

Once in the city, Manny managed to navigate his way back to within a few blocks of the central plaza. The streets were like a disaster area. Garbage was strewn about. Only soldiers could be seen. As he approached the plaza, Manny heard the staccato blasts of machine guns, saw the flare of cross-fire, and smelled the odor of burning rubber that emanated from all around. Exhausted, he tried to hide at the corner of one of the streets leading into the plaza.

Guaridan troops marched past him with arms drawn. Too close for comfort. He could have reached out and touched them. Fortunately, Manny appeared to be destitute; the troops had no interest in an indigent huddled on the street. He froze, held his breath, crouched down on the sidewalk, and prepared to make a dash across the street to an open abasto, a small general store. The troops passed, but he couldn't run yet. A large green army truck turned the corner and blocked his path.

231

As the truck moved in front of him, its tires squealing, and the engine sounded unmuffled. It backfired, spewed billows of smoke, and roared. The gears clanked as it changed speed.

When the truck passed him, Manny glimpsed twenty or so people standing shoulder-to-shoulder in its open bed. Scantily dressed, they appeared to be bound together. They chanted a haunting, melancholy sound, and Manny's heart dropped into his stomach. The Arawaks! He saw two children at the rear end of the truck, stuck behind the adults. He stood and spotted his little angels. Saba and Aichí were wedged against the rope that tied-off the truck bed, stoic expressions on their faces.

His heart pounding, Manny ran after the truck, tried to catch up, but it gained momentum. He could not keep up. The children saw him, lifted their bound hands as high as they could. As they were taken away, Saba and Aichí clenched their jaws and flashed brave expressions, as if to reassure Manny they would survive.

Manny felt sick to his stomach. There was nothing he could do for his friends. Those innocent children and their tribe were the reason he was alive. His head dropped. He stopped walking and stared at the sidewalk. Then machine gun blasts from across the plaza startled him. He felt the whoosh of an artillery shell, jerked his head, saw the orange flashes, and ran. The old farmer was right: the city was far from safe. There was no way he could traverse the Boulevard and make his way across town to the southern hills. The embassy was too isolated, too protected. It was probably closed anyway.

Manny caught a glimpse of the truck in the distance, moving toward the northern hills. He followed in the general direction, running as fast as he could, which was little more than a limping jog. He had to slow down and walk, but he kept moving as an act of sheer willpower. He didn't want to die in the cross-fire, and the image of Saba and Aichí was etched in his mind. He had to get out of the city and seek refuge somewhere. Whoever tortured him would be on his trail.

He looked back for a moment at the PI-dominated skyline, quickly turned, and decided to leave the city behind.

Ricardo Roldano sat on a leather sofa facing Bill McGeorge, who sat back in his chair behind a glass desk. McGeorge abruptly spun around and gazed out the window from his office on the top floor of the Petrol International Building in Guarida City. Fireballs flashed in the streets, and the rattle of machine guns was nearly continuous.

"Goddamn Guarida Libre! You truly screwed up, and now this, for Christ's sake. The last thing we need," he shouted, "is a bloody conflagration that destabilizes trade."

Roldano squinted and gritted his teeth. *Sure, the little Cuban failed,* he thought, *but there will be other opportunities.* What little confidence he had in McGeorge had been eroding rapidly.

"Harmon has justified military action on a singular incident that occurred on the high seas," McGeorge said, "possibly in territorial waters, but during a goddamn hurricane. I told him to get rid of Sánchez, but not like this."

"No one believes that Sánchez poses an imminent threat to the United States," Roldano stated. "His arsenal is as pathetic as his anti-American axis. An imminent threat means there would be impending peril, right? It's pretty far-fetched, don't you think?"

"You think this is about morality?" McGeorge sounded incredulous. "Americans will mobilize around any military venture. We're paranoid, you know. Any Orwellian-type enemy will do. You and I both know what this is about. As soon as that idiot Sánchez decided to deprive us of the energy that drives our entire friggin' economy—"

"Let's be realistic," Roldano said. "Sánchez has purchased weapons from the Russians. And what do we have? Our friend Case won't even come up with the paltry amount we requested. Without assault weapons, how can we stand up to the government's fire power, their AK-47s and their damn Security Police? We'll make a stand, but there are a bunch of new groups forming, and they support the effort to resist an American occupation. Ordinarily these people would be with us in opposition to Sánchez, but now he's the lesser of two evils. Politics makes for strange bedfellows, eh?"

"The issue is oil," McGeorge said. "Let's talk business. If Sánchez is ousted, can you assure me that PI will get preferential treatment? Can I count on you?"

"We'll talk if and when. But as long as we're being political realists, Bill, the invasion might be a way to divert public attention from your ineptitude in Iraq, huh?" Roldano did not like McGeorge, but he would work with the man at least until the country was stabilized.

"It's about oil, Ricardo, nothing more."

"I doubt if your troops know what the hell they're doing down here, but if they can get rid of Sánchez, more power to them," Roldano said. "Then we'll decide where to go from there."

"Guarida's falling apart," McGeorge said. "Our troops haven't been able to calm the situation. The airport is shut down. Now we've got factions crawling out of the crevices, we don't even know who's who anymore."

"Guarida Libre can assist. We'll get it right this time. We've got to get this occupation under control. There's a lot riding on it," Roldano said.

"I'm with you on that." McGeorge gave a curt nod. "Will you convince whoever takes over to give me a good deal?"

"I said we would talk. What's the worst that can happen? Either your troops put down Sánchez and restore stability—and then you'll get your deal—or they lose and withdraw. Cut and run, as you people like to say."

"What then?"

"We'd be left with exactly what we had before, only worse. So to be safe we're moving our money into the Caymans. We can always bring it back," Roldano said.

"We're hedging our bets too," McGeorge said.

"You Americans have a long record of not staying the course, as you put it. You wouldn't let Patton march into Beijing, allowed yourselves to be defeated in Vietnam, retreated from Bagdad in the first Gulf War, and wouldn't commit sufficient troops to get the job done in Afghanistan. And you've never engaged for very long anywhere in Latin America."

McGeorge shook his head. "Are we really going to sit here and debate history?"

"If Sánchez wins, our countries will become mortal enemies. Watch out, because his next step would be to proclaim every American citizen persona non grata in our island paradise."

⚘Chapter Twenty-Two⚘

Manny forced himself to follow the truck. He jogged as far as he could, but even at its slow pace, the vehicle outdistanced him and disappeared behind a stand of spruce pines in the northern hills. Why had they kidnapped the Arawaks? Where were they taking the people he had grown to love?

Manny's legs felt like rubber. He stopped, gulped at the humid air. He had to rethink his options. If the embassy had remained open—it would be closed if diplomatic ties had been broken during the invasion—Janey could help him. Was she still at her post or even in country? He hoped she was safe.

It really didn't matter if anyone was at the embassy. He couldn't get across the city anyway. And the compound was too damn secure in the southern hills. He wouldn't be able to rely on Tina, with all her bullshit about the CIA. She was a Guaridan, after all. Who knows, maybe she had something to do with his torture.

He felt so alone, so alienated. Dee would say that he was cut loose "like a rolling stone."

His pulse revved, reminding him that he couldn't remain where he was. So he kept walking. He stumbled upon one of the trailheads that led into the rainforest. Maybe he could make it up to a clearing. There, he would camp out and come up with a plan of action.

Manny began the steep ascent. Though he was breathing heavily, fear overcame fatigue as he dug his heels into the trail. The higher he got, the fainter grew the reverberations of the fighting, diminishing to cracking sounds rather than explosions. He looked over the escarpment next to a glade and saw the distant flares of gunfire in the city below—arcs of yellow, orange, and purple that could have been fireworks. But these colorful images were produced by lethal weapons.

The sun set, and he was no closer to finding a refuge. He was exhausted, hungry, and disoriented. He stumbled onto a path on the other side of the meadow that seemed wider than the others. The dirt trail was packed a bit harder, as if the volume of sparse traffic was greater there.

The wider path seemed less steep, and Manny walked easier now. A red-tail boa slithered across the path right in front of Manny's feet. He would have been petrified under normal conditions. Now he paid little attention to the serpent. He headed toward the pounding, gushing sounds of a waterfall farther along the trail. Perhaps there he would find a spot to sleep. The flowing water would have a tranquilizing effect, he thought. He had been running on adrenalin for too long.

The raucous flapping of wings, like a round of applause, distracted him as he approached the falls. *Probably a flock of guácharos coming out of the caves for their nocturnal flight,* he thought. He turned abruptly toward the source of the fracas and gasped. Two men walked toward him with rifles aimed at his chest. Manny froze. At their insistence, he raised his hands above his head.

"Come with us," the larger man said. He frisked Manny, made no attempt to take his Tag Heuer, the only thing that remained of any value. Not thieves, Manny realized.

"I'm an American," Manny said, "but I come in peace."

The smaller man led the way with Manny behind him. The larger man followed. They both had unkempt beards and wore olive fatigues—*perhaps the uniform of rebels*, Manny thought. Notwithstanding the rifles, he didn't feel in any danger. Quite the opposite. Manny felt as if he were being rescued.

After a short walk, they approached their destination. Armed guards who were perched on top of ten-foot-high boulders waved at Manny's captors, who waved back while passing through a corridor between the rocks. They entered a well-protected compound. Elevated behind the rocks, the site seemed artificially sculpted, like a movie set carved into the rainforest. It appeared to be a settlement, not a transient encampment.

More than a dozen large tents were positioned in a semi-circle around a campfire, surrounded by small rocks. He could see through the open flap of one tent that it contained supplies. The flaps on the others were closed. Men and women milled about, engaged in daily chores. The small village seemed self-contained and secure—a convivial place, Manny thought.

An old man with a grey beard approached. Unarmed, he studied Manny for a minute. There was a gleam in his eye, as if the intrusion amused him. "Who are you? And what are you doing up here?" the man asked in a gentle, non-threatening tone. The lines around his sparkling eyes intensified. He seemed to be interested as well as surprised to have found someone lurking alone in the hills.

"My name is Manny," he answered cautiously. Revealing as much of his bizarre story as he deemed necessary to gain the confidence of this man, whom he assumed to be a rebel leader, Manny recounted his role as a visiting professor and his frustration over the state of affairs in Guarida. He told the man that he was opposed to the invasion and had been tortured before being rescued by the Arawaks. He couldn't return to the city and didn't know where to go.

The old man nodded, appearing to digest the information. He looked into Manny's eyes. Then he dismissed the guards.

"Who are you?" Manny asked.

"Fair enough," the old man said. "My name is Gerónimo Esposito."

"And what's all this?" Manny looked around at the compound.

"We call ourselves the Freedom Front. This is our *guarida,* our hideout, within Guarida."

"What is your purpose?"

"The Front came into existence under Pérez Santo. After his demise, in which we played an instrumental role, the PDP and the NPG took over and were no better than the dictator. They held phony elections, alternated power among themselves, the same corrupt oligarchy that always held power. We had the puppet Baez for too long. Now we've got this buffoon Sánchez. He's a murderer, you know, a butcher. And he uses the Security Police to prop himself up."

"What about Guarida Libre? Do you support them?"

"They oppose Sánchez and his phony PPP, that's true. But those bastards would restore power to the oligarchs."

239

"Are you safe here?"

"The government knows we're up here, but doesn't consider us a real threat, haven't come after us for years."

"Do you think you're making any difference?"

"We have tried peaceful methods. They don't work in this country. We've seen some limited success only when we use the little force we can muster. It is very unfortunate. And much as we hate foreign influence, the American invasion might actually help us."

"Would you allow me to stay with you for a while?" Manny asked. He was too exhausted to stay on his feet any longer. "I have nowhere else to go, I'm really tired, and I need to figure out what to do next."

"Well, we can't just let you go. We'll need to corroborate your story. Then we'll see. What is your full name?"

"It's Emmanuel White Vidal."

"Vidal?" Gerónimo's expression changed. His eyes sharpened as he scrutinized Manny. "Anyway, you do not have a choice in the matter. You can sleep in that tent over there." He pointed to the tent nearest the massive boulders. Stationed behind the row of tents, a sentinel paced up and back at a leisurely clip with his eyes in constant surveillance.

Gerónimo offered a plate of beans, a piece of bread, and a cup of water before they retired for the night. Manny felt fortunate, not thinking of himself as a prisoner. He might have found what he had hoped for.

The next day, Manny awakened to the chatter of guards outside his tent. He stuck his head out and said good morning. They nodded and continued their conversation, something about a plan to raid a weapons depot.

The sun filtered through the high trees surrounding the camp. Dew still covered the grass. Manny crawled through the opening of his tent. He stood and stretched.

"Where do you—" he began to ask.

"Follow me," one of the guards said. He led Manny to a latrine that ran into a creek downstream from a high falls. After relieving himself and washing his face and hands next to the falls, Manny and the guard returned to the campfire. The strong aroma of fresh coffee offered a sense of domesticity.

A handsome woman who called herself Liliana offered Manny a cup. She poured from the large pot that had been propped over the flame. He sighed as he drank; it was the first coffee he had in many days. His last cup of coffee, on the plane with the man named Roberto, flashed into his mind, but he pushed the memory aside.

Manny looked around, searching for Gerónimo. He felt safe in the man's presence. When he did not see him, he asked Liliana where he was.

"He's gone over to one of our satellite camps and will return soon," she said. "He told me a little about you, but I don't understand why you are here. How did you find us?"

"I was wandering. Your guards found me. I can't go back to my place in the city with the war going on. How many are in your camps? Are there many women?"

"We have a couple of hundred, most are here. This is our main compound. Not many women, mostly girlfriends and a few wives who believe in the cause. The others would not join us."

"It must be a difficult life. How long have you been here?" Manny scrutinized Liliana's sharp facial features unadorned by cosmetics, her strong body clothed in a clinging sweatshirt and tight jeans, and wild hair tamed by a leather headband. She must be in her late thirties, he guessed.

"It's not that bad. The only times I have fear are when my boyfriend goes on a mission. I've been living here for around ten years. I left a comfortable home to be with the Front."

"I admire your resolve."

"Oh, there are difficulties. But we survive."

"Do you think you'll ever go home?"

"There's always hope, you know. But until things change, this isn't so bad."

Manny told Liliana about his injured left eye, and she inspected it. "It looks a little cloudy," she said. "Possibly damage to the cornea?"

They ate bread and cheese, drank coffee. The dew had dried. The sun rose sufficiently above the surrounding trees to brighten the compound. The guards remained at their posts on the boulders and behind the tents, but none had their weapons drawn. Manny felt as if he were in a scouting camp, rustic and very secure.

He asked Liliana how they were able to obtain provisions. She said a few of her comrades were from rich families. They managed to get things in.

"And Cristóbal, a boy who was born in the camp, acts as our courier," she said. "He sneaks my boyfriend's drawings down into the city, sells them, and uses the profits to buy supplies. At times he goes every few days, at times only once or twice a month. Fortunately, no one has ever followed him back to the camp."

Manny's eyes opened wide; he could hardly believe what he was hearing. With his heart racing, his hand jerked forward and knocked over his coffee. "Sorry," he said.

"What's the matter?" Liliana said. "You look like you've just seen a ghost."

Manny composed himself and asked her if the art studio was in the southern zone near the Block. Liliana didn't know where the drawings were sold. She only knew they commanded a decent price; not a lot, but enough to help the cause.

"Why?" she asked.

Manny studied her. Miraculous, he thought. Was it actually possible that the artist, her boyfriend, was his cousin?

"What's your boyfriend's name?" Manny was almost afraid to ask for fear that it might not be true.

"Rafael," she said. "Gerónimo went to get him."

Liliana offered Manny access to the group's makeshift library with a proud sweep of her hand. He selected *Diarios de Motocicleta* from the thirty or so books stacked in one of the tents. He had read Che's memoir, but under the circumstances, found it even more compelling. Manny identified with the young idealist, whose philosophical outlook before he became a revolutionary was similar to his own. They both sympathized with the plight of the poor and downtrodden.

And Manny thought he was beginning to look the part as his beard filled in.

Che had just crossed the Andes from Argentina into Chile when Manny's reading was interrupted. Gerónimo returned to the camp with a tall man at his side. Wiry and powerfully built, the man had a black beard and wore the olive fatigues that appeared to be the rebel uniform. His eyes projected intelligence and something more. He studied Manny.

Manny marked his place and put down the book. He greeted Gerónimo, then walked over to the other man and extended his hand. As they shook hands, the man said, "Gerónimo tells me your name is Vidal."

"I'm Emmanuel White Vidal—Manny," he said. "Who are you?"

The man gave Manny a bear hug. Then he held him by the shoulders at arm's length, looked him in the eyes as his own filled with tears, and said, "I'm Rafael. I'm your cousin." He reached into his pocket and brought out the Swiss Army knife that Manny had given him thirty years ago, when both men were only boys.

Manny laughed out loud. "I didn't recognize you at first. But I do now. You were twelve or thirteen when I stayed at El Retiro, and I was around fourteen or fifteen, I think. You've sprouted up, haven't you?" He gave his cousin another firm hug, and both men cried tears of joy.

"Time doesn't stand still, Manny."

"I know. So much has happened over the years."

Rafael shrugged, spread his hands. "Some good, some bad."

Manny said, "Many years ago I heard about the fire at El Retiro. Will you tell me about it?"

Rafael recounted what had happened to him and his parents three decades before. He spoke as if it were only yesterday, his voice still full of pain.

"Oh my God," Manny said. He hugged Rafael, told him he understood, although Manny knew he didn't, not really. His parents died suddenly, but they weren't murdered in his presence. Rafael's story was something you'd have to experience in order to truly comprehend. Manny had been through plenty, but it wasn't the same. "I appreciate the detail, Rafael. It's shocking. How are you coping after all these years?"

"I have nightmares every so often, but I've managed to survive. Gerónimo has helped. He is a kind and idealistic man, thrust by circumstances into the tough vocation of dissident in an unforgiving land. It was an unlikely role for him to play, but he had little choice. He's like a stepfather to me. And Liliana has been wonderful. You've met?"

"I like her very much, Rafael. You're lucky. Hold on to your woman. I've become an authority on the subject."

"It's good to see you, cousin. Tell me your story."

"You're strong, Rafael. I don't know what I would have done—"

"Same as me. Come on, tell me how the hell you found your way up here."

Manny highlighted his life as a scholar, the sudden death of his parents, his extraordinary sabbatical, and how he had been trying to find Rafael. He gave an account of his water boarding, loss of vision in one eye, rescue by the Indians, and trek through the rainforest to the city and then back up into the hills. "And here we are. Thank God we've found each other."

"You've been through a terrible time as well," Rafael said. He told Manny that the tribe had been relocated from their village which, along with the abandoned dock, was taken as a staging area for Guaridan troop mobilization.

"The Arawaks were good to me," Manny said. Tears filled his eyes as he recalled the faces of the two children in the truck.

"What did you mean when you said you've become an authority on holding on to your woman?"

Manny shook his head. The bizarre scene with Dee and Tina flashed in his mind. "I might have lost my American girlfriend because I made some foolish choices. I'll fill you in later."

The cousins discussed the invasion, theorized about who had tortured Manny—Rafael was certain that it had to have been the Security Police. Rafael told Manny about the camp, how long their supplies could last if they were attacked, and that the cave behind one of the boulders contained an escape route through a tunnel all the way to the sea. They reminisced and commiserated with each other. Rafael took out his drawing pad from his backpack and sketched while they chatted.

"What a stroke of luck for me to have wound up here," Manny said, "and to finally find you."

"We're both lucky," Rafael said. "You can stay with us as long as you want."

"I have some unfinished business," Manny said. He thought about his message to Sánchez; maybe he could end the fighting. And he had to reach Dee somehow. Meanwhile, he would live in the camp and contribute in whatever way he could.

In the days that followed, Manny fell into a comfortable routine. He helped find fire wood and prepare meals, tended to clean-up duty, and each evening entered into philosophical discussions with Rafael, Liliana, Gerónimo, and some of their comrades. In his free time, Manny exercised and read. He had finished *Diarios de Motocicleta* and was well into García Márquez's *Cien Años de Soledad*, which he had read years ago but now was beginning to comprehend in a different light.

He truly enjoyed the experience of compound life. It was a healthy existence, and he felt safe. The city seemed far removed, a distant reminder of his travails.

One afternoon, Manny sat on a rock near the campfire site reading the chapter in *Cien Años* in which Colonel Aureliano Buendía's men proclaimed him chief of the revolutionary forces. Cristóbal crossed in front of the campfire, distracting him. He stopped reading, closed the book, and watched the boy peek into Rafael's tent. Manny saw Rafael, who was conversing with Liliana, signal toward the pile of sketches on the table. Cristóbal grabbed the sketches and stuffed them in his rucksack.

Manny wondered about this arrangement. *Pretty risky,* he thought. Why wasn't Cristóbal followed back to the camp? The government was at odds with the Front, wasn't it? But Gerónimo must know what he was doing. He did say the Security Police left them alone for the most part, so he didn't consider them a serious threat. Manny had his doubts; the scheme worried him. It might be more dangerous than Gerónimo thought.

247

The sun would be setting soon, so Manny returned to his tent. He reclined on his camper's cot and opened *Cien Años*. He found his way back into Macundo, Márquez's metaphoric Colombian town. *Could have been Guarida City,* he thought. But he closed the book again after several minutes, unable to concentrate. Too many unresolved issues bounced around in his mind.

He wondered about Dee, hoped that he would be able to reunite with her one day. He assumed Janey was somewhere safe. Then his mind shifted to Tina. Where was she now? What was she doing? He didn't really want to see her. Yet, even if she had betrayed him, he hoped no harm had befallen her.

CΩChapter Twenty-Three℃Ωͻ

Tina moved in with Evita shortly after Manny disappeared. She had not returned to her Block apartment since her mother succumbed to a fever of unknown cause. Tina told Evita that she had done everything within her power to care for her mother, but felt guilty anyway.

"It's not your fault," Evita said.

"I wonder how Manny would have reacted if I told him I worked as an escort?"

"He wouldn't have understood. How could he?"

"I tried to tell him about Federico, but the timing never seemed right."

"Where the hell is Manny now? What happened to him?"

"God only knows." Tears welled in Tina's eyes. She harbored conflicting feelings. While she missed shacking up with the gringo, she knew it was an ill-fated relationship from the start.

Evita opened a bottle of Malbec. Tina had insisted on the Argentine wine. They toasted Guarida.

"Hope this damn fighting is over soon," Evita said.

"The sooner the better."

They took a few sips, looked at each other, and smiled. At least they were together, Tina thought.

"*Salud,* my love," Evita said.

They clinked their glasses together. Tina felt the wine soften her spirit, and she gazed into Evita's eyes. Loud knocking on the apartment door disturbed the moment.

"I'll get it." Evita walked over and looked through the peephole. "It's some tall guy in a suit. I don't know him."

Tina came to her side, glanced through the hole. "Oh, shit. I know him. He's the damn police."

Evita left the chain on and opened the door a crack. She held the door in that position while they peered through the opening.

"Hello, girls," Roberto said. Tina recognized them all. Álvaro, José, María Pilar, and Jorge stood a few steps behind him. She tried to push the door closed, but Roberto kicked it open, breaking the chain. They entered and looked around.

"Enjoying your wine?" Roberto said.

She looked at Álvaro and José. "You two were at El Farol," she said. Then she turned to Jorge and María Pilar. "You guys were at the beach. What the hell are you doing here?"

"You're under arrest, Señorita Reyes," Roberto said. "Come with us."

"What are you charging her with?" Evita said, standing in front of Roberto.

"This is ridiculous," Tina said. "There must be some mistake."

"There's no mistake," Roberto said. "Let's go."

Evita stood her ground, and Tina said, "Stay here, Evita. Don't interfere. They don't want you."

"That's right, dyke," Álvaro said. "Save yourself. We just want your lover-girl." He pushed Evita aside.

"Well, what in hell is the charge, you bastard?" Tina yelled.

Álvaro gave Tina a grim smile. "You are responsible for the death of your mother."

They dragged Tina to Security Police headquarters, where she suffered an excruciating interrogation. It was not about her mother.

"Where is the professor?" Roberto asked her repeatedly.

"Even if I knew, I wouldn't tell you," Tina shouted.

Álvaro smacked her face with the back of his hand. Tina stood and spit at him. José came from behind, clasped his hands around her shoulders, and forced her to sit. He bound her wrists behind her back with fishing line.

Álvaro stood in front of Tina, fondling the switchblade he had taken from her. He glared at her. "You are a whore," he snarled. "A puta."

"You bastard, Tina said, an angry grimace on her face. "You're nothing but a sniveling pendejo."

He hit her again, this time with a clenched fist to the jaw, followed by a flurry of jabs to her eyes. Blood spewed from the corner of Tina's mouth and she spit some out, then dropped her head. She tried to free her hands, but the line cut into her wrists.

"Here, suck this, you whore," Álvaro said as he opened his pants. He grabbed her hair so she could not look away. Tina lunged forward and bit down hard on Álvaro's member. He screamed, punched her head repeatedly, and then ran into the bathroom.

When he returned a few minutes later, he looked as if he was about to do something terrible with the switchblade. Tina cringed, but Roberto said, "That's enough" and positioned himself directly in front of her. "We'll find him sooner or later; make it easy on yourself."

Tina raised her head in defiance. Her hair was matted with blood. It stuck to her face.

José pointed at Álvaro, who was holding his crotch, his face twisted in pain. "Hey, amigo, does it still work?" he asked and started laughing.

Álvaro made a move toward José. Roberto stepped between them. "I said enough, and I meant it."

Unwilling and, more importantly, unable to reveal Manny's whereabouts, Tina surrendered only the name of Paulo Ferreira as a possible source of information. The bastard had been spying on her, and she hoped they would subject him to some pain.

"Lock her up," Roberto ordered. They grabbed Tina's bound arms, pushed and dragged her on the short walk over to the jail. She tried to break free even as they shoved her through the heavy gates. Her face was a ragged pulp, blood dripping from her mouth and nose, and her eyes were swollen.

"Stick the cunt in solitary," Álvaro instructed the guard.

Tina screamed, *"Carajo* assholes, what the *hell!* I need to speak to Claudio. You'd better damn well take me to the president. You'll pay for this shit."

They laughed.

Tina shouted, "Claudio won't like this. Claudio!" she yelled at the top of her lungs. "Claudio, Claudio!" Her voice faded as José slammed the cell door. The heavy metallic clank drowned out her supplications.

As they walked away, Álvaro yelled back at her, "Not such a tough bitch now!"

Álvaro and José met Roberto, Jorge, and María Pilar outside headquarters after they left the Retén. The entourage jumped into an unmarked van. When they arrived at La Ciruela, Paulo Ferreira was serving fresh pineapple juice to several school children.

Ferreira saw Roberto and his associates approaching, told the kids it was on the house, and walked toward the group. "What can I do for you?" he said.

"Cups of pineapple all around," Roberto ordered. "And some information. We're tracking down the gringo, Tina's friend—you know who we mean. He's CIA."

Ferreira told them to follow him.

"Where are we going?" Roberto demanded.

"You will see. It will be worth a short walk." Ferreira led them down the block, past El Salón de la Parrilla, and stopped outside the art studio.

"This better damn well be worth the effort," Roberto said.

"Look," Ferreira said as he pointed to the drawings in the window. "I saw the curator place these in the display on my way home from La Ciruela last night."

"Nice pictures—so what?" Roberto said.

"Look at this one." Ferreira pointed to the portrait. It was easy to recognize the professor, Manny Vidal, even with the beard.

"You will be rewarded for this," Roberto said as he waved his hand toward La Ciruela, sending Ferreira away.

"Where's the sketch I did of Manny?" Rafael asked Cristóbal. "I want to give it to him."

Cristóbal thought for a moment, then said he didn't know. Then his face turned red. "Was it in with the rest?"

"Oh, shit!" Rafael said. He hadn't intended for that sketch, the one he had done while he was chatting with his cousin, to be included in the delivery. It must have been left in the pile. The young courier had never been required to choose which of the drawings should be brought to the shop. He had just grabbed them all.

"I'll go back and get it," Cristóbal said.

"No, just leave it. It's too dangerous to return so soon." But the boy had already gone.

Álvaro and José trailed far enough behind Cristóbal to remain hidden when he returned to the camp at midday with the portrait of Manny in his satchel. They had shared a laugh at the boy's pathetic attempt to slip away from the art studio

254

undetected. Now they stopped behind a row of bushes on the downslope that led up to the boulders. José was out of breath.

They counted the guards sitting on the boulders. Two or three guards perched on top of each—maybe ten or eleven in all. One of the guards waved the kid into the compound, looked around, and resumed smoking and chatting with the other guards as if they were in a café on the Boulevard.

After their short surveillance, Álvaro and José headed back to town. The descent and return to the central plaza took them just under three hours. They stopped briefly for a couple of Nacionales at a pub next to the Security Police headquarters. Then they reported to Roberto.

Roberto said he would call Juan Carlos immediately. He would report that the professor has been located. Álvaro and José assured Roberto that they knew the trail. Not long afterward, Juan Carlos summoned Roberto, Álvaro, and José to the presidential palace. Claudio looked at Álvaro and smiled. "This will make up for your blunder," he said. Then Claudio turned toward the others.

"Assemble a strong team for a reconnaissance mission, Juan Carlos. I want our best Security Police to go up there. I'll send some of my guys as well." They all knew Claudio was referring obliquely to his buddies on the Escuadrón de la Muerte. "Do whatever is necessary, but I want the professor brought to me alive. Do you understand?"

Flapping wings and screeches disturbed the early morning calm and awakened Manny from a deep sleep. Parrots, toucans, and macaws burst into the air as if they had been rudely awakened by a predator. The uproar drowned out the usual gushing of the waterfall, cooing of doves, and buzz of insects.

Relentless rustling of leaves and fallen branches being crushed underfoot had caused the flare-up. The trampling grew louder as it approached the encampment. Soon, it became clear that the government's troops were moving in. The commotion alerted the guards. The Freedom Front mobilized in preparation for whatever was in store for them. They rapidly took up their positions on the boulders and behind the tents.

Approximately fifty armed police and soldiers marched toward the camp, carrying AK-47 assault rifles, Thompson submachine guns, bazookas, and grenades. The forces took positions on the hill below the boulders, within striking distance.

A guard summoned Gerónimo, who climbed one of the boulders in order to assess the situation. Another guard alerted the rest of the camp. Manny stood beside Liliana and Rafael, shaking, trying to calm himself by taking deep breaths, but it only made him lightheaded.

"This is it," Rafael said grimly. "Like Masada."

"Don't even think that," Liliana said, gripping his arm.

They heard a voice over a bullhorn call out, "We are here for Professor Emmanuel White Vidal. He is an enemy of the state, a spy. We only want the professor. Send him down and we'll leave you alone."

"We have no professors here. Go back to the city," Gerónimo yelled.

"We know he's there."

Gerónimo turned to his companions. "Prepare to fight, comrades," he said. "If they attack, we must defend ourselves. Mothers and children should get ready to enter the cave."

Manny assessed the situation. Although outnumbering the invaders by four to one, the Front faced far superior fire-power and had nowhere to retreat. They couldn't all fit into the escape route through the cave and would have to hold their ground for as long as possible, take down as many as they could. There was no alternative.

Manny realized he was the cause of this hopeless situation. Had he not been there, the Front would have remained safe. A wave of depression enveloped him, as if he were drowning. He felt as powerless as when he had been tortured. He had to do something.

"I'm giving myself up," Manny said. "It's me they want."

"No you're not," Gerónimo said. "We won't allow it, and anyway, it would do no good."

"We have all the time in the world," the voice called to them. "How long will your supplies last? Give us the professor now, and no harm will come to you."

Gerónimo shouted, "Join forces with us. The regime is corrupt. Together we can transform our country. Long live Guarida!"

Manny knew that they had nothing with which to negotiate, except him. He felt a strange combination of pride in the Front and personal guilt and fear. He was entirely responsible for putting his cousin and new friends in jeopardy.

"You do not have to die. We only want the professor."

"What professor? We have no professor here."

"We know he's there, old man. We will give you a few minutes to come to your senses, be reasonable, and do what you must—give us the professor!"

"I'm going down there," Manny said, and he meant it. He loved these people even in the short time he had been with them. He had to do something to save them.

"No, please, we'll figure something out," Rafael said, placing a hand on his arm. "You can't go—it would be suicide." The others agreed.

Gerónimo huddled with Rafael, Liliana, and two comrades. Manny heard their calculations. Food would last for three or four days, maybe they could stretch the supplies for a week. They had sufficient caches of rifles and bullets to last even longer. And they had a strategic advantage: the boulders formed a secure periphery from which to look down on their targets. The invaders would have to shoot at the rocks. But Manny sensed that they all knew it would be only a matter of time until they were overtaken. They couldn't hold out there forever.

"We will fight," Rafael said. Gerónimo and the others nodded and touched their clenched fists together, gave each other high fives, and raised their arms.

Manny, knowing that he was the cause of this tragic predicament, shook his head and took a deep breath. Then he said, "I'm going down there. Don't try to stop me—I'll be all right."

"No, Manny, that is not an option!" Gerónimo and Rafael said almost in unison. Rafael looked into Manny's eyes, put his hands on Manny's shoulders, and gave him a strong abrazo. Liliana then put her arms around the cousins, and so did Gerónimo.

The first shot was delivered by the government forces. It ricocheted off one of the boulders, sounded like a percussion symbol. Then a flurry of shots and machine guns rat-tat-tatted like drum rolls. The orchestra had no violins, no wind section, just bass drums. The round caused no damage.

"Send down the professor!"

Retaliatory shots fired by the Freedom Front exploded from the compound and ripped through the trees below. One must have found its target; a loud cry of anguish punctuated the first barrage of shots. The invading forces responded with a salvo of bazookas and grenades that landed within the camp. A tent was set on fire. It had to be doused before it could catch the others. One of the guards was hit, bleeding profusely from his stomach. Liliana attended to him in a tent.

Rafael grabbed another rifle, moved to a more aggressive position on a front boulder, and fired without hesitation. He could see movement below. Sweating profusely, he went through his ammunition and grabbed more. This was all-out war. Blasts, flares, trees cracking, bullets rebounding off the rocks, fire. The odors of cordite and smoke permeated the humid air. Chaos and insanity reigned for nearly twenty minutes. Then there was silence.

The unexpected lull was broken by Rafael, whose voice echoed through the clearing. "No!" he yelled at the top of his lungs as he watched Manny walk down the hill with his hands raised above his head. "No, no, no!"

Manny walked as if in a dream past the boulders into no-man's land. Time and place disappeared, everything turned surreal. The only way to save his cousin and the rest of the rebels, his extended family, was for him to surrender. They had protected him and he would return the favor. The choice filled him with joy.

And then, at the bottom of the hill, joy faded and the clock ticked once again. His heart beat wildly as he was met by two armed Security Police. They cuffed his hands behind his back and led him away, toward the trail. One stood on either side of him with pistols drawn. At that moment, he resigned himself to being executed on the spot. He closed his eyes.

One of the officials slapped the back of Manny's head. "Open your eyes, let's go," he said.

Shocked, Manny gaped as they pushed him along the trail. It was quiet as they walked, but for the breeze sweeping through the trees.

Then suddenly, the whistling of mortar shells careening through the air, rock-crushing blasts, and piercing explosions broke out. Manny stopped, looked back, and saw flames. He knew immediately they had betrayed him. His anger rapidly turned to sorrow, and again, a feeling of impotence flushed through him. "They said no harm—all they wanted was me—"

The officials looked at each other and laughed. They pushed Manny, shoved him hard. "Keep walking, fool."

"Lying bastards!" Manny yelled out in anguish.

One of the officials slammed the butt of his rifle into Manny's back. "Just keep walking," he repeated.

As Manny walked on, it occurred to him that his only hope might be to deliver Stark's message to Claudio Sánchez.

ᴄᴡᴑChapter Twenty-Fourᴞᴄᴞ

President Sánchez prepared for his televised appearance by brandishing his Louisville Slugger. He grabbed the bat with one hand, hit his other hand on the sweet spot, and then clutched the bat with both hands. He took several fast cuts as he calculated what he wanted to include in his statement.

The speech would be delivered unscripted, as always. Although officially retired from the army, he appeared in his military fatigues and refused any make-up. He placed the bat behind his desk and took a seat.

"All right, let's roll," he told the TV crew. He saw the "on-air" signal and began. "My fellow citizens, the blood-thirsty Imperialists sent their spy boat into sovereign Guaridan territorial waters to attack us. We retaliated. Now they have invaded. The yanquis want your democratically elected president defeated by force," he said, expressing grave concern with a controlled cadence. "The North American military is in collusion with *gusano* turncoats who are in bed with foreign businesses that want to rape us. But they can't defeat courageous Guarideños. We will prevail, my friends. With this in mind, I have an important announcement."

Claudio breathed into the moment. Time for something dramatic. The tide was turning. The Guaridan public was beginning to see the conflict in a different light, to blame the administration for the havoc and uncertainty in the streets.

He signaled to one of his assistants. Then he thrust his right arm upward, pointing his index finger at the ceiling. "Our Security Police have captured one of our key enemies," he roared, "whose subversive activities have led to the state of war in which we now find ourselves." A photograph of Prof. Manny Vidal—taken after the long descent from the hills—flashed on the screen. The camera magnified his disconcerted expression, making him look like a bearded revolutionary or a dangerous criminal. Claudio continued as if sharing secret information with a friend. "Emmanuel White Vidal is a CIA operative, a spy living among us. His cover was that of university professor. He had even infiltrated a presidential advisory committee."

The camera shifted from the photo back to Claudio. "Señor Vidal is clever. He fooled me for a while. But now he is in our custody. His contacts with Guarida Libre have come to an end, and the Freedom Front has been destroyed. Their main compound in the hills was blasted, burned to the ground, and the subversive organization has been decimated."

Claudio went on to say that Vidal would be treated as a prisoner of war. "He will be accorded all the protections of the Geneva Convention—something the Imperialists choose to ignore when it suits them. Guarida is a civilized country that protects individual human rights. We do not merely give lip-service to these high ideals; we carry them out because they are inherent in our peaceful revolution. The prisoner is subject to our jurisprudence. Justice will be served and Guarida will prevail, my loyal citizens. Long live the patria!"

The speech ended, the bright lights dimmed, and the cameras stopped rolling. "Now let's see if Washington wants to deal," the weary president said to Juan Carlos. "We'll see if they want him or not. Meanwhile, keep him in solitary. Let the embassy personnel come over if they want. But that's it. No other visitors. I'm going to talk to the professor tomorrow, and we'll see if your plan will work."

"It'll work. My calls are always correct, no?" Juan Carlos said, as if he were behind the plate signaling to his pitcher.

After being held prisoner in a holding cell for forty-eight hours, Manny was blindfolded and led through the halls of the Retén, where the horrific sounds of the incarcerated were burned into his brain. He heard the cries and curses of caged animals—schizophrenic rumblings of those who had lost touch with reality, and sexual innuendoes grunted by those who had been in for far too long. The place stunk of human feces covered by bleach.

Manny's mind raced. It was difficult to think logically. Why was he tortured? Why was he arrested? Tina must have believed the CIA myth. What did she want from him? Or maybe, he admitted to himself, he should be asking what he really wanted from her. What had happened to Rafael and the others, and what would happen to Guarida?

The calculated process of dehumanization continued when they took his clothes and hosed him down with cold water. The orange jumpsuit was too large. It made Manny feel like a clown.

The guards walked him through a long corridor, past the rattling of metal objects over cell bars; more cries and taunting. They came to a halt in what sounded like a quieter section of the prison. A cold metal door clanked shut behind him.

Then they removed his blindfold. At first he couldn't see. It took several minutes for his good eye to adjust to the light.

Thank God I'm not in with those others, Manny thought. But after they shoved him into his cell and left him there, the walls seemed to close in on him. He was confined in an area that was approximately ten by ten feet square with a very high ceiling and no window. A tiny opening near the ceiling let in a trickle of light.

Through a round hole on the door slightly below eye level, guards could look in to observe Manny's every move. Manny, however, was unable to see much more than a small portion of the hallway through the hole. The cell offered a rudimentary cot and a bucket. The walls were marked with scratched lines that must have represented weeks. Every sixth parallel was crossed by a seventh. There were hundreds of them.

Manny sat on the cot, motionless. He heard his father's voice: *Never say die, up man and try.* He stood, stretched his arms out, and swung his hands in circles. Then he did a few push-ups on the dirty floor. That's what a prisoner did in a novel Manny had read, but he wasn't sure why. Was it supposed to divert his attention?

How the hell did Nelson Mandela survive Robin Island for over twenty years? Manny wondered. He got up and sat down again. Angry and frustrated, tears formed in his eyes, but he couldn't cry. All he had ever wanted was to see his mother's country prosper, to advise his own country to facilitate rather than impede Guarida's development, to find his cousin, and have a bit of adventure along the way.

Jane Kelley-Noel ran upstairs to the ambassador's makeshift office. She chose the stairs rather than wait for the elevator. Kingfield's door was ajar. Janey charged in and saw the ambassador gazing through a large window toward the skyline. The PI towers cast shadows across the Presidential Palace and the Retén.

"Frank, they've got our professor in jail," Janey said, out of breath. "Sánchez is holding him as a spy, a political prisoner—a prisoner of war, for the love of God! Manny White Vidal is innocent of those ridiculous charges. He wasn't one of our operatives, was he? He sympathized with the goddamn revolution, for mercy's sake!"

"I know all about this. Please, sit down. We're both fond of Manny."

"We've got to do something."

"You know the protocol as well as I." Kingfield held up the small Swiss flag from his desk and studied it, as if searching for a solution. "This white equilateral cross represents peace and honesty," he said, "and it sits in the center of a red background that stands for bravery, strength, and honor."

"I'm familiar with their flag, Adam." The Swiss consulate had provided the office.

"Look, Janey, we have no jurisdiction here. And now we're at war, or rather an emergency military action. We've invaded Guarida, for God's sake!"

"And Manny is in the Retén. We have to come up with something—go outside of channels. Maybe you can cut a deal with Sánchez, talk to Washington. There must be something we can do for him. This is completely outrageous. The poor man must be suffering. Can we at least make sure they adhere to the rules of the Geneva Accords?"

"We'll do what we can. I'll call the Secretary, get approval to issue a formal protest, see if Sánchez will meet with me. Meanwhile, go over there and talk to Manny. They'll let you in. Assure him we'll do everything in our power."

"I'll get back to you after I've seen him."

"Just remember your last visit over there, Janey."

"I'll be careful," she reassured him, but she was more than a little anxious. She remembered two young American women who had languished hopelessly in that same prison on a drug charge simply to prove that Americans were not above the law.

Janey ran back to her office and arranged for the bullet-proof limousine with diplomatic plates to drive her to the Retén, a block away from the Presidential Palace. The area was besieged by random assaults and flaring crossfire. She told her assistant to inform the Guaridan authorities that she was going to visit Professor Emmanuel White Vidal. Then she gathered a stack of books, magazines, and newspapers and took the limo to the gates of the Retén. She showed the guards her diplomatic passport.

"Hola, Señorita Janey," one of the guards said. He winked at her and waved her inside, where he led her through the dank, stinking corridors.

Previous experiences had not inured Janey to the squalid conditions within the Retén. Although she tried hard to camouflage her disgust and pity, she felt like she had entered purgatory. When they finally reached Manny's cell, the guard opened the cell door. It squeaked and hit the wall with a dull thud, startling her.

"Hi, Manny," she said with a bright smile, as if she were greeting him at a social gathering. The guard waited at the door.

Manny got up from the cot. His face was grim, his eyes vacant. "Thanks for coming here, Janey," he said, and she could hear the hope in his voice. "I hope you're not in danger."

Janey gave him a hug. "We can talk," she said as she glanced at the guard, "he doesn't speak English."

"I feel like a fool. I'm sorry you had to come. But I'm very glad you're here."

He held on tight until she pulled back gently. "Hey, don't worry, Manny. I'm here because I want to be. We'll do everything in our power. Here's something to read." She set the reading material on the cot.

"I appreciate it. But you really don't have much influence with Sánchez under the circumstances, right? It seems I'm royally screwed. And I don't even know exactly why. How the hell did I get into this mess? What's going on?"

"Sánchez claims you were involved with Guarida Libre. And the Security Police say they have proof you've been conspiring with our intelligence community. They say you're CIA. The trip to Washington, tennis with young Roldano, hiding out with the Freedom Front—that appears to be their proof. We're preparing a response."

"I'm being set up, Janey. And unless he escaped, they killed my cousin."

"I don't know about your cousin, but I'll try to find out."

"Are we winning the war?"

"Our troops are pounding away at the periphery of the Presidential Palace. They're making progress. What do you mean set up, Manny?"

267

"First they held me in some godforsaken oil dock down on the coast. I was tortured, waterboarded. The Indians rescued me."

Janey stepped back and raised her hand, unable to hide her shock. Her eyes opened wide and her jaw dropped. "Hold on, Manny. Slow down." She fumbled for the pen and the notepad she always carried in her purse. "Tell me exactly what happened."

Manny recounted his experiences with as much precision as he was able to muster, given his poor physical and emotional condition. Janey wrote as fast as she could. She kept shaking her head, asking him to stop a few times so she could catch up.

"You lost the vision in one of your eyes. Stayed with the Freedom Front. Found your cousin."

"That's right."

"The ones who tortured you, did they speak Spanish?" Janey tapped the pen on her pad, trying to piece together what he was saying.

"For all I know, it was Torquemada himself." Manny attempted to inject a little humor, reassuring Janey that he retained his sanity.

"Come on, Manny, this isn't the Spanish Inquisition."

"It feels like it. Please get me out of here."

"We will. Now let's think this through. If they were Guaridans, that might mean the Security Police. They were probably directed by the administration in that case. But it could have been Guarida Libre. They might have connected you with Sánchez. Isn't that possible? They might have wanted to know what you know about them."

"I don't know. I suppose Sánchez thinks I'm CIA. Everyone else does."

"But you aren't, right? And Guarida Libre should've known. They're supposed to be on our side. Couldn't they have misinterpreted your support for reform of the system as collaboration with the regime?"

"I believed in the revolution but never participated. I was an advisor, for God's sake. I was living under an illusion that Sánchez could do some good. Where does that leave me now? I can't last much longer in this hellhole, Janey. It's driving me crazy."

"Please do your best to hold on." Janey put a hand on his shoulder. "Sánchez will try to use you to his advantage. He might deal; we don't know. We're working on it. Rest assured that I'll do as much as I can to get you out of here as soon as possible."

"I appreciate it. And I'll do my best to maintain my sanity and some semblance of reason, of hope. It isn't easy, though. I don't know if you noticed on the way in, but this isn't the Ritz." He laughed at his own joke, and she heard an edge of hysteria in his voice. "Listen, there's something I need to add to my account of what happened to me."

"You should tell me everything."

"You probably know about this already. But when I was in Washington, I met with Adam Stark and Jim Brownfield."

"I knew about State and INR."

"They cornered me at a Department function. It was at a cocktail party they threw for a bunch of us academics and think-tankers. Stark said they wanted me to act as a liaison, to offer Sánchez a deal. Something like what they did with Raul

Cédras to get him out of Haiti." Manny paused, scrutinized Janey, and took a deep breath. "I don't know how I could communicate this, especially now; maybe this is where you could help. Sánchez probably won't go for it, but at least it's worth a try, if you could arrange a meeting or something. It might be my only play. I'm grasping at straws here."

The revelation that INR had employed a civilian, rather than a governmental operative, as a liaison surprised her. She felt a bit overwhelmed by this new information. Yet, she believed him and thought, if she could contact Sánchez, it might provide Manny an opportunity to negotiate his release.

"We—or at least I—am unaware of any of this. Let me speak with the ambassador. This could be something."

"It might be my only hope."

"Gut it out, okay? Hang in there while I check on this."

"I don't have many options, do I?" Manny's face was pale. His hands were trembling.

Chapter Twenty-Five

Manny hadn't slept since Janey's visit two days earlier. He sprawled on the cot as if hypnotized or comatose. So little light squeezed through the tiny hole in the ceiling of his cell that he couldn't tell what time of day it was.

A loud metallic clank—must have been the lock being opened—snapped him out of his trance. The coldness of the sudden sound sent chills down Manny's spine. He rose shakily from the cot and stood watching the door. Janey must have returned. She would rescue him, get him out of this inferno.

The heavy cell door squeaked open slowly. Manny's one good eye had to adjust to the light filtered into the cell from the hall. The shadowy outline of a stocky man stepped through. The apparition held what looked like a club in one hand. Manny squinted and finally regained his focus. He could hardly believe what he saw: Claudio Sánchez stood before him.

Sánchez told the guards to wait outside. They questioned the order but obeyed when the president insisted. Then he turned toward Manny, and the prisoner took a step closer. What in hell was Sánchez doing here? Manny tried to calm down, think this situation through. *Play the ball, don't let it play you,* he thought. Why the club? No, not a club: it was Sánchez's infamous Louisville Slugger.

"Mr. President, this is a big mistake. Please get me out of here." Manny blurted. *Not a good start,* he thought.

"Professor, I'm deeply saddened by the turn of events that has resulted in your detention. But we are at war. Your role as an agent of our enemy has required this unfortunate action."

"Sir, you know I'm not a spy. I've got nothing to do with the CIA. I'm an academic, a scholar. You've heard my views. I served on your team. This is all a colossal error—I never supported an invasion."

The president studied his prisoner for what seemed to Manny to be several minutes. He appeared to be weighing the facts and calculating his response. Manny waited, gaining hope that the president's presence could be a positive sign.

"Well, Professor Vidal, we—or better said, I—must now make the next move. You're a prisoner of war and you represent what's wrong with imperialism. The international community sees this. Americans think they can come down here and call the shots?"

"With all due respect, sir, I don't see how my imprisonment can help your cause. If anything, it'll hurt because—"

"Oh no, professor, I'm not here for a lecture. You'll listen to me. Now, listen carefully; your life depends on it." He cradled his bat, patted its sweet spot, and rubbed its handle. He took a deep breath, looked around the cell, and returned his attention to Manny. Their eyes met.

"Please," Manny pleaded, "let's be reasonable."

"Oh, yes. That's exactly what I propose. We will both be reasonable. I need to expose your government's hypocrisy and corruption."

"What do I have to do with that?"

"And I'll do so with the magnanimous gesture of granting your freedom. You advised me to be diplomatic, didn't you?" Sánchez scrutinized Manny, then his eyes narrowed, and he licked his lips and smiled. "That is, after you've recanted. If you don't, you'll never be heard from again."

Sánchez repeated the ritual with his bat—gripped the handle in his right hand and caressed the thick part with his left—as he stared at his prisoner. Manny began to shiver and sweat all at once. Oddly, his stomach growled. At the same time, he was encouraged to hear that freedom could be in the offing.

"You'll appear on television," Sánchez continued. "We'll arrange for CNN and international coverage. You're an excellent public speaker, very persuasive. It'll be like conducting a class on the evils of Imperialism. I expect you to expose the folly of this invasion into our sovereign territory. After all, that's what you said you believe, no? You'll also illustrate the progress my regime has made in making inroads into what you people call developmental problems. I've heard you speak on this topic many times. And I've read your excellent articles. So, you'll denounce your government's evil intentions and admit to your own complicity. Then I'll let you go. Agreed?"

"I've been sympathetic to your so-called revolution. But I can't lie about—"

"You know that your hot little puta sold you out, don't you? Her duty to country prevailed."

Manny looked at the floor, realizing how unstable Tina must be. What had he ever seen in her? Her naked ass flashed in his mind. "Is that how you found me?"

"Our snitch at your favorite fruit store led us to an art studio with your portrait displayed in broad daylight for everyone to see. A very good facsimile, I might add. We tracked you up into the hills, to the Freedom Front. By the way, that subversive group no longer exists."

Manny knew that whatever he said might seal his fate. He envisioned—wished, hoped, prayed—that Rafael and a few of the others had escaped through the cave. He pictured Paulo Ferreira chatting with customers at La Ciruela, and his mind raced. When his eyes met the president's again, Manny saw clearly that the power relationship was no longer that of idealistic professor and reformer-in-chief. Now he was prisoner and Sánchez, jailer. They stared at each other. Yet, despite the peculiar circumstances, there was still a modicum of mutual respect.

He won't swing that thing at me, Manny hoped.

"We'll win this war. And do you know why?" Sánchez asked. "We'll win because we are fighting to preserve our independence, our fundamental essence as a nation. We have just as much right to our revolution as you had for yours."

Manny heard himself saying, "Mr. President, I have a message for you. It's from Assistant Secretary Adam Stark." The words seemed to flow involuntarily from his lips.

"You see! I knew you were connected to the CIA."

"Stark's with the State Department, and I'm actually *not* CIA. I was in contact with Stark when I was in Washington. That's the truth. They asked me to convey the message even before the invasion."

Claudio scrunched his forehead, locked his jaw, and knocked the bat on the ground a few times. He didn't speak, just made a "go on" gesture.

"They want to offer you a deal, one that will make you a wealthy man, a very wealthy man. You could live in Panama, or any neutral country, for the rest of your life."

"Do you think I would betray my country? What do your people think they have to bargain with? They're fools—"

"You don't want to follow in Noriega's footsteps, do you? Or spend the rest of your days in Guantánamo? Or even worse, if you don't take their extremely generous offer, they'll crush you. They're prepared to use overwhelming force, what they call 'shock and awe.' Raúl Cédras took the deal after Colin Powell convinced him. And oil wasn't even an issue in Haiti. Anyway, there's unfortunately no way in hell they'll withdraw troops in exchange for my release. They don't even like me. And you know that the American government won't negotiate under pressure. You know that."

"I'm a patriot. I'll fight to the death." Sánchez smiled, clutched his bat, and took a little swing in the air. "You're clever. And how do I know you aren't just making all this up as we speak? You will go on the air and talk about how wrong it is for the Colossus to march into an independent country, merely for access to its resources. All you need to do is speak your mind—be honest."

"I couldn't go home." Manny shook his head; it was the truth. "I'd be perceived as a traitor. No one would believe I was coerced, so there would always be a stigma."

"Ah, but Guarida is your new home. You have put down roots here. And I doubt if you want to go for another swim." Sánchez's thinly veiled threat exposed him as the intellectual author of Manny's waterboarding session at the

275

dock. "In fact, I can guarantee that you will be very uncomfortable for the rest of a very short and painful life—"

"You need to corroborate my message, Mr. President. You'll have to speak with Stark directly. I just informed the embassy. Jane Kelley-Noel was here yesterday, and I told her about the deal. They, or at least she, didn't even know about it. But I imagine they're also confirming the offer right now."

"You're giving me instructions?"

"Please think about this, sir. You're a realist. Think this over and don't act in haste. It's not only for my own life that I plead: it's for yours as well."

Sánchez shifted from side to side, scratched his head, and smiled. "That's very shrewd. I will leave you to consider my offer. If you truly believe in my revolution, you'll have no problem in articulating your position in front of the television cameras, no? Just think—you can alter the course of history simply by telling it like it is. You could change the tide and shift the balance in favor of the underdog. More important, you can save your ass and the more beautiful one of your little amiga. We've got her down here too." He took another practice swing.

Manny winced and stepped back. Was Claudio Sánchez using Tina to threaten him? The bitch had facilitated his capture. Perhaps the president wasn't so cunning after all. "You're the clever one," he said. "You want the idealist to face reality, right?"

"Just remember one thing: your theoretical distinctions between realists and idealists might prove to be artificial constructions. These concepts are good for academic discourse, but this cell isn't a classroom. Think it over. I'll return on Monday."

Sánchez knocked his bat against the door frame as he walked out of the cell. The door squeaked shut and the lock clanked, as if to punctuate the president's dictum. The guards sealed off the small portal in Manny's cell door. Manny lay down on his cot, covered his eyes with his arm, and let out a sigh.

Over the weekend, Manny spent hours stretched out on the cot, intent on figuring things out. But his mind refused to focus. Had he gone crazy? He forced himself to concentrate, attempted to predict the president's next move. Then his mind drifted, and suddenly he imagined being engaged in a classroom debate.

What would his parents have thought of him now? What would Rafael have thought? Dee, Ray, Janey? What did they think? How the hell did he manage to get himself into this mess? What would happen if he didn't comply with Sánchez's offer? Check that—his demand. In his head, he heard Janey telling him to avoid trouble, Dee giving him his space, Tina telling him to choose, his father assuring him that *only the Shadow knows.*

Manny's body shuddered along with his brain. He felt as if he were caught in an overpowering river, losing a battle with its strong current. All he could do was ride it out, see where it would carry him. *What harm,* Manny thought, *would be done if I appear on television? I'll simply tell the truth, explain my beliefs.* He really did oppose American military intervention, unless its purpose was to defend against an imminent threat. But that, sure as he was still breathing, was not the case in Guarida.

Then in complete contradiction to his rationalizations, Manny had a defiant afterthought: He would use the public forum to expose Sánchez, the calculating bastard, on live TV and tell the world how he was tortured and bribed. At least that way he would die a heroic death. But he didn't harbor that illusion for long. He had tried to act courageously to save his cousin; where did that get him? Would defiance be worth it? Of what value would his painful demise be?

As much as he wanted to believe that a decision to comply with Sánchez's proposition rested on reason, deep down Manny knew the threat to subject him to another session with the Security Police moved him to capitulate. He had nightmares about the way they had covered his face with a wet cloth until the natural instinct to breathe ruled over his knowledge that breathing meant certain death. No way could he go through that again.

Yet he didn't want to capitulate. He now understood what Gandhi meant when he said, "Compromise on mere fundamentals is a surrender."

On Monday morning, two guards led Manny to a chair behind a table in the entrance hall of the Retén. Twelve microphones were set on the table, forming a horseshoe into which Manny would speak to the world. A crowd of reporters gathered behind a line of television cameras facing the table. Bright lights flashed on as Manny arrived. He was momentarily blinded, had to squint. His mind raced. It was as if his whole life, his entire history, had led him to this place. This was to be his defining moment—his moment of truth.

Why, he thought, *did it take a series of bad choices, an odyssey of trouble, to bring me to this?*

The TV crews prepared for the event, touted by Guaridan officials as a definitive exposé of American Imperialism and a feather in Sánchez's cap. Manny would admit to espionage and condemn the U.S. invasion into sovereign Guarida. Sánchez would then magnanimously pardon the professor, used as a dupe for the nefarious CIA, and deport him from Guarida. There would be no safe haven for an undercover agent of the Colossus of the North.

Manny tried to imagine a way in which he could somehow make a universal appeal, one that would serve the interests of both sides. He would state that the United States of America stood for peace and justice and freedom. Desperate, he looked around for inspiration, attempted to gather his thoughts. The hot camera lights caused beads of sweat to form on his forehead. He tried to distract himself, thought how he would explain that the ideals of harmony, fairness, and liberty had made his country great. The beads of sweat began to drip. Manny grabbed a handkerchief from his back pocket— included with the clothes they had given him for the performance—and wiped his face. He would say that Guarida aspired to the same ideals as the U.S., and President Claudio Sánchez, in launching progressive developmental reforms, deserved support.

Daunted, Manny looked out at the crowd of reporters beyond the glare of the lights. They were poised to take notes, snap stills, and raise questions. He took a deep breath, wiped his forehead again. He readied himself to speak out against an invasion that had caused turmoil and bloodshed. He would urge U.S. policymakers to withdraw American troops immediately. He would keep his remarks brief and to the point, not say anything he didn't believe. Wasn't it the individual citizen's obligation to make judgments about his country's policies? Or should the collective wisdom prevail— defend one's country, right or wrong? Certainly this wasn't the proper forum for such a debate.

Now Manny had to make a choice. But he had to comply with the Guaridan president's demand, didn't he?

There was no escape. Reason dictated that he should surrender. Defiance would be foolish. Perhaps fatal.

The countdown began. Five, four, three... Manny prepared to speak. Then a moment of dead silence stifled the befuddled journalists.

"I am *not* a spy," Manny stated clearly into the microphones. "I am an American professor. To my government I say, do not negotiate—" Before he could finish, a guard rushed to his side, grabbed his arms, and put him in a hammer-lock while he pulled Manny away from the microphones. As he was being hustled out of the room, Manny shouted, "They tortured me!"

An announcer took over in a feeble attempt to explain what had just happened.

Manny's epiphany, if that is what it was, belied all logic. His better judgment had suggested some form of compromise. Sell his soul to the devil? A Faustian deal? Hostages almost always succumbed, and he knew that his noncooperation would incur his captor's wrath. Yet he could not do it; he was not, and never would be, a puppet. At the end of the day, he would have to live with himself. *If I am not for myself, then who will be for me?* he thought. *And after all is said and done, what would remain of my humanity?* He felt a pang of pride. *If I am for myself alone, what am I?*

Something deep inside him—his heart?—had reasons he had not been able to understand until that instant. He would not act out this farce. He had been jerked around enough. First Stark and now Sánchez had tried to use him as if he were nothing more than a pawn in a game he had no intention of playing. The time had come to take a stand. *If not now, when?* Manny had never expected to react this way. He had surprised himself and immediately had doubts about what he had done.

Three guards with their weapons drawn surrounded Manny and took him back into the Retén. Every member of the press squawked paparazzi-style questions as he passed through the gauntlet. He remained silent.

His bravado faded as he grew more painfully aware of what he had just done. Once again, just like up in the hills, there was no turning back. In defying Sánchez, he had to be willing to face the consequences. Manny was frightened that he would show weakness. His hands trembled and he felt paralyzed. In that awful moment, he was a fly caught in a spider's web.

What was in store for him? He was deathly afraid of torture of any kind, but especially waterboarding, and he did not want to die. But at least he would go down with his honor intact.

After Manny had been led back into his cell, Claudio Sánchez appeared in the hallway before the press. He took the seat that was designated for Manny. The camera lights were still on, and it took a moment or two for his eyes to adjust to the glare.

Claudio spoke into the microphones, commenting with a laugh that the professor had put on quite a show. He called Prof. Emmanuel White Vidal a pathetic liar and a coward. He stated that his intelligence had disclosed a definitive connection between Professor Vidal and the CIA.

Then he raised his right arm and pointed to the sky in a manner reminiscent of his idol, Castro. "Even as we are under attack, Guarida lives by the rule of law."

Claudio's eyes scanned the room and found Juan Carlos, who stood on the side of the entrance hall. Claudio then made the sign of the cross three times across his chest, paused, took a deep breath, and cried, "Long live Guarida!"

Juan Carlos saw the signal. The contingency plan would be set into motion immediately.

✑Chapter Twenty-Six✎

C laudio Sánchez landed in Panama a few hours after the press conference. He skipped down the steps from the jet, stood on the tarmac, and shaded his eyes as he looked around for Juan Carlos.

It's a pity I had no time to use the professor for batting practice, he thought.

A shiny black Mercedes Benz S-550 limousine with darkened windows and adorned with Panamanian flags pulled up beside him. The driver got out and gathered the ex-president's luggage, explaining that the limo was designated to transport Señor Sánchez to the palatial mansion once owned by Omar Torrijos.

Claudio had fled after thinking long and hard about what was happening in his country. A tragic incident the day before the press conference, in which government forces had fired into a crowd and killed twelve innocent bystanders, and Prof. Vidal's betrayal on international television had been game-changers. The collateral damage had caused public opinion to turn against the regime. No longer did his people consider him their messiah.

Political factions had been springing up in the barrios as well as in the suburbs. Guarida Libre had been unable to unite these diverse elements. Some wanted Claudio out; others called for an immediate American withdrawal. Some advocated new elections while others demanded a return to autocracy. Racial and class divisions had fractured the country. Unable to unite, the factions, nevertheless, had begun to find a common cause in their opposition to the status quo. Aside from providing an additional measure of ballast for anti-American sentiment, his capture of the CIA spy had gained for Claudio no strategic advantage in the war on the ground.

Fighting had flared up in the downtown streets, but not with the intensity that had characterized the initial landing of U.S. forces. Many activities had returned to an appearance of normalcy. Life had to go on. Even in wartime, people had to eat, drink, sleep, and make love.

U.S. troop levels had remained constant because President Harmon had expended political capital in defense of what he characterized as "a simple operation that would be over in a few days, cost little, and result in very few American casualties." As the conflict lingered, the American public had become more critical of the rationale for war. Congress had refused to authorize its expansion.

The real war, Claudio knew, continued in the editorial columns as well as in policy-making circles. Public discourse revolved around issues of democracy, human rights, terrorism, and nation-building. Yet, everyone was aware that the underlying concern was access to oil.

Time had run out. If his increasingly embattled forces could not win, Claudio realized that he would find himself between a rock and a hard place. He needed some kind of maneuverability. He planned to use the American money offered by Stark, as well as the amount Juan Carlos was able to secure from the National Treasury, to finance a counter-coup. He and his friends would march back into Guarida and resume the revolution. *Just like Fidel did,* he thought. Next time, the *escuadrón* would get the job done and the masses would rally around him.

All of these thoughts ran through Claudio's head while the limo driver loaded the luggage. When the driver opened the rear door, as if to usher Claudio inside, two men in dark business suits quickly stepped out and caught Claudio by his arms. They pushed him into the back seat. Someone sat there waiting for him, but it wasn't Juan Carlos Guerrero.

"This is it, Mr. President," the man said. A nine millimeter Walther PPQ rested on his lap. A bracelet of skulls adorned his wrist. "Let's go for a ride."

The former president of Guarida cried, "Who the hell are you?"

"Mission accomplished," U.S. Secretary of State Pham-Dixon said. "Sánchez has fled. American forces are being withdrawn." The Secretary appeared on all the major television channels to announce that the war was over. The American public gave a noncommittal shrug and went back to watching their regular programming.

"We are here at the Presidential Palace with Mr. Ricardo Roldano," an excited local reporter stated. "Mr. Roldano has been installed by the High Military Command as the interim president of the Republic of Guarida. He is the patriarch of one of Guarida's most prominent families. As director of Guarida Libre, Mr. Roldano led the most active opposition to the Sánchez regime. He was accused of conspiring to organize a coup and alleged to have been implicated in the failed assassination attempt against Claudio Sánchez." He turned to face the man standing next to him, and shoved the microphone at him. "Are these allegations true, Mr. Roldano?"

Ricardo Roldano wore the type of pin-striped business suit common among chief executives. The colors of the presidential sash worn across his chest clashed with those of his tie. He did not smile, and he spoke with the intonation of one who is used to being in charge. Juan Carlos Guerrero stood beside him.

Roldano raised his fist to his heart and spoke clearly and calmly. "Long live the Republic! First, I would like to thank the High Command for its significant role in assisting with an orderly transition of power in our country. Second, I am grateful to Juan Carlos Guerrero for his crucial support in this process. Dr. Guerrero's allegiance to the patria as well as his oversight of our Security Police provides the continuity we need in these difficult times. The Roldano and Guerrero families have had a long history of close ties. Finally, we are reunited."

"Recent events," Roldano continued, "have confirmed to us all the need for a stable government in our country. Guarida Libre has been steadfast in championing law and order in our society. We believe that our traditions must be revered and preserved. We will remedy the irresponsible and foolhardy policies of the previous administration. We will renew our heritage, honor our commitments, and live up to our promise as a great nation."

Roldano looked around the room filled with military officers—Juan Carlos had brought along members of the PPP who shared his political aspirations—and members of the press corps. Even Colonel Heráclio Romero y Romero, Claudio's esquadrón mentor, and El Gordo stood among them.

Then Roldano gave Juan Carlos a strong abrazo before he turned and saluted the Guaridan flag. "My goal," Roldano said, "is to restore stability and order."

To that end, he told his people, the transitional government would not tolerate subversive elements infiltrating Guarida's institutions. Radicals would be expunged from the government, the university, and the press. He would administer a curfew and a state of emergency under martial law. In due course, general elections would be conducted.

"Until then, my fellow citizens, Guarida counts on your support and allegiance. Long live the patria. Thank you."

"Were you involved in the attempted assassination?"

Roldano ordered the reporter to have the cameras turned off. "We've got work to do," he said.

Juan Carlos shook the new president's hand and said, "Well done, Mr. President."

Roldano was pleased that Juan Carlos had seen the writing on the wall even before Sánchez had informed him of Stark's deal. He knew Juan Carlos had no intention of relinquishing the position he had managed to secure through sheer cunning.

"Let Claudio believe I'll meet him in Panama," Juan Carlos had told Roldano.

"I've got a much better deal." Roldano knew his support as well as his leadership of the Security Police would be instrumental in making the changing of the guard a peaceful transition. He thought of their extraordinary coalition as a grafted political hybrid that might or might not "take," but was glued together—at least for the moment.

"Together, we will restore order in Guarida," the president declared.

Two uniformed Security Police who looked like they could have been prize-fighters or heavyweight wrestlers accompanied Manny through the gates of the Retén to the street outside. He looked around, took several deep breaths, gulped in the fresh air, and felt a bit lightheaded, as if a giant weight had been removed from his shoulders. Ricardo Roldano, at the insistence of his son Raimundo, had pardoned Manny.

As the officers drove Manny to his apartment, he gazed out the window at people going about their business, picking up the pieces, restoring order. Life went on. He saw Paulo Ferreira peer out from the remodeled façade of La Ciruela.

One of the officers had keys to Manny's Las Palmas apartment, which he used to open the locks on the wrought-iron gate and the door. "Nice and safe, professor, very secure," he said. The other let out a fit of gruff laughter.

Once inside, the officers looked around. The first officer dropped the keys on the table, and said, "Get your things. We're going to the airport."

The officer who had laughed said, "It might be a good idea to stay the hell out of Guarida." Then Manny watched them station themselves in the hall outside his apartment.

Inside, Manny was alone for the moment. The place remained exactly as he had left it: a few dishes in the sink, the bed unmade. The only difference was that Tina's things were gone.

He sat down on the couch and stared at the living room walls, feeling as if someone had just administered a powerful drug that had removed all sensation from his body and mind.

It was the same feeling he'd had during his ill-fated attempt at heroics.

Manny tried to piece everything together, figure out this liquid jigsaw puzzle in which events seemed to run together. In a strange way, he felt immune to the consequences of his own irrationality, as if nothing could defeat him— almost as if he were invincible. *No, just plain lucky,* he thought. Only one eye, but he could see.

Ironically, Manny thought he saw things more clearly now. Guarida was what it was; same with the good old U.S.A. Game, set, and match. Next week was Thanksgiving, and he had a lot to be thankful for, despite everything.

He got up, paced around the apartment, stopped at the window, and gazed out at the sill where Tina had balanced herself on the edge that night. What the hell was she trying to prove? She was nuts.

He idly picked up the telephone handset. The line had gone dead, but the electricity was still on. Manny checked his laptop, wished the battery had not died, wondered why the police hadn't taken it and searched it for evidence against him. He turned on the TV and watched in amazement as a news blurb showed Claudio Sánchez stepping off a Guaridan Air Force jet and onto Panamanian territory. Stunned, he slapped his right palm to his forehead.

One of the policemen stuck his head through the door and shouted, "Hurry up!"

"Just a minute." Manny threw his clothes into a suitcase and gathered his tennis equipment. Then, with his gear over his shoulder and the suitcase in his hand, he left the apartment. "I need to get my things from UG."

Once at UG, the officers parked at the university entrance and waited there. Oddly, even these two would not enter the autonomous university campus. It was one of the few Guaridan traditions that seemed sacrosanct.

"Which is your building?"

"That one next to the big tree. You can see it from here."

"Go get your shit. You've got ten minutes. Then we're going directly to the airport."

Manny walked down the palm-lined pathways, past the café, and was about to enter his building when a group of students congregated under the old live oak tree caught his attention. They stood motionless, as if in a trance. Manny couldn't hear what they were saying. What was going on?

He walked closer to the group, looked up and saw what they were staring at. An effigy, strung from one of the tree's larger limbs, hung over the pathway. It might have been a ragdoll, with its dangling legs, upturned head, and flowing hair. The hair—

Manny felt his heart drop into the pit of his stomach. He could see that it was not a doll. It was the body of a human being, a woman. Her arms were tied behind her back, the noose tight around her neck. That hair... no, it could not be.

The hair covered her face, but Manny knew. He hurried over.

A University Safety Patrol guard reached up and put his arms around the lower limbs and hips of the inert body as if hugging it. He lifted it while another guard released the noose. For an instant, the hair fell back, revealing the bluish-grey face. A cross had been carved into her forehead. The guard cut the fishing line that bound her hands, and they dangled loosely. Together the two men laid the body down on the cement path.

Manny stood over the motionless corpse—a body that was once filled with vitality—and felt a strong urge to vomit, but could not. He ran up to his office, his entire body shaking. He sat at his desk for a moment, got up and stared out the window. He saw the guards carry Tina's body away.

Hanging Tree, Manny thought. A bolt of lightning seemed to penetrate his body. The tree stood in the midst of the country's center of higher learning, yet symbolized all that was wrong and corrupt in Guarida. Its roots were deep, its limbs strong. Must have been where Guerrero's grandfather was hanged, and now Tina, a humble product of the Block, who had just been trying to survive. *Guarida needs radical surgery,* he thought. *The Freedom Front was on the right track.*

Manny decided he wouldn't leave the country just yet. He had to see Ray first. Maybe Ray knew what had happened up in the hills.

He gathered some papers and left his cubicle, dashed down the stairs, and ran out the back door of the building. He sprinted through the palm-lined paths within the UG to a secondary exit on the opposite side of campus from where the Security Police were waiting for him.

An hour later and a couple of miles from the campus, Manny called Ray from an abasto, told him he had evaded the Security Police and left his things in their car. "They were taking me to the airport," he said.

Ray insisted that Manny meet him at Campo Alegre. They both knew it would be their last meeting for a long time. Perhaps it would be the last time the friends would ever meet at the club, or anywhere for that matter. "I'll take you to the airport later," Ray said.

Manny walked to the club and took a seat at a table beside the stadium court. He stared into space, still in shock. He couldn't get Tina's grizzly execution out of his mind. Could he have been any more naïve?

"Happy Thanksgiving," Ray said as he approached the table.

"Yeah," Manny replied.

"Sorry I'm late. How're you doing?"

"Wonderful."

"I'm really sorry, Manny. I think I know what you've been through."

"I don't want to talk about it." How could Ray know what had happened to Tina? Or that he felt a sense of responsibility for her demise?

"You don't have to talk about it, my friend," Ray said.

"I'm out of here, Ray. I can't stay here; can't work at the university."

"What did you expect? My father had to take action."

"You don't have to answer for your father. And I understand his position on the matter of my job, although I don't agree. I didn't want favoritism, anyway. Thank him for getting me out of the Retén."

"Please don't take this personally, Manny. UG is a public university. The government funds its operation. I asked the old man to look at your case, but there's a general policy."

"Against subversives. I know. But do you see me as a subversive? Who am I, Socrates? Do I corrupt young minds? Did I create Claudio Sánchez?" Manny realized he had raised his voice and was attracting attention. He lowered it again. "My God, if I had that kind of influence—"

"Listen, Manny, it's not what I believe. You advised Sánchez before he turned on you, my friend. That's just reality. No matter how much you insist it isn't, everything—every word uttered and every public act—is political. Either you're with us or against us. That's just the way it is." Ray took a sip of his drink, swirled the ice cubes in his glass. "What will you do now?"

"I'm going to change my life. From now on, my own choices will decide my future. I'll go back to New York. Then I'll fly to Texas, talk to Dee; see if I can put our life back together. Otherwise, maybe I'll get a position at an English university. Or maybe I'll go to Spain. What about you?"

"Someone has to run the Roldano businesses while Dad's taking care of the country."

"Do you know what happened to the Front?" Manny asked. "Did some of them get away?"

"Sánchez claimed that he wiped them out," Ray said.

"Some of them could have escaped. They had a tunnel that led to the sea," Manny said. Without proof to the contrary, he would not give up hope that Rafael had survived.

Ray shrugged. "I don't know, but I'll see what I can find out for you."

The doubles match on the stadium court was in its last phase. "Five–three," called the next server, a tall wiry man of around seventy with an aristocratic bearing.

"Look at that guy, Ray." Manny gestured toward the court. "He and his ilk are back in the driver's seat. No need to worry about those poor masses anymore. Your dad will protect—"

"My old man knows what he's doing. And it didn't take much for him to convince Guerrero. Actually Guerrero came to him. Our families go way back, you know? Anyway, it's safe now. The country is protected from revolutions that change nothing, just make things worse."

"You might need a real revolution, pal, not the crap we heard from Sánchez. He didn't mean a word of it, did he? But I think he might have wanted to believe. I'm getting the picture all right. Power is all that matters."

"No, Manny, it's precisely because of the power of ideas that Socrates had to drink the hemlock. I understand your idealism, my friend. But that's not the way people think. They've got to blame someone, you know. And it seems that you were in the wrong places at the wrong times."

The group meandered off the court. Ray stood and gathered his rackets, along with a can of balls. "Come on, my friend—let's hit a few. It'll take your mind off things, at least for a while."

"How the hell can I play tennis now?"

"Come on, let's go. I've got extra gear. Use my locker, change clothes, get out there and give it a try, see if you can still hit the ball."

Manny was skeptical; his heart wasn't in it, but he changed and met Ray on the court. Surprisingly the match did allow Manny to refocus his energy. His monocular vision seemed to have adjusted instantly. *A miracle,* he thought; he was playing almost as well as before.

The strategies were definitive, dependent on geometry. The ball was angled and spun over a net that separated the competitors, each attempting to outwit the other. Cross court drives, then down the line. Force the opponent to run one way, then hit behind him into the open court. Bring him in with a drop shot and lob the ball over his head out of reach. Serve hard and volley the weak return on an angle for a winner.

Unfortunately, Manny thought, *the rules of life aren't as clearly defined as the rules of tennis.*

As usual, the match was close. Ray was about to serve for the match. He yelled over to Manny, "This is it, pal. Here we go again."

Manny didn't respond. *Never say die, up man and try...* He broke Ray at love. He fought back and went up six–five on his own serve, able to end the match if he held. Instead Ray broke back. Now it was six–all in the third set.

"Shall we play a tie-break?" Ray was enjoying himself.

"Sure, why not?" He had come from behind and wouldn't give up now.

They both became very serious. Neither Ray nor Manny wanted to lose this one. It might be their last contest for a long time, and it seemed as if the outcome would reveal who was right or wrong about everything. Why didn't countries resolve international conflicts on the basis of a soccer match or tennis or any other sport, Manny wondered? Although it was supposed to be an informal match, a casual game among friends, the intensity level was equal to that of a Wimbledon final.

The tie-break was close, but Manny held on to a mini-break. A tremendous sense of relief washed over him, remembering the time they played the finals of the club championship when one lucky shot gave Ray the match. This time there was no crowd in the stadium court, no one to claim a Guaridan victory against the U.S.

"What happened to you in the stretch?" Manny asked.

"Well, I felt sorry for you, my friend. You were identified as a spy by your great populist leader, interrogated by our Security Police, and now kicked out of the UG as a subversive. I couldn't add tennis to the list, so I had to tank it."

"That's not funny, Ray. This is no joke."

"I know, Manny. I know—"

"You don't really, but I know you. You wouldn't tank. You couldn't, especially to a one-eyed bandit."

"It's nearly Thanksgiving, my friend, and you should be thankful you are able to play. I'll tell you the truth if you will level with me."

"I'm thankful to be alive, believe me. Level with you about what?"

"Admit that the revolution was a farce," Ray demanded.

Irritated, Manny said, "Was it?" Even now Ray had to make a point.

"You know it was."

"I overestimated Sánchez. But the country needs a progressive leader, maybe a true revolution," Manny said.

"Still a dreamer, eh?"

"So, did you tank?"

"No, I didn't."

"I'm not sure I believe you," Manny said, and he handed over the racket for the last time before taking his leave of Ray and Guarida.

Chapter Twenty-Seven

anny returned to New York, where he was able to reconstitute his tenure committee at NYU. After all he had been through, he was back where he had started. Yet he felt like a different person.

And he missed Dee.

Within a couple of weeks, he was summoned to a meeting in Washington. "We're concerned about Roldano," Stark told him.

Then, to Manny's astonishment, Stark presented him with a State Department award, signed by the president: *Certificate of Commendation for Exceptional Public Service in Promoting Mutual Understanding between the People of Guarida and the United States of America.* Manny's activities on behalf of his nation were no longer secret. Part of him was proud of the recognition; he would display the certificate in his office. Yet, deep down, he resented its superficiality. Would he have received an award had the outcome in Guarida been different? And how, precisely, had he contributed to mutual understanding?

After the sparsely attended ceremony in Stark's office at the Bureau of Intelligence and Research, Stark accompanied

Manny to the canteen in Foggy Bottom's basement. "Let me buy you a cup of coffee," he said.

They sat at one of the tables near the elevator. The doors opened, and several INR officers walked through and peered at Manny, who had become a cause célèbre of late. Manny recognized a few of them and nodded. "I'm truly surprised by the award," he said to Stark. *Mutual understanding,* he thought. *What a farce!*

"Of course, we know you were under some pressure," Stark said.

Some pressure, Manny thought. *That has to be the understatement of the century.* He trembled when he remembered the waterboarding.

"And not everyone was enamored with the idea for an award, you know. Some of our more conservative colleagues would have had you tried for treason for serving on that advisory committee. INR didn't see it that way. Your statement to the press was courageous, indeed. You took a stand for your country."

On his way back to the Georgetown Inn from Foggy Bottom, Manny passed the shop at the corner of M and Wisconsin where he had bought Dee the chocolate-covered espresso beans. It seemed like yesterday. Then, as he walked up Wisconsin toward N, he did a double-take, wondering if he could believe his eyes. Janey was on the other side of the street in front of a furniture store. She carried a book bag and walked alone.

Manny jogged across through the traffic. "Janey!" he shouted.

She saw him and stopped. They hugged. "It's good to see you, Janey. You've been assigned to DC?"

"Well, something like that." Her bright smile lit up her face. He had never noticed that before. Or maybe she hadn't smiled at him like that before. "Got time for a coffee? I'll explain."

They turned toward the Inn, walked across the street, and ducked into the restaurant. At a small table next to the window, Manny gazed at people strolling by. But his attention was quickly drawn back to Janey, who settled in her seat and reached across the table toward him. "It's nice to see you, Manny." She asked if he was okay and what he was doing in Washington.

Manny brought her up to date. "Crazy what's happened in Guarida, eh?" he said. Then he asked her about her assignment.

"I left the Foreign Service. I felt like a hypocrite, articulating policies I didn't believe in. I couldn't take it anymore. Anyway, now I'm assistant professor of national security studies at Georgetown. I like it. Gives me a chance to think a bit—and I'd like to write."

"About what?"

"What else? Aren't you supposed to write about what you know best?"

"Experience can be a great teacher," he said. "Publish or perish, huh?"

"It's more than that," she said, sipping her coffee. "The story has to be told. American intervention is counterproductive."

"I've been thinking of doing something as well," he said, surprised and energized by this turn of events. "Why don't we collaborate? I've come to believe that ideas really can change things. You can be a realist without giving up your ideals."

"We could produce quite an exposé, don't you think?"

"Might be more appealing if we wrote it as fiction," Manny said. "We can be creative, tell the tale without getting caught up in the drab pseudo-objectivity of academic discourse. The lie that tells a truth, right?"

"Count me in," Janey said. "This could be fun and illuminating at the same time."

"We'd be working very closely together, you know."

"I wouldn't mind that at all." She smiled, meeting his gaze, and he noticed for the first time how blue her eyes were.

The best he could come up with was, "I've always valued our friendship," but he meant so much more. If he was unable to reconcile with Dee, why shouldn't he see where his relationship with Janey might lead?

"So have I." She touched his hand lightly, tentatively.

"You're an attractive, intelligent, and good woman. Let's see how things go. We've got a lot of work to do."

"Don't say things you don't mean, Manny."

"You know me better than that." He grasped her hand and held it.

A week later Manny attended a luncheon at the dean's penthouse on Washington Square West. The fare consisted of an American smorgasbord with Boar's Head deli and fresh fruit. It was accompanied by dated bottles of Cotes du Rhone and Champagne.

Several professors and their tenure committee members grazed and chatted while Dean Rhoades and his wife circulated around the large living room. Manny stood alone next to a window that overlooked the square.

"Hrrumph." Rhoades cleared his throat as he approached. "I say, congratulations are in order."

"Thanks," Manny said. "Beautiful view." The pompous ass had argued against Manny's tenure on the basis of insufficient continuity in the department. Fortunately, his colleagues had voted for him unanimously.

"We like it here. Hrrumph." Rhoades cleared his throat again. "I hear you are in demand in Washington these days, and that you're writing a memoir." The dean took a sip of his wine.

"Actually, it's fiction."

"Of course, certainly. But naturally your experiences will be infused in the narrative?"

"We'll let the readers come to their own conclusions," Manny said. The dean pissed him off. He was an ostentatious political animal through to the core. And he had eyes for Dee.

"Hrrumph. I look forward to reading whatever it turns out to be," Rhoades said and then added, "What else might you be up to, my friend? Another escapade, I presume."

Manny almost said, *You pretentious, superficial bastard,* but instead he reached into his pocket and pulled out an open round-trip ticket for a flight from Kennedy to Dallas-Fort Worth International Airport. His hand tingled at the feel of the paper. He had come to value Dee now more than ever. He would fly down there as soon as his schedule would permit and try to convince her to come back to New York with him. "Heading for Texas, actually."

301

"Ah, yes." Rhoades turned away and walked toward three female psychologists who kept glancing at Manny during their animated conversation. "Good luck," the dean said over his shoulder.

Manny assumed the remark was directed at him.

Manny and Janey worked together for a year to piece together an entertaining account of Caribbean life through the eyes of their characters. Beneath the surface it was an imaginative behind-the-scenes look at American influence abroad. They decided to use fictitious names for the country and characters. But the story was theirs.

Manny suggested that they begin with an epigraph, a quote from Samuel Johnson's *The Vanity of Human Wishes.* "This really expresses what we're getting at, Janey," he said. "Listen to this:

Deign on the passing world, to turn thine eyes,

and pause awhile from letters, to be wise;

There mark what ills a scholar's life assail;

Toil, Envy, Want, the Patron, and the Jayl.

It was written in the eighteenth century!"

"I love it," Janey said, "but I hope we don't wind up in jail, seriously. You've already seen the inside of the Retén."

"Don't worry about that," Manny said. *Never again,* he thought.

The writing process was cathartic. They travelled back and forth from DC to New York, used Skype, and transferred files. They spent countless numbers of long hours revising and trying to incorporate an edifying conclusion into their manuscript. They both still believed in the existence of goodness and love, despite everything, but were hard-pressed to come up with a happy ending.

Manny called Janey. "Several agents expressed interest in our manuscript," he said. "One said that *mea culpas* sell and was able to parley that idea to a large New York publishing house."

"We did it!" she yelled into the phone.

"The manuscript sold for a generous advance," he told her. Manny would use his share of the money to initiate the Rafael Vidal Scholarship Fund as well as an advocacy group devoted to the abolition of waterboarding. "Working with you has been like a dream come true, Janey."

"Yeah, it's been great."

As long as he remained hopeful about Dee, he made sure his partnership with Janey was purely professional. They enjoyed dining together often, but he had declined more than one offer to come up to her apartment after dinner. He remembered what had happened with Tina.

"I suppose that's it, then," she said.

"Let's see how our masterpiece is received. Then we'll go from there." He could easily fall for her, were it not for Dee.

A month later, Janey came to Manny's NYU office. She set her leather tote on the floor and took a seat in his guest chair. "What's up, professor?" she asked with a grin.

"Look here," Manny said. He opened the New York Review of Books and pointed to a pre-release critique of *Operation Empty Nest by Emmanuel White Vidal and Jane*

Kelley-Noel with a foreword by former ambassador Frank Kingfield.

Manny read aloud to her. "Here's what they say: 'It's the story of an academic and a Foreign Service Officer used as political operatives...'"

"Well, they got that much right," Janey said.

Manny laughed and continued:

...a potent sub-theme that foreign intervention into the affairs of sovereign nations is explosive, especially when such action is designed to enhance the economic interests of powerful nations, infuses the novel. And the hero unwittingly steps into a political minefield. It is a page-turner...

Manny stopped reading. He and Janey nodded at each other, silly grins on their faces. She asked him to read some more. He skipped down the page and found what he was looking for.

...The story includes America's complicity in an assassination attempt against the president of a small Caribbean nation...

"Uh, oh." Janey grinned. "Hope this doesn't wreck your career, Manny."

"I've got tenure."

"I mean with the INR," she said.

"They gave me an award," Manny said. "And what about you?"

"No problem, Georgetown welcomes all points of view. They love that I'm a former FSO. They're going to promote me to associate professor. Anyhow, our book is fictional, right?"

"More important, the book's a success," Manny said.

"Are you ready for the lecture circuit?" Janey said.

"Yes! I can't wait to get out there and speak my mind."

Adam Stark smiled when he read the review. He was secretly pleased that the genie seemed to be out of the bottle. The president wasn't happy with Stark's performance and had passed over him in choosing the next Secretary of State. Stark remained at INR and continued to bring Manny in for consultation from time to time.

"You made a wise choice in not naming names in your book," Stark told Manny. "And up on Capitol Hill, there's talk about your depiction of waterboarding. A rose is a rose, I guess—by any other name it's torture. The so-called conservatives rationalize its use. Only by us, of course. And the Hawks don't like the way you portray military interventions."

Manny raised his hands. "It's just a novel," he said.

"Well, I'll try to keep them off your back. No telling what Congress will do, though. You have a good lawyer?"

"Don't worry about me. I won't be pulling any punches. Someone's got to speak up."

"Just be careful. By the way, your account of the plight of the Indians was illuminating." Stark had been impressed enough to take action. "We put a little pressure on Roldano, made sure that the Arawaks were allowed to return to their tribal lands."

"Thank God!" Manny thought about Saba and Aichí and the trauma they had been through. He hoped they were all right. He wished he could see them again, and he vowed to do something for them. "What happened to Case? I'm almost

305

certain I saw him in the background of a *Times* photo taken in Tripoli. What the hell is he doing in Libya?"

"I saw the article. It was about Halliburton's links to Blackwater." Stark adjusted his glasses. "The guy gets around, doesn't he?"

"Who does he work for?"

Stark did not respond.

Manny dropped the subject and took a sip of his watered-down American coffee. *Not like the rich blend of Guaridan café,* he thought. What he really wanted was a cup of fresh tropical fruit juice. A guanábana or parchita would really hit the spot. He wished he could find something like La Ciruela in the States.

I miss Guarida, he thought.

༺Epilogue༻

"THE SOULS IN TORMENT, WHO MUST GATHER UP THEIR SINS WHERE
THEY WERE COMMITTED..."

~ RÓMULO GALLEGOS

Bill McGeorge stood next to his office window and stared down at what looked like a bleak rectangular trough cut out of New York City's mountainous skyscrapers. The trees in Central Park had lost their leaves. He walked to his desk, stared down at a copy of *Operation Empty Nest*. He sat down, leaned back in his swivel chair, rested his feet on his glass desk, and hit the speed-dial on his cell phone.

Someone in the White House finally connected him to the president. McGeorge spoke into the microphone attached to his headset. "I thought we were back in business, Timothy," he exclaimed. "Roldano told me we were going to have a deal."

A pigeon lit on the outside windowsill. The bird stared at McGeorge with its head cocked. McGeorge stared back.

"I thought so too, Bill," the president said. "Who would have expected Roldano to carry through on Sánchez's nationalization plan, eh? At least the world's a safer place now, and we've got contingency plans. Soon we'll have those supply lines open for you again, don't worry. By the way, there's a close senate race up in South Dakota. I wonder if you'd be willing to chip in. And can I put your name on a short list for ambassador to Guarida?"

"Well, Timothy, I suppose I'd be honored..."

After the call ended, Bill McGeorge stood, removed his headset, and paced around the office. He had shifted his assets, protected himself. PI had made a killing in the oil commodities market by first selling off reserves as the price skyrocketed after Sánchez was gone and then shorting the market. But he hoped Harmon was right. PI still wanted all the business it could get in Guarida.

McGeorge reached into the cabinet for one of several bottles of Chivas. He poured a double shot and downed it in one gulp.

The pigeon left a glob of white droppings on the ledge and flew away.

An orange liquid ball of fire melted into the skyline. Álvaro, José, Jorge, María Pilar, and Roberto had gathered on the pool deck at the Meliá Caribe in Panama City. They watched the sensational sunset and drank from a bottle of Ravenscroft.

"Claudio should have been here by now," Roberto said.

The entourage had consumed large quantities of the aged single malt scotch. Slurring his words, Jorge said, "He'll show."

Roberto said, "I'd like to get my hands on Guerrero—that worm."

"I never would have guessed," María Pilar said.

José lifted his glass and toasted. "To Claudio, wherever he is, to Panama, to Guarida." Tears welled up in his eyes.

"Panama, Guarida," Álvaro said, "what's the difference? They are all the same puta. Countries are whorehouses. No?"

"We tried to do the correct thing," María Pilar said. "The revolution could have improved the lives of our peasants, our masses. Hah. Those goddamned arrogant sonsofbitches up there in that Imperial Colossus—"

"We need to plan our return," Roberto said, "for Claudio, for Guarida."

"It won't be easy," Jorge responded.

"Fidel did it." José gulped a shot of the single malt.

"We can do it," Roberto said. "Claudio managed to start a few good programs, and he made a fool of that gringo professor."

"We'll need to pay off the Panama police," Álvaro said with a smile.

"That won't be a problem," Roberto replied.

"Then we'll need a boat," María Pilar suggested, "like Granma, eh?"

"We'll have to get arms. We can do this, no problem," Álvaro said. Roberto, José, Jorge, and María Pilar nodded, all becoming more animated as they plotted, slurring their words increasingly as they drank. The volume of their chatter rose. And the few remaining hotel guests on the pool deck shook their heads as they walked away.

Again the raucous group toasted, this time to their patria. "Viva Guarida!" Then they finished off the bottle and sang a drunken version of their national anthem.

The sun had dropped beneath the horizon as if seeking a hiding place. Darkness engulfed the deck.

Gentle waves lapped up on the sandy shore of the barrier-island on which Rafael, Liliana, and a few other Front members had taken refuge. Up in the hills, they had fought courageously until Sánchez's forces began annihilating their compound. They had ducked into the cave just in time, detonated a blast that covered the cave's entrance, and plodded through the cavernous tunnel all the way to the sea. Their canoes were ready for a run across the channel to the uninhabited cay.

Gerónimo had taken a bullet and died before they made their escape. Rafael had lifted him in his arms and wept. As he entered the cave, Rafael had looked back and caught a glimpse of the entire camp going up in flames.

Just like El Retiro, he thought.

"Where do we go from here, Rafael?"

"We'll see, Liliana. You know the Arawaks used to come out here to fish," he said as he gathered driftwood for a fire.

Manny walked across Yale's main quad toward the MacMillan Center, where he was scheduled to give a talk at 7:00 that evening as part of the Castle Lecture Series on Ethics, Politics, and Economics. A couple of students stopped beside him on the path next to the glass-enclosed bulletin board. The students were young, he thought. An athletic-looking fellow with long flowing hair and a sweatshirt that bore an image of Ché Guevara asked a pretty coed, "Going to the lecture?"

"Yeah, totally, it'll be awesome." Her pink sweater had fluorescent purple outlines of hands emblazoned over each breast—a fashion statement of sorts?

"Hear the guy was in the CIA," the athlete said. Both students slung their book bags over their shoulders.

"That's what I've heard. And he was involved in the coup in Guarida."

"Oh yeah, it'll be awesome. Want to meet me there?" The guy seemed more interested in the girl than the subject of the lecture.

Manny smiled. *I'll give them a good show,* he thought as his eyes homed in on the bouncy fluorescent purple outlines. Then Manny shook his head, silently reprimanded himself, and looked away.

After the lecture, Manny responded to a variety of questions, only a few of which were hostile. He walked away from the Macmillan Center, noting how peaceful the campus was at the late hour. He sat on a bench, stretched out his legs, and put his hands behind his neck. The stars shone above.

His life seemed to have come full circle. Events had taken their toll. But Manny was alive and, except for his left eye, he felt stronger than ever. Wiser, too.

He rubbed the back of his neck, thinking about how he had told Stark, in no uncertain terms, that he would return to Guarida only if there was definitive proof Rafael had survived. And, if that were the case, he would not step on Guaridan soil without a personal bodyguard.

Yawning, he looked at his Tag Heuer. Time to head out. It would take a couple of hours to drive back to the Village.

On his way home, Manny thought about his recent trip to Texas. He should have gone sooner. *Better late than never,* he thought. As he turned off FDR onto East Houston, a jolt of adrenalin darted through him, as if he were awakening from a deep sleep. His body gained strength; his vision, although monocular, seemed to sharpen.

Choices do have consequences: that he had learned beyond all doubt.

Smiling at the sight of a parking space on Bleeker Street, unusually close to home, Manny pulled in, locked the car, and strode to the front steps of his brownstone. Before he could reach for his key, the door swung open. She stood directly in front of him, tossed her hair over her shoulders, and opened her arms.

"Morning, hon! Want some breakfast?" Dee said as the sun rose on a new day.

About the Author

R ichard S. Hillman has traveled around the world on the Semester-at-Sea faculty, served as a Fulbright Scholar in Venezuela, participated in a People-to-People delegation in Cuba, and consulted at the U.S. State Department. An avid reader, his lifelong love of books has resulted in a voluminous personal library and inspiration to write.

313

He has published non-fiction works, but finds crafting a novel more creative. Born in New York City, he has lived in Long Island, Maine, Scotland, Spain, Brazil, and Venezuela. He and his Jamaican wife reside in Florida. Their son is a U.S. Marine and daughter, a computer tech and teacher. When not reading, writing, or traveling, Hillman can be found on a tennis court or kayaking around Caladesi Island. Currently, he is working on Finding Rafael, a sequel to Tropical Liaison.

For more information about Richard, please visit:

http://richardshillman.com/index.html